NO FUNERAL FOR NAZIA

NO FUNERAL
FOR NAZIA

Taha Kehar

NEEM TREE
PRESS

Published by Neem Tree Press Limited, 2023

Copyright © Taha Kehar, 2023

Neem Tree Press Limited
95A Ridgmount Gardens, London, WC1E 7AZ

info@neemtreepress.com
www.neemtreepress.com

A catalogue record for this book is available from the British Library
ISBN 978-1-911107-74-3 Paperback
ISBN 978-1-911107-75-0 Ebook UK
ISBN 978-1-911107-32-3 Ebook US

Printed and bound in Great Britain

For Pashi and in loving memory of Naz.

Contents

My Darling Noori,

    I know I have greatly tested your generosity and patience over these years. As I slip into the next life, I ask you for one last favour: no funeral, but rather a party. My blue diary, the one I have kept by my side all these months, has the details.

    All my love,
    Nazia

The Final Wish

Naureen rose from her wicker chair and sauntered through the cobbled tracks along the lawn – like Nazia used to. As she approached the bougainvillea creepers, she smoothed the creases on her off-white cotton kurta, stopping to light a cigarette. Naureen drew in the woody fragrance of smoke and then exhaled audibly. She craned her neck and inspected the creepers, running a finger through their thin, papery texture – a riot of pink against an azure Karachi sky.

The stab of a migraine jolted through her head. Naureen pressed her thumbs against her eyelids, then massaged her temples. Within minutes, the pain dissipated, and she inhaled deeply.

'What's the matter?' Asfand's voice broke through the distant call of crows and the soft murmur of a grasshopper. 'Are you not feeling well? Why are you wandering through the garden like a ghost?'

His gaze turned towards the pack of Marlboro Lights clumsily tucked into her fist. Asfand gasped in terror.

'Noori, what are you doing with Nazia's cigarettes?' he fumed, snatching the pack from his wife's hand. 'Are

1

you planning to follow your sister to the grave? Stop smoking at once.'

A defiant scowl appeared on Naureen's face, deepening the creases on her forehead. She traipsed towards the wide wicker chair, threw her portly frame on to its thick yellow cushion with a gentle thud and continued to stare at the creepers.

Asfand shuffled towards her, placed the cigarettes on the mahogany table and knelt next to his wife. 'Noori,' he said, 'you need to be strong. I know it's only been a few hours since you lost Nazia, but you have to keep yourself together. There are so many arrangements we need to make for the funeral. This is no time to be smoking because you're stressed.'

'I'm not smoking because I'm stressed.' Naureen turned her head away, her furrowed brows meeting above her nose. 'I was just trying to climb into my sister's skin and understand how she felt during her morning walks. She always walked down to the bougainvillea creepers, stopped to smoke, and then repeated the lap a few times.'

Puzzled by his wife's reaction to her sister's death, Asfand was tempted to remind Naureen about the friction that had laid siege to the two sisters' relationship. It seemed like the perfect antidote for Noori's troubled mind, to prevent her from slipping deeper into her grief. Instead, he opted for a few platitudes one would expect from distant relatives and unwanted guests.

'Noori, it's best to start the process of forgetting the dead soon after they die,' he said, placing his hand heavily on Naureen's shoulder.

She moved it away briskly and jumped to her feet.

'We have so much to do before the funeral,' Asfand continued. 'Your sister was quite popular. I'm sure I'll be busy entertaining lots of heartbroken *aashiqs* today.'

'There will be no funeral,' Naureen stated firmly, ignoring her husband's dig at her sister's character. 'Nazia wanted us to throw her a farewell party that gives people an opportunity to say goodbye to her without all the hysterical displays of crying that we see at funerals. She prepared a guest list and left instructions for what to do after she died. The burial has to be a quiet affair, Asfand. Nazia didn't want any of her friends to be present when her body is lowered into the ground. You and I can make the arrangements to have her buried later today. I have to make a few calls and invite guests for the party. We'll do it this Saturday night.'

Frozen at this news, Asfand struggled to find the words to express his shock over the preposterous suggested arrangements for Nazia's last rites. Naureen picked up a blue pocket diary from the table and distractedly flicked through it.

'Noori, this is … this is … outrageous,' Asfand said warily, struggling to disguise his irritation and anger. 'What will people say? Your relatives will expect a *janaza* and *soyem*, not a bloody party. Some of them will demand prayer meetings every Thursday and a *chehlum*.

How will we tell them that we're hosting a *party* instead of a *Qur'an khwani*?'

'Our relatives haven't visited us in years, Asfand,' she responded calmly. 'Most of them still love to hate us. Besides, Nazia was a sly beast. She knew how to keep them in their place.'

Stifling a grin, Naureen pulled open the diary and pointed, directing Asfand's gaze towards a passage written in red ink – Nazia's messy cursive.

Lie to them. Tell them that I died by suicide. That'll keep our relatives at bay. God-fearing Muslims won't show up for my funeral if they think I downed a bottle of paracetamol.

'Are you out of your mind?' Asfand snatched the diary from Naureen's hand and flung it towards a lone bare spot in an otherwise luscious garden. 'That is entirely and totally and wholly inappropriate. Your sister was always so bloody insensitive. She cared so little about what people had to say, and did whatever she pleased. But you were always the saner one, the good daughter, who always did the right thing. Please be rational. We'll never be able to show our face in public again if we follow Nazia's instructions. Try to understand, Noori. People will talk.'

Naureen heaved a sigh as she stood up to walk to where the diary lay. She bent down to pick it up.

'Asfand, this is none of your business,' she said as she cleaned a film of mud from the pages filled with

4

the curves, tails and tunnels of Nazia's handwriting. 'All I need is your cooperation. Call the *maulvi* sahib who manages the mosque at the graveyard and make all the arrangements for the *ghusl* and the burial today. You and I will go over in the late afternoon and do the deed.'

Naureen dabbed a finger on the last trace of mud that clung to the pocket diary and flicked it off. She pressed the book against her chest and walked into the house.

Asfand tutted, but reluctantly plodded behind her. 'Burying someone isn't the same thing as taking a walk at Zamzama Park,' he muttered. 'There are rules to be followed. I doubt they'll let you into the Gizri Graveyard during the burial.'

Naureen glared at Asfand. It was a gesture that told him more about her predicament than any long conversation with his wife could offer. Twenty-eight years of marriage had taught Asfand the art of reading each frown or grin that flooded her face. It was the only shred of intimacy that hadn't eluded them over the years.

Defeated, he whispered, 'I'll find a way, Noori.'

'Thank you,' she hissed. 'Don't disappoint me.'

Asfand waited for the click-clack of his wife's heels against the marble floor to subside. Once he was certain Naureen was inside the house, he walked back out to the garden. He placed a cigarette between his lips and raised an old Zippo lighter that he carried in his pocket, holding the flame against its tip.

The bougainvillea swayed in the light breeze and let out a soft whistle, mingling with the discordant call of birds and the din of the traffic on Sunset Boulevard. Asfand strutted down the cobbled pathway and made a mental note to have the gardener trim the grass and remove the creepers.

It's all over, his inner voice cried out. Even memories didn't seem enough to comfort his broken heart.

*

The fierce blue flame diminished under the steel pot as Bi Jaan turned down the dial on the stove. Gingerly, the old housekeeper tossed boiled rice, saffron, coriander and mint into the biryani and covered the lid.

'Sorayya!' she hollered as she readjusted the dial and left the pot on a low flame. 'Come here at once.'

Bi Jaan clicked her tongue in disapproval as her niece ambled in through the door, the clink of her brass bangles growing louder as she approached the kitchen counter. The girl hummed a song from a Sunny Leone movie that always drew her aunt's ire. Sorayya's long, matted tresses cascaded down her left shoulder, the right side of her neck visible to the prying eyes of the neighbours' servants, who would often climb on to the boundary wall and peep at her. Driven by a sense of propriety, Bi Jaan tugged at a handful of her niece's hair and flung it against her right shoulder. Sorayya's eyes twitched in mild pain, but she didn't protest.

'How many times have I told you to dress modestly?' Bi Jaan exclaimed. 'Why must you reveal your neck? Which one of the neighbours' servants are you trying to seduce?'

'*Wah*, Phuppo.' Sorayya pointed at her aunt. 'If you don't cover your head or neck with a dupatta, it's all good. If I don't, it's a sin.'

'Enough!' the old housekeeper shouted. 'How can you talk to me in this way at a time like this? Nazia Apa did so much for you. Have some respect for her memory.'

Sorayya flinched with disgust, a childlike contempt for her aunt's hypocrisy.

'She did a lot for you too,' she said, huffing. 'I don't see you mourning. All you're doing is telling me how to mourn.'

'Hurry up already,' Bi Jaan said, ignoring Sorayya's petulance. 'We must prove to Naureen Bibi that you're still needed at the house. I don't want her to tell me that your services are no longer required now that Nazia Apa is dead.'

'So what if they throw me out?' Sorayya replied nonchalantly. 'I don't even want to be here, especially when I'm not wanted. Everyone in our village thought I would become a famous actress one day. Don't you realise that my acting and dancing skills can put even the best heroines to shame?'

'Of course,' Bi Jaan said with a sarcastic lilt. 'How can anyone expect our modern-day Madhuri Dixit to leave her films, lock herself in a kitchen and perform housework?'

Sorayya's face reddened at what she thought was a rare compliment from her *phuppo*. Once the girl caught sight of her aunt's unimpressed furrowed face, her broad grin sobered into a half-smile. Her aunt had practically raised her after her mother died in childbirth. Yet, Sorayya still couldn't tell when she was angry or cracking a joke.

'When will you learn?' Bi Jaan said, her tone sharper than it was before. 'If you lose your job right now, your orphaned brother will have no one to support him. Your father, may he rest in peace, will never forgive you.'

Bi Jaan's words stung her, but she made a conscious attempt to conceal her anger. Despite her efforts to remain silent, Sorayya felt the need to say something – anything – to convey her distress and discourage her aunt from being so insensitive.

'Raqib isn't the only one who's been orphaned, Phuppo,' Sorayya stammered, still anxious about being cruel to her aunt. 'You always forget that I was orphaned too when Abba died in that bus accident.'

'What did you say?' Bi Jaan bellowed. 'Don't take that tone with me, *chokri*. Now, go wash the dishes and set the table. I want Naureen Bibi and Sahib to eat before they go to the graveyard.' Bi Jaan removed the lid from the steel pot and stirred the lumps of rice with a ladle.

'Phuppo –' Sorayya blurted out the words with an unusual fervour – 'why hasn't anyone come to the house for Nazia Apa's *janaza*?'

'Naureen Bibi said there won't be a *janaza*.' Bi Jaan shifted uncomfortably, her anger forgotten. 'She said there will be a small gathering or *party* in a few days that will be attended by Nazia Apa's close friends.' She shook her head and fussed over her pots – a burst of activity at the bizarreness of what she had just uttered. 'I think it's very strange that no one has turned up,' she continued, as

Sorayya walked over to the teak cabinet. 'Nazia Apa had many friends. But, over the last few years, they stopped visiting her.'

'Why did they stop?' Sorayya asked, without thinking, her question triggered more by curiosity than genuine concern. She took out a plate from the cabinet and began wiping it with a cloth, waiting for Bi Jaan to answer.

The old housekeeper lowered her gaze, let out a loud wheeze and pinched the skin between her fading eyebrows. Sorayya watched the expression on her face transform, puzzled by the way her innocent words had wounded her aunt.

'Don't waste my time with such questions!' Bi Jaan yelled, raising a finger at her niece to show her exasperation. 'I want you to make sure that the forks and spoons are clean. If I spot any stains, you'll be in trouble.'

Bi Jaan scurried out of the kitchen and hid inside the cavernous storeroom next to the servant quarters, her dupatta pressed tightly against her mouth. It wasn't long before Sorayya heard her muffled cries. A tremor ran through the girl's heart, beating against the walls of her chest and threatening to tear them down. She skulked towards the sliding door that led to the servant quarters, peeped through its dusty netting and watched tears roll down her aunt's bloodshot eyes.

Sorayya felt the urge to comfort Bi Jaan, but struggled to understand the source of her phuppo's distress. From what she knew, Nazia Apa and Bi Jaan were adversaries who sought pleasure in quarrelling over everyday matters. Ever since Sorayya had started working at the house, she'd heard Nazia Apa complain about how Bi Jaan always forgot to add chopped scallions in her avocado salad, how she broke antique vases and other trinkets when she cleaned her room, and burnt her Banarasi saris when she ironed them before a special soirée. Bi Jaan found ways to pay her back in the same coin, by tossing rotten avocados into her salad and ironing her designer saris mere minutes before Nazia was expected to leave for a party. Why was Bi Jaan crying over the death of someone she clashed with so often?

'Bi Jaan! Sorayya!' Naureen's voice disrupted the flow of her thoughts. 'Please hurry. Sahib and I are leaving to go to the graveyard.'

'Yes, Naureen Bibi,' Bi Jaan said, wiping her eyes with her dupatta as she returned to the kitchen.

While the old housekeeper spooned biryani into the serving dish, Sorayya observed the tears that clung to her aunt's eyelashes, despite her repeated attempts to blink them away. She pitied her aunt, even though it was hard for her to explain why.

'I think it's a silly idea to have a party instead of a funeral,' Bi Jaan said, as she placed the ladle back into the pot. 'Naureen Bibi is making a big mistake.'

'What's there to celebrate about death, Phuppo?' Sorayya asked in disbelief. 'Isn't death all about grief, the usual *rona dhona*?'

Bi Jaan placed a finger on her lips to silence her niece. It was the only way to warn Sorayya against overstepping her bounds and interfering in matters that were of no concern to the hired help.

As Sorayya carried the tray to the dining room, she felt the weight of the serving dish, cutlery and plates in a gnawing ache against her elbows. The pain reminded her of something Raqib had told her after their father's funeral.

I insisted on holding the bier along with the others, her brother had said. *Sameer Mamu had told me that I wouldn't be able to handle it. But I insisted.* Baji, *you wouldn't believe that Abba's body was still heavy.*

Raqib's words were etched in her mind like a scar. As the young girl laid the table, she wondered if she and Raqib should have celebrated Abba's death instead of carrying the weight of his lifeless body long after it had been buried. If they had, she was sure their lives would have been different, if not happier.

*

The afternoon sun prickled Naureen's skin as they drove to Gizri Graveyard. She wiped the beads of sweat from her forehead with a handkerchief, switched on the air conditioner and breathed noisily. Why did Nazia have to die in summer? Naureen thought. She always knew how to inconvenience people, especially those who loved her.

'Is the van following us?' she said, turning back to check on the Suzuki that carried Nazia's body. The van jostled for space amid the wailing cars, buses and motorcycles that clogged Sunset Boulevard.

'Don't worry,' Asfand said, as he steered their way up the road leading to the graveyard. 'You told them to follow our car. Stop fussing over all this and enjoy your sister's funeral.' As the words left his lips, Asfand immediately regretted their acidic inflection. Tormented by a mix of guilt and rage, he honked at an errant rickshaw-driver who was trying to overtake their car.

'This isn't a funeral,' Naureen said, overlooking his snide remark. 'Please stop calling it that.'

'I'm sorry for being so insensitive,' he said, appearing more compassionate than usual. 'You know I didn't mean that. I was just ...'

'This isn't a funeral,' Naureen repeated herself, her words soaked in an unexplained fury.

There was a brief interlude, during which the silence between them became unbearable. 'Have you thought about who you'll be inviting for the party?' Asfand asked, just to say something.

'Nazia left a guest list that has six names on it, apart from the both of us.'

Asfand nodded, then quickly changed the topic to avoid talking about a party that he didn't approve of. 'You're a lucky woman,' he said. 'You're perhaps the only woman in the country – maybe even the Muslim world – who has been allowed to enter a graveyard for a funeral service. The *maulvi* sahib was quite reluctant at first. But I handed him a crisp five-thousand *ka* note and assured him that you're not one of those emotional women who'll cry like an injured bird.'

Nazia greeted this backhanded compliment with silence and a grunting cough.

'You've been smoking again, haven't you?' Asfand grumbled. 'I could smell it on you when we were leaving the house.'

'Don't start with me again,' she snapped, shuffling in her seat to face the traffic out of her window. 'This isn't your business. Besides, Nazia did it all the time.'

'And look where she ended up,' Asfand said remorsefully. 'After today, she'll be six feet under. And she wasn't even fifty yet. What's the point of smoking and flirting your life away, when all that'll be left of you is a gravestone?'

Asfand feared that she would misinterpret his comment, but Naureen threw a sideways glance at him and smiled unexpectedly. Asfand drew her hand towards his mouth, kissed it and released it before anyone caught a glimpse of this rare display of affection.

'Nazia truly knew how to draw the attention of men,' she said, with a quiet laugh. 'All kinds of men. Young, old, rich, poor, single, *married* …'

Asfand cleared his throat and pressed his fingers tightly against the steering wheel to stop his hands from shaking. Naureen rolled down the car window, plucked out a cigarette from Nazia's packet of Marlboros and lit up. Asfand didn't stop her.

The Mourners

The trill of her mobile phone wrenched Parveen Shah out of a deep slumber. She uttered an exasperated groan and awkwardly rose to her feet. 'No one lets me sleep anymore,' Parveen grumbled to herself as she stretched her arms in the air. *I should have put my phone on silent before taking a nap.*

'Hello,' she said, as she placed the phone on speaker. She stifled a yawn and silently cursed the caller.

'Nazia's gone, Pino,' Naureen whispered on speaker. 'It happened last night.'

'What?' Parveen said, her heart pounding against her chest.

Forgetting her fatigue, she plodded towards her desk by the window, pulled open a drawer and rifled through its contents – an old pot of ink, an unused Parker pen, and stacks of brown envelopes. She held up one of the envelopes, opened the flap and pulled out a sheet of paper that was torn at the edges. Parveen inspected the stick-figure sketch of two girls with pigtailed hair scribbled above their oval faces in black crayon. *To my best friend Parveen, love Nazia*, read the untidy scrawl above the illustration. Tears filled her eyes and flowed down to her cleft chin. She covered her mouth to suppress a shriek, but couldn't control her emotions.

Sensing Parveen's despair, Naureen sighed deeply and waited for her to stop crying.

'We buried her an hour ago,' she said finally. 'You know how rebellious and difficult she could be. She never wanted a funeral. She wanted us to throw her a farewell party. It'll be at my house, this Saturday night, Pino.'

'This is such distressing news,' Parveen said, dabbing her reddened eyes with a tissue. 'How did it happen? She seemed in good health. Last week, someone I met at Mrs Daud's dinner was telling me about how well Nazia was doing. She told me about the new manuscript Nazia had completed and submitted to her publisher. What a tragedy.'

'She died in her sleep,' Naureen continued. Her words were uttered with practised ease, a soothing whisper. 'What can we do now, other than accept reality?' she said. 'The least I can do for my older sister is fulfil her wishes. Please do come over on Saturday, Pino. She'd want you to be there.'

'I … uh … will,' Parveen said, struggling to form coherent sentences. 'A party …?'

'Bring Sabeen too,' Naureen added. 'I would have called to tell her the news. But I don't think she wants to speak to me.'

Parveen gasped as a fresh fear lodged in her mind. 'But Noori, how will I break the news to her? I can't do it. I can't.'

'Pino, don't be silly,' Naureen snapped. 'You've been like a mother to Sabeen, especially since you convinced her to abandon Nazia three years ago. I'm sure you'll know how to handle her.'

'Don't blame me,' Parveen raised her voice, the veneer of cordiality between them now shattered. 'I didn't do anything. Sabeen chose me over that mother of hers.'

'Pino,' Naureen spat out, 'have some respect for my sister. If you won't tell Sabeen, I will be forced to tell her some things about you that she ought to know too. I'm sure you'll like that.'

'I'll tell her,' Parveen said abruptly, fearing Naureen's threat had the power to sabotage her delicate bond with Sabeen. 'I'll also make sure that she comes with me.'

When Naureen ended the call, Parveen dabbed her eyes and cheeks with a tissue, placed the drawing on her dresser and took a deep breath before she went over to Sabeen's room.

For months, she had deluded herself that removing Sabeen from Nazia's clutches was one of her key accomplishments. Parveen hadn't realised that Sabeen would become a burden on her. She wasn't prepared to be a doting mother – especially not to Nazia's daughter. Ever since she had left her mother's house, Sabeen had struggled to keep a job and had, over the last two months, stopped working altogether. Instead, she was often spotted along the streets of Karachi, sitting on the back of a Careem bike, riding side-saddle, with her fingers wedged into her Captain's armpits. Parveen was astonished by her unladylike conduct, but didn't have the courage to confront Sabeen with her objections. Her experience with heartbreak had taught her that people often resorted to strange coping tactics. But she couldn't ignore the realities. Bereft of a steady income, Nazia's daughter had become a financial liability on Parveen. With Nazia's death, Parveen's responsibilities would expand to other domains, and she wasn't prepared to deal with the consequences.

*

Parveen poured herself a glass of cold water and took slow, cautious sips. She had instructed the maid to bring Sabeen a bottle of water, along with a glass, as the girl had sat disbelievingly silent on the sofa upon hearing about her mother, but Parveen soon realised that she was the one who felt dehydrated, especially after being woken up from her long nap by the news of Nazia's demise.

'How did this happen, Pino Aunty?' Sabeen asked, burying her tear-streaked face in Parveen's new Sana Safinaz kameez. 'Was Mama ill? I bet that man did something to her. He's not to be trusted.'

'No, no, *beti*,' Parveen said, resting her head against Sabeen's forehead in a comforting gesture. 'This was Allah's wish. All we can do is accept His wishes.'

Overwhelmed with grief and anger, Sabeen wasn't satisfied with Parveen's logic. 'I'll never forgive that Asfand,' she said angrily, her eyebrows creased in concentration. 'He's to blame for Mama's death.'

'Don't say that,' Parveen said, stunned by Sabeen's proclivity for melodrama. 'He and his wife gave you and your mother a place to live for so many years. Why would he try to harm her?'

'You know very well what he did to her, Pino Aunty.' Sabeen stared into the distance. 'In exchange for a roof over our heads, he made her do vile things. She eventually gave in and had an affair with him.'

As she flattened Sabeen's hair with her palm, Parveen wondered if she should tell her that Nazia's affair with Asfand was little more than a rumour, a neighbourhood scandal that had never been proved. *I can't tell her the truth,* she thought. *If Sabeen finds out that I lied to her, she'll never forgive me.*

'The least he could have done was ask me if I wanted to attend my own mother's burial,' Sabeen said, her voice cracking. 'I bet that Asfand told Naureen Aunty to keep me away.'

'Let's pay our respects,' Parveen said. 'Your mother never wanted a funeral. She wanted us to have a farewell party for her.'

'Mama was always eccentric,' Sabeen sniffed, and then shouted in fury, 'but still, I should have been there! It's all Asfand's fault.'

Parveen eyed Sabeen with a mix of incredulity and concern, half hoping that her silence alone would console Nazia's daughter.

'What will we do at this party, anyway?' Sabeen continued, once she had regained composure, a few minutes later.

'Let's hope we don't starve,' Parveen said, in a flippant effort to comfort Sabeen. 'Your Naureen Aunty is a terrible cook.'

Ignoring Pino Aunty's attempt at humour, Sabeen rose from her perch and returned to her room. When she slammed the door, Parveen instinctively pressed her hands against her ears to protect herself from the sound. *She truly has her mother's temper*, she thought.

*

Light from the streetlamp filtered through the iron bars of the window and threw oblong patterns on the desk. As she returned to the room, Parveen realised this sight was the only bright spot in her long, hapless days. Her fingers squirmed against the wall as she struggled to find the switch for the ceiling fan. She observed with a lopsided smile the intricate web that had formed on her desk. When she finally switched on the fan, the sheet of paper trembled under the sudden blast of air. It fell on the Afghan carpet, its edge flapping against the smooth surface of the handwoven material. Parveen picked it up, flicked on the table lamp and studied the note once again.

She had kept this sketch because it was a souvenir from a peaceful childhood spent with Nazia. Their friendship had been cultivated through those gawky teenage years when they learned to be each other's confidantes. Although their camaraderie had not withstood the blows of adversity, Parveen wanted to be reminded of the days when she wasn't a casualty of her friend's small mutinies. The note was the only proof that Parveen had of Nazia's guileless charm, her innocence.

The phone rang, pulling Parveen out of her thoughts. She checked her mobile to see who was calling – an unknown number appeared on her screen. Parveen answered the phone with a sullenness.

'Pino.' A husky male voice seeped through the receiver, frantic yet firm. 'She's dead.'

'How did you find out, Saleem?' Parveen responded indifferently as she straightened up, now holding her phone with both hands. She tried to sound nonchalant, despite her heartbeat quickening and her breathing getting noticeably shallower and faster. She'd recognised the voice immediately.

'Naureen called,' he said, unfazed by her abrupt response. 'How is Sabeen? Can I talk to her?'

Parveen pondered his question for a moment. 'She doesn't want to talk to you,' she answered coldly.

'I'm her father, Pino,' Saleem said. 'Why are you doing this? You kept Sabeen away from her mother. And now you're trying to sabotage her chances of building a relationship with her only surviving parent. What are you trying to prove—?'

'Wait a second,' Parveen interrupted him, knowing that she would regret what she said next. 'Let me clarify a few things. I'm not keeping you away from Sabeen. You were the one who pushed her away, when you abandoned Nazia, all those years ago. Now you've come back for her and expect her to just open up to you?'

'My daughter isn't a child, Pino,' Saleem fumed. 'She's old enough to understand that what happened between her parents is none of her business. But you've prevented that from happening. You've turned her into a child – an unaccomplished brat, who is still haunted by her parents' relationship. She's been foolish enough to believe you and the lies that you've fed her about Nazia.' Saleem paused to clear his throat.

'Anyway, I'll talk to her at Saturday's party,' he said. 'I hope you'll be bringing her to Naureen's house for Nazia's final farewell.'

'You're invited?' Parveen said cuttingly. 'I knew Nazia wasn't the brightest woman in town, but I wonder why she'd be stupid enough to invite her ex-husband to her funeral.'

'It's not a funeral,' Saleem responded triumphantly, a petulant attempt at dulling the sting of her words. 'Naureen wants it to be a small party, where we remember Nazia. My dear wife left instructions on what we must do at the party.'

'*Ex*-wife,' Parveen corrected him. 'One shouldn't harbour delusions, my friend. They take us nowhere.'

'You should heed your own advice rather than tell me what to do.' With that, Saleem disconnected the call, and Parveen was left burdened with a debilitating guilt.

'I should have been nicer to him,' she murmured, placing Nazia's note and her mobile on the desk. 'But he doesn't deserve my kindness, especially after he's made me wait so long to hear from him.'

As she paced the floor, Parveen was shocked at her resentment towards a man whose phone call she had anticipated for decades. Saleem had been her infatuation when they were younger, and it came as no surprise to Parveen that he still left her feeling giddy. Over the years, she had overcome the youthful gawkiness that had inhibited her from speaking to him with ease when they were briefly engaged. But not all of her past insecurities had eluded her. Saleem had eventually married Nazia and later abandoned her, but Parveen's feelings for him were like an incurable disease that consumed her.

Parveen had spent many years trying to find the perfect distraction to pull herself away from thoughts of Saleem. In an attempt to forget the man she secretly loved, she had a string of affairs with cricketers, *zamindars*, businessmen, doctors – anyone who could help her believe that Saleem was not a suitable match for her. But these romances were nothing more than fleeting inconveniences. Instead of helping her forget Saleem, they reminded Parveen of him. She had even saddled herself with a rich husband – a PPP politician with far too many scruples for her taste. His death in a car accident some years ago had persuaded her that Saleem couldn't be replaced in her heart and mind. Saleem was the panacea for all her problems.

Parveen switched on the ceiling lights in the room. Memories of Nazia's betrayal pierced her mind, erasing all traces of compassion she had felt towards her friend. She thought about the question Saleem had asked her: *What are you trying to prove?* 'Poisoning Sabeen's mind was my way of winning him back from her,' Parveen mumbled to herself. 'It was my way of getting back at Nazia.'

*

'Do it properly, Sorayya,' Naureen said, as the maid pressed her forehead. 'Scare the pain away with your hands!'

Sorayya recoiled in horror as her employer's soothing voice rose to a loud, rasping grunt. Her fingers squirmed against Naureen's forehead, tugging at the supple skin above her frontal bone. Bi Jaan had urged Sorayya to avoid the threat of unemployment by putting her many talents as a housekeeper, carer and silent confidante on display for Naureen Bibi. Sorayya had even brought her a cup of tea that she'd placed on the glass table next to the bed.

But Naureen Bibi was far more demanding than her sister had ever been. Since her efforts to look after Nazia Apa's basic needs had always been sluggish at best, Sorayya found herself somewhat ill-prepared to fulfil Naureen's endless demands. She soon realised that her inadequacies disadvantaged her, and Naureen would eventually sack her. She wasn't ready to face a bleak future if the threat of being sacked was acted upon, not when Raqib's school fees had to be paid. Bi Jaan hadn't spared any opportunity to remind Sorayya that she bore the responsibility of ensuring her brother's well-being. Earlier, as she stirred two spoons of sugar into Naureen Bibi's tea, Sorayya had told herself to keep her reckless impulses in check and to mould herself into the dependable servant that Naureen Bibi expected her to be. It would be a difficult task, but one that would help Sorayya put an end to her family's ordeal.

'Sorry, Naureen Bibi,' Sorayya stammered. 'Nazia Apa never made me press her head. So, I'm not very good at it.'

'I'm surprised,' Naureen laughed. 'My sister was very demanding. She used to order all the servants in our old house around. In her own way, Nazia was nothing short of a *rani* with an attitude problem.'

'No, no,' Sorayya answered rapidly, aware that she wasn't telling the truth. 'She was anything but demanding. She used to talk a lot. In fact, she would always tell me stories.'

'What stories?' The softness in Naureen's voice returned as her curiosity took hold.

'She told me about her husband and her daughter,' Sorayya said.

She leaned forward carefully to see if a frown had emerged on Naureen's face or if her mouth was quivering with impatience. Though it had been months since Sorayya was hired, the young girl had yet to carve a niche for herself in Naureen's home. Until she had earned her employer's respect, every word that Sorayya spoke was a liability and stood the risk of being considered a transgression.

'Bibi,' Sorayya said, 'did Nazia Apa's husband really flee the country with all the other MQM leaders?' As the question tumbled out of her mouth, Sorayya realised how blunt it may have come across. Racked with guilt over Bi Jaan's tearful outburst earlier that day, she didn't want to cause her further distress. She muttered an apology, but her employer ignored it.

'Those were different times,' Naureen said. 'It was the 1990s. An operation had been launched in 1992 to rid Karachi of antisocial elements. Many MQM leaders were arrested or went missing. Some of them, including their chief, had to leave the country. Saleem Bhai wasn't safe in Pakistan anymore.'

Sorayya nodded, not giving away how little she actually knew of Nazia's personal history.

'After the operation ended two years later, Saleem Bhai started disappearing for several days at a stretch,' Naureen continued, as if talking more to herself than Sorayya. 'By that time, the MQM was locked in a battle with the paramilitary forces. Nazia was frustrated with Saleem's constant disappearances but remained devoted to him. In 1996, Saleem Bhai vanished without a trace. This time around, he didn't return after a few days and even his fellow party members had no clue about his whereabouts. That's when Nazia and her daughter Sabeen came to live with us. They were a lot safer here, as the government had started carrying out search operations at the houses of MQM activists.'

'Why didn't he take them along with him, Naureen Bibi?'

Naureen registered the question with a smirk, walked over to the dressing table and unscrewed the cap from her jar of night cream. Sorayya watched the steam rise from the teacup. Fearing the tea would cool down before Naureen Bibi got the chance to drink it, she hurriedly placed the cup on the dressing table. Naureen greeted the maid's gesture with a silent nod. She pressed her fingers into her jawbone, resting her plump face on the tips of her polished nails, and inspected her reflection in the mirror. Her weary eyes twitched as she moved her neck sideways to study her right profile. She then smeared the cream against her dimpled cheeks.

'Saleem Bhai ended his marriage with Nazia before he left the country,' Naureen said. 'He probably left her for another woman. I think his troubles with the MQM were an excuse to leave Nazia and Sabeen.'

'What do you mean? Didn't he love them?'

Naureen moved her hands away from her face and let out a pensive sigh.

'I wanted to ask you something,' Sorayya said, with some hesitation. 'Nazia Apa gave me a sari, some days before she died. She told me that she'd worn it on her wedding day. I didn't feel comfortable taking it, but she insisted that I should keep it. She told me to ask you what I have to do with it after she dies.'

Relieved at the sudden change of subject from Nazia's failed marriage to her wedding dress, Naureen pinched her fingers against the ridge of her nose and took a deep breath. Then, seeming to remember that Sorayya was also in the room, she cast an enigmatic smile at her.

Still uncertain about the gravity of her question, Sorayya felt a sudden pang of guilt. Once again, the fear of losing a job that would pay her bills and open doors for Raqib's future perturbed her. *Why can't you think before you speak?* she chided herself.

'Sorayya,' Naureen said, 'you can keep the sari. Nazia Apa just wanted you to wear it at Saturday's party and serve the guests. Bi Jaan will be busy in the kitchen. So, I'll need your help. I'll give you detailed instructions tomorrow.'

'Whatever you say.' Sorayya nodded, unsure if she should be smiling at Naureen Bibi at such a tragic time.

'One more thing,' Naureen said. 'Tell Bi Jaan to style your hair like Nazia Apa used to do hers.'

If Sorayya was perplexed by her employer's strange demand, she didn't make it apparent. She nodded and silently marched out of the room, like a soldier accustomed to taking orders.

When Sorayya had left the room, Naureen opened the drawer of her dressing table and took out Nazia's pocket diary. She flipped through the pages, carelessly twisting the book's spine, and settled on an entry scrawled in red ink.

My life is a story with many narrators, each with a different perspective on what matters and what doesn't. When I die, I want all those narrators to be heard.

Naureen closed the pocket diary, pressed it against her fingers and returned to rubbing night cream on the skin below her cheekbone.

Just then, Asfand barged into their bedroom in a frenzy. 'You're making a mistake, Noori,' he said.

His unexpected remark exasperated Naureen. *Was he eavesdropping on my conversation with Sorayya?* she wondered.

'How can you let that girl serve the guests while wearing Nazia's sari?' Asfand snapped, confirming her suspicions. 'I don't know what you're trying to achieve with this party on Saturday night. But this is getting all too unnerving. I—'

'You're sticking your nose in matters that have nothing to do with you,' she said. 'I shouldn't have expected any less from you. After all, you had the audacity to stick your cock where it didn't belong for almost fifteen years.'

'Enough, Noori!' Asfand hollered.

'I've told you not to interfere,' she replied sternly. 'I'm simply following my sister's instructions. Why don't you understand what I'm trying to do?'

'Your sister is dead,' he said. 'You have to stop paying attention to the instructions that she left in that diary. You can't possibly know what she wanted through a notebook.'

'Oh, now I should ignore her commands, huh, Asfand? I'm sure you knew what she wanted,' Naureen said, staring at his reflection in the mirror. 'You thought I didn't know what the two of you were up to. But I did.'

'You're the one who let it continue,' Asfand said softly, as if he were disclosing a secret. 'You could have stopped us.'

Naureen rose from the dressing table, flared her nostrils and moved towards the bed. 'You're right,' she said, as she lay down and switched off the table lamp. '*I* should have stopped you. How silly of me to expect my husband to know that he shouldn't cheat on his wife – and that, too, with her own sister!'

'Noori, stop being so dramatic.'

Naureen threw herself into the comfort of her pillow, burying her face deep into its belly. Asfand walked slowly to the airy veranda and lit himself a cigarette in an attempt to calm his nerves. A short while later, the sound of Naureen sobbing morphed into that of her gently snoring instead, reminding Asfand of his wife's unsettling presence, her anger over his past mistakes.

Conflicts and Condolences

Sorayya sat on a thin patch of manicured grass, its stubble pricking against the soft skin of her hands. The *pallav* of Nazia's red sari was carelessly flung behind her. An ant had crawled up to her shoulders, but Sorayya wasn't troubled by the tingling sensation that coursed through her back. The evening sky, mottled with patches of pink and grey, held her in a trance and she momentarily forgot how uncomfortable she felt in her sari.

'Stupid girl,' Bi Jaan snarled at her from the servant quarters. The old housekeeper waddled down to the garden and waved her hands in the air.

Sorayya lowered her head and spun it towards her aunt, the spell broken.

'Why are you sitting on the grass?' Bi Jaan said, her tone becoming more menacing as she drew closer to Sorayya. 'You'll ruin Nazia Apa's red sari. How can you be so careless? Do you know how much she cherished this sari? She insisted on wearing it at her wedding, even though her mother was against the idea.'

'It's not Nazia Apa's sari anymore!' Sorayya exclaimed, waving her hands in the air, as if batting away Bi Jaan's words. 'It belongs to me, now. Don't I look like a heroine from an Indian film?'

'Don't ruin the sari by sitting on grass!' Bi Jaan barked, pulling her niece up from the ground and brushing off any traces of dirt from her sari. 'I need to do your hair. Nazia Apa loved her bouffant hairdo. Come on, don't waste my time. I want to see you inside our room in less than a minute.'

Bi Jaan detected an edge to her voice that irked her as she walked over to the servant quarters. In her long years of service, the old housekeeper had dutifully complied with Naureen's dictum, leaving any qualms she may have had in a secret corner of her heart. But Nazia Apa's death had forced Bi Jaan to question her allegiances and doubt her employer's intentions, albeit silently.

'Now, remember,' Bi Jaan said, as she combed Sorayya's hair in the scant room of the servant quarters, where they sat on the *charpoy* that functioned as their bed, sofa and dining table, 'Naureen Bibi wants you to serve tea to the guests and then sit in Nazia Apa's room.'

The housekeeper was alarmed by the calmness with which her employer had issued these orders. They seemed foreign and formidable – rules that could be neither bent nor broken.

'Why does she want me to do that?' Sorayya questioned, echoing her aunt's unspoken concern. 'All of this sounds very odd.'

'You'll do as you're told,' Bi Jaan said, instantly regretting her sternness. 'Don't you want to stay in this house?'

Sorayya inhaled deeply and closed her eyes, holding her breath for a moment before exhaling and opening her eyes once more. She caught a glimpse of herself in the small mirror that hung from a rusted nail in the wall.

'I've never worn a sari before,' she confided to her aunt. 'What if I can't walk in it?'

'Nazia Apa asked me the same thing on her wedding day,' Bi Jaan giggled. 'I told her that she should listen to her mother and wear the *jora* they had paid that famous designer Bunto Kazmi a fortune to prepare for the event. What Pakistani bride wears a sari at her wedding, anyway? But she was adamant. She told me that the sari belonged to Saleem Sahib's mother and *dulha mian* wanted her to wear it.'

The old housekeeper trailed off as she shared trivial details about Nazia's wedding day. From the glint in her aunt's eyes, Sorayya realised that Bi Jaan shared a connection with Nazia that went beyond the petty arguments she'd had with her. Before bitterness settled like an intruder into their relationship, there had been love. Was it so difficult to celebrate that love with a party, instead of mourning Nazia's loss?

*

'Are you sure you won't stand out?' Farid whispered as they parked the silver Civic outside Naureen's house. 'I don't know if it's in good taste to wear an emerald-green sari to a funeral.'

Dolly rummaged through her purse, pulled out a strip of Panadol, popped a pill and washed it down with a sip of water from the steel thermos she always kept in the car. 'Don't be silly,' she said, raising her head and frowning at him. 'Noori said this isn't a funeral. She called it a farewell party for Nazia.'

'Sounds like a load of crap, to me,' Farid commented. 'I've never heard of such a thing. Who else is going to be there?'

'Noori mentioned six people were invited,' Dolly said. 'I'm told Pino will be attending. I'm not sure about Sabeen, though. I've heard through the grapevine that the poor thing is still offended about not being invited to her mother's burial. Saleem might show up too.'

'Saleem?' Farid said, his hand tightly clutching his forehead. 'I didn't know ex-husbands were invited to such affairs. Who else?'

'Noori didn't mention who the other guest was,' Dolly responded. 'She said it's a surprise.'

'No funeral, a party with a surprise! *Wah!*' Farid tossed his hands in the air in confusion.

Dolly patted his knee in a conciliatory gesture, but her eyes wore a look that betrayed her misgivings. After thirty years of marriage and two prodigal children, Farid had become more unbearable than he was before. Over the years, she had learned, with much difficulty, how to curb his foul temper. But, as her husband inched towards old age, Dolly realised that she could no longer use the same tactics to appease him. Farid's mood swings now verged on a quiet aggression that terrified her. Dolly had to put herself through the ordeal of unlearning her old ways, upsetting the practised rhythm of her married life.

'I thought we were going to pay our respects,' Farid said, after a pregnant pause. 'It sounds odd to have a surprise, as well as a party, at a time of tragedy.'

'Let's not be critical; let's go along with it for Nazia,' Dolly said, choked with emotion. 'We owe her a last goodbye.'

Farid opened the car door, pressed his hands against his ear to blot out the cacophony of traffic, walked towards the wrought-iron gates and rang the bell. *You need to say goodbye to her*, he told himself. *She never let you say goodbye to her after you betrayed her.*

*

Parveen Shah was happily ensconced on the black Natuzzi sofa in Naureen's high-ceilinged drawing room. Clad in a white kaftan, with a string of pearls dangling from her wide neck, she looked like a woman who was accustomed to death – or, at least, knew how to dress for it. Sabeen sat next to her in a beige shalwar kameez, her ash-brown tresses tied into a messy ponytail draping over her slender shoulders. She silently inspected the room where she had, as a teenager, seen her mother locked in Asfand Uncle's embrace. Naureen Aunty may have redecorated the drawing room, replacing the hand-carved settees with leather-upholstered Italian sofas, but Sabeen still remembered the exact spot where she had seen them – next to the wooden floor lamp. She had seen them in other parts of the house as well, but had never dared to confront her mother about it. In all these years, Naureen hadn't removed that lamp from its place near the window. Its presence made Sabeen nervous.

'What a tragedy, Noori,' Parveen said. 'Nazia was my childhood friend. Remember the time when we made a tent under the palm trees in your old house in PECHS? Nazia threw the both of us out and declared that she was the queen of the tent.' She paused to sip from her wine glass.

The hint of a smile flashed on Naureen's face and just as quickly disappeared.

'She did the same to us later in life, too.' Parveen nudged Naureen and let out a shrill laugh. 'She had no qualms about stealing our men.'

Our men? Naureen wondered, startled by the comment.

As she spoke, Parveen wished that she could take back her words. She should have bitten her tongue before making such an irresponsible statement about Asfand. After all, Nazia's affair with him was little more than salacious gossip that was discussed in the drawing rooms of their friends and neighbours.

'Go easy on the wine, Pino,' Naureen whispered into Parveen's ear. 'Have some consideration for Sabeen. What will she think? The poor girl's mother has just died. The least you can do is show some respect.'

'Don't worry,' Parveen said, her guilt forgotten. 'She knows what her mother was like. She can take care of herself – can't you, Sabeen?'

Naureen winced. How could Pino be so insensitive?

As if to escape Parveen's scrutiny, Sabeen shot to her feet and walked towards the door. 'Can I go upstairs?' she said, turning back to face her aunt. 'Is Mama's room still where it used to be?'

Naureen nodded, stunned that her niece would ask her for permission to walk around the house she had grown up in. 'Nothing has changed since you left this house, my child,' she said with motherly warmth. 'Go ahead – you're no stranger to our home.'

Naureen waited for the sound of Sabeen's shoes to subside before she turned back to Parveen and berated her.

'Are you out of your mind, Pino?' she said, with a scowl painted on her face. 'Why must you insist on making that poor girl's mother seem like a bloody villain?'

'Because she was,' a voice rose from the entrance of the drawing room.

Naureen spun around towards the door.

'She's a villain for having left us,' Dolly said, tears flowing like small rivulets down her cheeks.

Farid stood behind his wife as she sobbed, flushed with embarrassment at her sudden outpouring of grief, wondering why she couldn't be more stoic and composed instead of being so unabashedly sentimental.

'Hello, Dolly, darling,' Naureen said, rising from the sofa to hold her guest in a comforting embrace. 'We've been expecting you. How are you, Farid?'

'Not too bad,' he replied, his hands pressed against his belt. 'I'm so sorry to hear about Nazia. How did it happen?'

'She died in her sleep.'

'What a way to go,' Parveen said, taking another swig from her glass. 'And there's no better way to remember her than through a party like this. I always cringe at the sight of *janazas*. Who needs to see all that morbid stuff? Crying over death distracts people from the flavours of life. It's best to celebrate death, not get bogged down by it. *Haina?*'

'I see you've had an early start on the booze, Pino,' Farid laughed.

Dolly mopped her tears with a handkerchief and smiled a little. *Farid seems to be going along with everything amiably*, she thought. *I just hope it stays that way.*

'The tea will be ready soon,' Naureen said. 'Pino thinks it's too hot to have chai and requested a glass of wine.'

'I can't do without my red wine in this heat,' Parveen chuckled.

Dismissing her remark with a frown, Naureen signalled to her guests to take a seat.

Spurned by her hostess, Parveen shifted her focus towards examining the folds of Dolly's sari. Wasn't she a bit overdressed for an event like this? Parveen wondered.

'Where's your husband, Naureen?' Dolly asked.

'I think he's checking on the generator,' Naureen said. 'Load-shedding has started once again in Karachi, particularly in this weather. I don't want Nazia's farewell party to be ruined by a power cut.'

'It's tough to mourn in summer,' Parveen piped up, dismissively waving her hand in the air. '*Waise*, Dolly, I love your outfit. It's very ... colourful.'

Naureen flinched with anger. Dolly self-consciously folded her arms over her chest, protecting herself from Parveen's harsh scrutiny of her attire.

'I was going to wear my new purple suit from Élan,' Parveen sighed. 'But I couldn't insult Nazia by dressing extravagantly at her memorial party.'

Dolly lowered her head in embarrassment and fidgeted with her silver bracelet. Parveen's snide remark smoldered in her heart, but she didn't attempt to retaliate. *I am here for Nazia*, she told herself. Tonight, those five words were a balm for her restless thoughts.

'I think it looks lovely on you,' Naureen said, tapping Dolly's knee and smiling reassuringly.

'Whose idea was it to have a party instead of a funeral?' Farid asked. 'I think it's absolutely brilliant. You must have saved a fortune.'

'Don't say that, Farid,' Dolly responded, mortified by her husband's insensitive remark, especially after their conversation in the car on the way over.

Naureen stared impassively at her guests and heaved a loud sigh to indicate her displeasure. Farid's smugness was irritating, but hospitality prevented her from telling him off.

'I think you did the right thing,' Parveen's voice ricocheted through the drawing room. 'People spend so much on funerals, these days. They're such impersonal affairs. You can't even grieve openly.' She paused, tilted her neck back and chugged her wine, leaving red drops on her chin. 'Mrs Sadiq, my neighbour, attended a male colleague's funeral, some weeks ago,' she continued, sloppily rubbing her knuckles against her lips. 'They had worked together for twenty-nine years at the bank and had become good friends. But poor Mrs Sadiq just couldn't cry at the funeral. She didn't want her colleague's wife to become suspicious. As it is, Mr Sadiq is the jealous sort and had insisted on accompanying her to the funeral. Imagine what he would think if he found his wife crying at some other man's funeral!'

Naureen guffawed happily as she heard the story. Something about Mrs Sadiq's dilemma seemed to make her lose her equanimity and urbane refinement. Had she been hosting a funeral, such behaviour would have been frowned upon as a sign of disrespect towards the deceased. But this was different. Through her unconventional demands, Nazia had released her from the constraints of mourning and its etiquettes. For the first time, Naureen admired Nazia's benevolence: the freedom that her death had provided them. She could be herself, or whoever else she wanted to be.

'Are you writing anything new?' Dolly asked Parveen, giving Naureen the time and space to recover from her fit of laughter.

'I ... I am,' Parveen stammered. 'It's still a work in progress. I'm not sure where the story will take me. For now, I'm just writing.' *This woman has some nerve*, she thought in her drunken stupor. *She knows perfectly well that I haven't written anything since her publishing house dropped me.*

'That's nice,' Dolly said, smiling. 'I just hope you've moved on from writing those dreadful fables from Sindh. You should start writing like Nazia did. Her books are racy, complex and funny. I simply adored her previous novel, *Cold War* – the one about Karachi's high-society neuroses. She truly knew how to write realistic characters.' Dolly turned to Farid and gently tapped his knees. 'Did you know Nazia sent me her manuscript last month? It's such a beautiful novel. I'm going to publish it next year.'

Farid acknowledged her comment with a smirk that belied his agitation.

Parveen placed her wine glass on the coaster laid on a wooden table. How could Dolly compare Parveen's eloquent words with Nazia's patchy narratives? She wrote modern-day renditions of Sindhi folklore, whereas Nazia's work was laced with accounts of people who lived on the 'right side' of Clifton Bridge. There was no plausible basis for a comparison between Parveen's fables and Nazia's trashy novels. Parveen believed that she was a far better writer, even though she hadn't earned the recognition and praise that Nazia had received for her work.

'Nazia mentioned it to me once,' she lied.

'Is that so?' Dolly said in disbelief. 'I'm surprised that she even spoke to you, after ...' Before she could continue, Dolly noticed that Parveen's hard face had turned ashen with rage, and she quickly bit her tongue.

'Tell us what it's about, Dolly,' Naureen said. 'She was very secretive about her writing. I was curious about her new book, but she'd never tell me anything.'

Why would Nazia tell you, anyway? Dolly thought. *You and your husband always gave her so much trouble.*

'It's about three men who fall in love with the same woman,' Dolly said. 'Nazia explores the woman's relationship with the women who love these men.'

Farid pulled out his phone and squinted as he checked his messages. He rose from his seat, pressed his phone against his ear, shouted a brisk 'Hello' into the receiver and plodded out of the room. As he slammed the door behind him, he moved the phone away from his ear and placed it in his pocket. Perspiration trickled down his forehead and soaked the rim of his glasses. He nervously removed the spectacles and dabbed them with a handkerchief.

Am I one of the men Nazia has written about? Farid asked himself as he placed his handkerchief back in his pocket. After taking a few deep breaths, he dismissed his fears as the product of his guilty conscience – the paranoia that had stayed with him ever since he fell in love with Nazia. Dolly wouldn't publish the book if it was about my affair with Nazia, he told himself.

Farid exhaled loudly and began pressing the keys on his phone, reluctant to go back into the room and hear people speak about the alleged secrets and lies that Nazia had weaved into her final book.

Back in the drawing room, the conversation veered in the direction that Farid had expected it to go.

'I can't wait to read her last novel,' Parveen said with an enthusiastic grin that disguised her apprehensions about Nazia's book. 'But it sounds slightly autobiographical, don't you think? Or am I reading too much into Dolly's synopsis?'

'Pino!' Naureen bellowed, disapprovingly shaking her head. 'Please don't say such things. Nazia is dead. We ought to respect her and stop dwelling on her mistakes.'

'She isn't wrong,' Dolly said. 'It is semi-autobiographical. And yes, Pino – it's about us.'

'And you'll be publishing this book?' Parveen asked grimly.

'Calm down, Pino,' Dolly said. 'I'm taking out the parts of the book that are untrue.'

Parveen glared at her, unconvinced that Dolly could make Nazia's side of the story palatable for publication. She had a looming fear that the book would omit the injustices Nazia had committed. '*Acha*, and who made you the custodian of truth?' Parveen roared. 'How will you know what the truth is and where she's using her wild imagination?'

'I know that I'm doing the right thing,' Dolly said impatiently. 'Don't you dare try to patronise me just because you're jealous and bitter! Moreover, it's fiction and authors quite rightly let their imaginations fly.'

'Jealous?' Parveen said, aghast at Dolly's accusations. 'I have nothing to be jealous of.'

'But you're bitter,' Dolly growled, pointing a finger at her. 'You're still upset because I rejected those ghastly stories that you wrote. I think you don't realise that readers are better off without your romantic sagas from Sindh. Who cares about your attempts to write a contemporary adaptation of *Umar Marvi*, anyway? People want to read more glamorous stories, these days. What would you know about glamour? You're nothing but a second-rate writer with no grip on reality.'

Dolly's words pulled Parveen deeper into a web of insecurities about her failings as a writer. She shot to her feet, livid at being subjected to yet another bout of cruelty by a woman who found pleasure in demeaning her.

Naureen held her hand and lowered her back down on to the settee. 'Enough, both of you,' she glowered. 'This party is our way of saying goodbye to Nazia. It's no time for us to fight.' She faced Parveen and then turned her head in Dolly's direction. 'After tea, I'll read you the note that she left for us in her pocket diary. I think that'll help us resolve this problem.'

*

Sabeen sat on the rocking chair in her mother's room and peered out of the window at the charcoal sky. Tears swam in her kohl-rimmed eyes, but didn't flow down her cheeks. Her mother's room hadn't changed. The wooden bed rested against the bumpy orange walls of the room. A pink bed sheet had been neatly tucked into the mattress and covered with the matching pink duvet Nazia had bought from a shop at Zainab Market during one of their secret excursions when Sabeen was a child and Saleem was still part of their life.

'Pink is my favourite colour,' Nazia had told her four-year-old daughter, while haggling with the shopkeeper. 'This will look great in our bedroom.'

But this wasn't the room for which they had bought the duvet and bed sheets. That bedroom existed in a house that no longer belonged to them. The only claim Sabeen had to that room was through a hazy childhood memory of her mother sprawled on the bed at night, with a pillow wedged below her elbow and her feet tucked into a quilt, waiting for Saleem to return home. Sabeen would lie next to her in deep sleep, woken only by the sound of the door creaking like a mischief of mice when her father walked into the room. She could vividly recall a conversation her parents had on one of these nights.

'Where have you been?' Nazia had said with the vehemence of someone who had lost all patience.

'We were deciding our next move,' he'd responded with rehearsed poise. 'Things haven't been the same for some years now, especially after those false Jinnahpur maps were found and that army major claimed he was kidnapped by the MQM. Don't you remember when they captured more party members after they discovered the party's armed caches and torture chambers? Things will get worse, Nazia. We're not sure who'll be their next target.'

Before Nazia could reply, Sabeen had fallen asleep. Much like her relationship with her mother, the conversation had been abruptly cut short.

Unlike Sabeen's childhood room, Nazia's bedroom brought back dark memories that were difficult to overlook. It was another facet of her childhood that Sabeen could not forget. Once, she had woken up to find her mother hugging Asfand near the door. Still young, she didn't know how to broach the subject with her mother and resorted to a long spell of silence that ultimately strained their relationship. As she sat in her mother's room, Sabeen realised she would now remember this room as the place where her mother had spent her final days.

Unnerved by this cold fact, she stared at her reflection in the mirror, her cheeks now glistening with tears, her deep brown eyes bloodshot. Sabeen tried to push away the dark memories with some happy childhood recollections of this room, but couldn't.

'Sabeen,' a shrill voice broke her reverie. 'Is that you?'

She turned to face the door and smiled as Bi Jaan staggered towards her, arms outstretched, and hugged her.

'How are you, *beti*?' the housekeeper asked, sobbing incessantly. 'I just can't believe it. She was so young.'

'I know, Bi Jaan,' Sabeen said, hugging the housekeeper who had watched her grow from a sprightly girl to a cynical, mistrustful young woman. 'Was she peaceful when she died?'

'I don't know,' Bi Jaan said. 'She was very troubled after you left her and moved to Parveen Bibi's house.'

Sabeen nodded, uncertain about how she should respond to this remark. When she was a child, Bi Jaan had been her carer, the woman who could understand her silences and comfort her with a quick glance, a joke or a fable filled with all the trappings of reality to put the young girl's anxieties to rest. Her nurturing ways led Sabeen to believe, or at least imagine, that Bi Jaan was her real mother – a tendency that had always irked Nazia.

'Why did you leave?' Bi Jaan asked with an accusing look in her eye. 'She didn't deserve that.'

Sabeen kissed the housekeeper's forehead and allowed the tears to stream down her face. Just then, she heard a gruff voice – 'Bi Jaan, can you give us a minute?' – dangerous yet familiar. Her knees stiffened and her heart raced with the fear of a confrontation.

The old woman freed herself from Sabeen's embrace and scurried out of the room.

'Hello, Asfand,' Sabeen said, her low pitch making her appear calmer than she really was.

'Since when do you call me by my name?' Asfand said, gazing into her eyes to spot any trace of her tears. 'What became of Asfand Uncle? You seem to have forgotten how to respect your elders. I'm guessing Pino has something to do with this.'

'Don't drag Pino Aunty into this. How dare you demand respect from me when all you've ever done is disrespect me and my mother?'

'I have no idea what you're talking about,' Asfand said. 'I think that Pino is poisoning your mind against me.'

'Pino Aunty has done nothing wrong,' Sabeen answered firmly. 'You were the one who was wrong.'

'Oh, come on,' Asfand sneered. 'Must you be so harsh with me? You're not a child anymore, Sabeen. I think you should do away with all these senseless theories you've concocted about me and your mother. All of us must grow up at some point.'

'I think you're the one who needs to grow up, Asfand *Uncle*,' she snapped at him. 'Why don't you begin by explaining why I wasn't asked to attend my own mother's burial?'

Asfand buried his face in his hands and let out a loud groan. 'I knew I'd be blamed for this,' he said, clicking his tongue and holding his brow below his receding hairline to express his discontent. 'Sabeen, *beti*, your mother wanted it to be this way. Nazia told your Naureen Aunty that she didn't want a funeral. She wanted a quiet burial and then a party.'

'I don't care what she wanted or didn't. I'm her daughter. I had every right to be present when they buried her. In fact, I had more of a right to attend the burial than you, or even Naureen Aunty.'

'Don't take your anger out on your aunt, Sabeen,' Asfand said. 'She's been through a lot.'

'I'll say,' she sneered at him. 'She's suffered enough with a husband like you, who couldn't keep his hands off her older sister.' Unwilling to let him respond to her accusations, Sabeen stormed out of the room.

Asfand inhaled deeply, threw himself on the bed and closed his eyes. 'Nazia is d-dead,' he said, stuttering as the words fell out of his mouth. 'I have to put this behind me.' With that, tears streamed down his face and gathered in a wet patch under his chin. It didn't take long for his silent tears to morph into audible sobs. Asfand knew then that he was mourning a loss that he could never acknowledge

– at least not publicly. His brief conversation with Sabeen had drawn him out of the dense grove of fantasies he had nursed about Nazia for all these years. Sabeen had questioned his motives and carelessly ignored the fact that he had loved her mother deeply. She had made him seem like a troublemaker, a casual interloper who had shattered all traces of calm in Nazia's sheltered world. For Sabeen, Asfand had no claim to her estranged mother's memory. He was the villain of their story, who didn't deserve even a smidgen of sympathy.

But Sabeen doesn't know the truth about my relationship with her mother, Asfand thought, convinced, especially in death, that theirs was a mutually sought-out affair.

'Asfand!' Naureen thundered from the upstairs lounge.

When he heard her approaching the room, Asfand hurriedly wiped his tears, rose from the bed and smoothed out the creases he'd left on the duvet.

'What are you doing here, Asfand?' Naureen asked as she entered the room. 'We have guests over for the party. Farid has been asking about you for such a long time.'

'I'm just coming, Noori,' Asfand said, suddenly calmer than he was before. He walked over to the window and peered out at the dark sky. 'This room was getting a bit stuffy,' he said, as he reached out for the lock on the window. 'I just wanted to open—'

'Let it be,' Naureen rebuked her husband. 'There's no need to open the windows. Sorayya will be sitting in here. You just come down … it's getting late—'

'Noori,' Asfand interrupted her. 'Are you sure you know what you're doing? That girl will steal Nazia's pearls if you leave her in this room alone.'

'Stop worrying,' she said petulantly. 'Just come downstairs. I think I saw Saleem Bhai enter through the gate.'

'He's coming too? Noori, you've got to be kidding me! Do you realise how awkward this party is going to get?'

Pretending she hadn't heard him, Naureen left the room in a restless huff. Asfand noticed that his wife seemed nervous – like an actor who was performing on stage for the first time.

Reunion in Death

Saleem gave himself a quick look in the mirror next to the entrance and self-consciously tucked a wisp of his silver locks behind his ear. In the early days of their marriage, Saleem had tied his shoulder-length mane into a neat ponytail to avoid a severe reprimanding from his wife.

'Men look shabby with long hair,' she would tease him, stroking the split-ends of his curls with her fingers. 'You should crop it short. I'm surprised Altaf Bhai hasn't told you to get a haircut.'

At first, Saleem was tempted to scold her for making such a shallow remark about Bhai – his misunderstood messiah, who was struggling to ensure the well-being of a disillusioned Mohajir community. His wife's casual cynicism made him acutely aware of how little she knew about his struggle and motives. Had she probed deeper, Saleem would have told her more about the cause that kept him away from home and how it was rooted in decades of oppression.

He would have told her about his older brother, who was disparagingly called *hindustani* by the Sindhi elite during his days at Sindh University, because his family migrated from North India after Partition. Saleem would have mentioned his brother's struggle to safeguard his cultural identity by refusing to take his exams in Sindhi instead of Urdu. Had Nazia asked him questions, she would have learned about Saleem's early days at Karachi University, when he joined the All-Pakistan Mohajir Student Organisation and took an oath to protect Mohajirs against exploitation. She would have known how students had taunted him when he asked them for donations for the organisation. From the outset, there had been so much that Nazia just didn't know or attempt to understand about Saleem.

When Nazia's remarks became more frequent and were followed by playful laughter, Saleem realised there was no malice in her observations. Sometimes, he would feign outrage at her jokes and the two of them would break into childish giggles. Swayed by the persistence of Nazia's lighthearted comments, Saleem agreed to a compromise and fastened his unruly tresses with one of his wife's elasticated hairbands. But this was long before their happy marriage had been eclipsed with sadness. Circumstances were different now that his past loyalties toward the MQM had eroded and Nazia was dead.

Since he and Nazia hadn't been together in years, Saleem didn't feel the need to follow her standards of propriety. But, as he strolled into Naureen's drawing room, Saleem had a nagging suspicion that, if Nazia had been alive and still cared about him, she wouldn't have been pleased to see his hair growing like tall thickets of grass in an untrimmed lawn. Though her jokes about

Altaf Bhai would seem irrelevant at a time when the MQM no longer reigned over Karachi, Nazia would have found a way to scold him for letting his hair fall clumsily down his neck.

'Hello everyone,' Saleem said as he walked into the drawing room.

'Well, well, if it isn't the ex-husband,' Parveen mocked Saleem, desperately trying to conceal the fact that she was delighted to see him. 'I'm surprised you came.'

'Don't be rude, Pino,' Naureen said, rising from her seat to greet Saleem. 'Welcome, Saleem Bhai. Thank you for coming. I hope you didn't have any trouble finding the place.'

Naureen hasn't changed at all, Saleem thought. *She's still as cordial as she was the day I married her sister.* 'I haven't been here since the nineties,' he said, holding her in a tight embrace. 'By the time I crossed Ghani Sons, I forgot which side of Sunset Boulevard your house was on.'

'Maybe, if you'd visited us more, you wouldn't have lost your way,' Sabeen said.

Saleem turned to his daughter, his eyes gleaming with delight. 'Sabeen,' he said, his heart galloping at a feverish pace. 'Is that you? I haven't seen you since you were a little girl. You'll turn twenty-seven in September, right?'

'October.'

'Of course.' Saleem gently slapped his forehead. 'I meant—'

'It's all right,' Sabeen cut in. 'I don't expect you to remember my birthday.'

'Don't say that, Sabeen. You're my daughter and I love you. Besides, the year you were born was tough for me.'

'Is that supposed to make me feel better? That excuses everything, does it?' Sabeen scoffed.

Parveen rose from the sofa and stood behind Sabeen, though it wasn't clear if she was trying to prevent her from attacking her father or protecting her from Saleem.

Sensing the accelerating tension in the room, Naureen made every attempt to distract her guests from the drama she feared would ruin the entire evening. 'Sorayya, bring the tea already!' she called out, her eyes transfixed on Saleem's crestfallen face.

In her clumsy curiosity, Dolly sat up on her seat and cast a sideways look at Sabeen, her father and the woman who once loved him, eagerly awaiting their next move. While Dolly had heard about the conflict between Parveen and Nazia that had left many unsuspecting victims in its wake, she had never witnessed it so closely. Now, as the drama was about to unfold before her, she couldn't resist the temptation to pry.

Reluctant to allow a brief confrontation between father and child to become the source of malicious gossip, Asfand hurriedly pulled out his packet of Dunhill Switch and offered a cigarette to Farid.

'So, how's the newspaper business?' he said. 'I've heard Imran Khan has really muzzled the press with his new policies. Has that affected you?'

'Oh, yes – the price of government ads has been reduced,' Farid said, blowing grey smoke rings that vanished into the air. His animated voice distracted Dolly. She turned to her husband and watched his frown disappear as he began a tirade on the media crisis. Farid was never so chatty at home. Even when the children were back in Karachi for their vacations and their house was clamouring with laughter and loud chatter, her husband found any excuse to remain in his study and avoid having a conversation with them. Could he possibly be having a good time?

Naureen smiled at her husband, grateful for his efforts to divert Farid's attention. With his gaze on Naureen, Asfand nodded as Farid spoke, took a generous puff of his cigarette and winked at his wife.

Saleem dragged his daughter by her arm out of the drawing room and into a secluded, sparsely furnished corner of the downstairs lounge. Parveen lurked behind Sabeen like a bodyguard, unwilling to let her speak to her father without any supervision.

'Can you give us some privacy, Pino?' Saleem said, when he saw her standing behind his daughter. 'I think Sabeen and I need to clear the air.'

'I'm sorry,' Parveen said, holding her wine glass in her left hand as she tipsily placed her right arm around Sabeen's shoulder. 'Sabeen's my responsibility. And I need to protect her from people who can harm her.' As the words spewed out of her mouth, Parveen noticed how unusual they sounded, almost as though someone else had uttered them. For a moment, she feared the sudden onset of a maternal instinct towards Sabeen. It took a few seconds for her to dismiss these new feelings and remind herself that she was here to protect herself, not anyone else.

'I'm her father,' Saleem retorted, turning to face his daughter. 'Don't listen to this woman, Sabeen. She didn't approve of your mother's marriage to me. And now she wants to shut me out of your life too.'

'Saleem,' Parveen responded curtly, 'why would I do such a thing? I've never meant to harm you or Nazia.'

Parveen knew that this wasn't the truth. If there was anyone who'd harmed Nazia – deliberately or otherwise – it was her. But she didn't feel guilty for being dishonest. With time, her lies had emboldened her, giving her the strength to survive the onslaughts of people who had only disappointed her. Parveen's obsession with Saleem had made her immune to the cruel things people said to and about each other.

'Sabeen,' her father said, 'you must hear what I have to say. Please don't jump to conclusions without listening to me—'

'Stop badgering her,' Parveen cut in. 'She's capable of making her own choices. And she has decided not to listen to what you have to say.'

Sabeen strode back into the drawing room, unwilling to prolong her conversation with a father who had walked out on her without any qualms. This was her chance to repay him in the same currency: to flee when he needed her the most.

'You've got some nerve,' Saleem said to Parveen. 'My daughter deserves to know the truth. You've corrupted her mind against both her parents. I still don't understand why you're doing this. All I know is that it's downright petty and despicable. I'll see to it that you—'

'Why did you choose her over me?' Parveen interrupted him, her words veiled in a sadness that had brewed within her for years.

'What do you mean?' Saleem said, perplexed by her question. 'Who did I choose over you?'

'Nazia – who else? Why did you marry her instead of me?'

'Is this why you've turned my daughter against her parents?' Saleem replied softly. 'Are you poisoning my daughter's mind against me because I broke our engagement all those years ago?'

'Don't be silly,' Parveen said, taking a sip from her glass and seductively stroking a finger against Saleem's chest. 'It was my way of being closer to you. I wanted to win you over.'

'You're insane,' he spat out. 'I'm surprised that you don't know why I chose her over you. She was intelligent, witty and charming. You were dull, foolish and deluded.'

'If she was so perfect, why did you leave her?' Parveen lashed out at him.

Saleem drew a deep breath and plopped himself on a nearby settee. Parveen placed her wine glass on a teak table and watched his face turn pale with worry.

'I had no choice,' he said in a fierce baritone. 'The party was …'

Saleem stopped speaking when he heard the glass door of the lounge open with a thud. Naureen emerged from the room and threw them a puzzled glance.

'What's going on over here?' she said as she walked over to them.

Saleem mumbled an apology for arguing with Parveen in the drawing room. Though Parveen remained silent, Naureen threw a suspicious look at her, wary of her scheming ways.

'Please don't forget that you're here for Nazia.' Naureen glowered at Parveen. 'She wanted this party for a reason. Stop quarrelling and come back into the drawing room. I don't want the two of you to argue in front of Dolly and Farid.'

'Why?' Parveen said, holding up her glass and taking another sip from it. 'It's not like they don't know what's happening. They knew Nazia very well. I doubt they'll discover anything that surprises them.'

'Pino, what's wrong with you?' Naureen retorted, snatching Parveen's wine glass. 'You've been drinking all evening and talking nonsense. Go back into the drawing room. We're serving tea.'

Outraged by Naureen's audacity, Parveen sneered at Saleem and hurriedly wandered back towards the glass door. Before going through, she spun around to face Saleem and scowled at him. Parveen only went into the drawing room when Naureen, with her lips pursed and eyes glaring, pointed a finger at her and then at the drawing room entrance.

'Maybe I shouldn't have come,' Saleem said. He took out a handkerchief from his pocket and wiped it against his clammy forehead.

'Nazia wanted you here,' Naureen said, with a lopsided smile that made Saleem question whether she was happy to see her brother-in-law after so long. 'You have no reason to worry.' Continuing in a different tone, she added, 'You really need to start ignoring her, Saleem Bhai. She'll make constant attempts to provoke you today. She seems to be in a foul mood.'

'I'm sorry. It's just that she's turned Sabeen against me. How can you expect me to stay quiet?'

'Try not to respond to her cruel remarks,' she said evenly. 'We'll find a way to win Sabeen over – together. For now, let's have some tea.'

Reassured by her level-headedness, Saleem hurried back into the drawing room to join the other guests. Naureen trailed behind him, stopping at intervals to guzzle down the remnants of wine in Parveen's glass. Tonight, she would need a little Dutch courage to survive the chaos that Nazia's guests had brought into her home. If she wanted her guests to get along, Naureen would need to step out of her shell and take charge.

'Nazia's letter will distract them from all their grievances,' she murmured. 'I just need to deal with all this drama for a few more minutes.'

*

Sorayya entered the drawing room with a tray crammed with cups, a sugar bowl, and a teapot that emitted a faint wisp of steam. Behind her, Bi Jaan wheeled in a serving trolley loaded with plates of samosas and chicken cutlets, a platter of club sandwiches with toothpicks jabbed into them, and a serving bowl filled with spaghetti bolognese.

'Oh my!' Parveen said smugly. 'Did you prepare this meal all by yourself, Noori? If yes, then we have something to worry about.'

Naureen frowned at Parveen in an attempt to silence her. Parveen lowered her gaze and cleared her throat.

'You've certainly gone all out, Naureen,' Dolly said, her mouth agape with wonder. 'You shouldn't have put yourself to the trouble.'

As she handed Dolly a cup and poured her some tea, Sorayya had to fight back the temptation to clarify that Naureen Bibi hadn't slaved away in the kitchen throughout the afternoon to prepare the delicacies. The credit should have gone to Bi Jaan. But Dolly was right about one thing: Sorayya's aunt shouldn't have gone to the trouble of cooking for this party if the lady of the house was going to take all the credit.

'I did nothing,' Naureen said, as she signalled Bi Jaan to pass the plates to the guests. 'That's the advantage of having well-trained staff. They know how to put together a decent meal.'

'The dollar has shot up to over a hundred and fifty-five rupees!' Farid said. 'Imran is losing his grip over the government.'

Stubbing his cigarette into an ashtray, Asfand seized two plates from the housekeeper's hands, offered them to Farid and Saleem, and motioned towards the trolley. Farid rose from the sofa, confident that his views on the PTI government's maiden stint in power would receive loud approbation.

'I'll say,' Saleem said. 'I'm surprised that the party was able to win elections in Karachi and defeat the MQM.'

'Are you?' Parveen said, her words soaked in cynicism. 'Your beloved MQM is dead, my friend. It has been smashed into pieces after the Rangers' operation. Quite frankly, it's payback for terrorising the city for decades with wheel-jam strikes and targeted killings.'

Saleem nodded slowly, unsure if he should defend a political party that he had fallen out of love with.

'I still think Imran has some potential,' Parveen said, as she took a plate from Bi Jaan and spooned out a generous helping of spaghetti.

'I didn't know you were a closet PTI supporter, Pino,' Farid teased her. 'Your late husband Sardar Wajid Ali probably turned in his grave as you said that. Isn't it sacrilege for a PPP supporter to suddenly become a fan of Imran Khan?'

Parveen giggled, her ego unscathed by Farid's banter. 'I'm surprised you journalists can think about any party other than the PTI,' she scoffed. 'All I see on TV and read about in the paper is how Imran is the great saviour.'

'We have no option, Pino,' Farid answered. 'We can't even present critical opinions about the government of the day. It's a tragedy.'

'The only thing that's tragic is how those *youthias* who voted for the PTI are suffering,' Parveen said. 'If we wanted another failed government, we would have stuck with the baldie brothers.'

With her limited grasp over English, Sorayya struggled to understand what they were saying. But the resounding laughter that spread through the room confirmed that Parveen had cracked a joke. She felt the urge to smile because it seemed like the only way she would feel included in something that was foreign yet funny. Instead, Sorayya adjusted her sari, then bent over and handed Saleem a cup with a placid smile.

'Isn't that the sari Nazia wore at our wedding?' Saleem pointed at Sorayya's clothes, suppressing the urge to accuse her of theft. 'The one that belonged to my mother.'

'Nazia Apa gifted it to me a few weeks before she died,' Sorayya said, her smile faltering.

'Why would she do such a thing?' Saleem asked indignantly as he took the cup from her. 'She loved that sari. And what about her hair?' He looked to Naureen. 'Who told her to do her hair like Nazia's? This is shocking to me, Naureen!'

'Did you expect her to save her wedding dress from a marriage that didn't even last?' Sabeen asked, with a smirk on her face.

Naureen shot a cold glance at her niece, goading her into silence. When the grin disappeared from Sabeen's face, Naureen felt gratified in the realisation that she had finally established the power to control the actions of her guests.

'Nazia was a bountiful woman, Saleem Bhai,' Naureen said. 'She always gave presents to the servants. And Sorayya was her carer, the only woman she could trust. That's probably why she was given the sari. Nazia also wanted Sorayya to have her hair match how she would have worn it with the sari for tonight.'

Saleem's brows twitched in agitation, his eyes fixed upon Sorayya as she poured tea for each guest, appraising her movements with the persistence of a stalker. Sorayya avoided his piercing gaze as she left the drawing room, exulting over the compliment that Naureen Bibi had paid her. But a fresh anxiety swept over her, leaving her head full of questions.

She had harboured the illusion that the red sari was a gift Nazia Apa had decided to give her on a whim. Now, as she climbed the stairs, Sorayya realised that her employer had never done anything that was even remotely impulsive. She knew that Nazia Apa's gift wasn't just a goodwill gesture towards a young girl who had given her company during her final days. It was a calculated step, imbued with hidden meaning and a purpose that Sorayya didn't quite understand. And yet, she wasn't afraid to follow the instructions Naureen Bibi had given her, because she was curious to know how people forgot the dead by celebrating their life, instead of mourning it in the ways custom dictated.

*

'Did you see Saleem Sahib?' Bi Jaan hissed, once Sorayya had clambered up the stairs and was within earshot. 'He was Nazia Apa's husband.'

'I thought as much,' Sorayya said. 'He seems a lot older and very moody. Did you see how he reacted when he saw me wearing the sari and saw my hairdo? Also, was that woman Nazia Apa's daughter?'

'Yes,' Bi Jaan beamed. 'That's Sabeen Beti. I raised her.'

'Phuppo, you seem to have raised everyone,' Sorayya said, with a simpering smile. 'Me, Raqib and Sabeen Bibi. Is there anyone who has been spared from your smothering love?'

'Shush, don't act this way with me,' Bi Jaan said, her face contorted with mock irritation. 'Go to the room and wait for Naureen Bibi.'

Sorayya strolled into the room and sat on a wooden armchair – the only one she had been allowed to sit on by her employer. When Nazia Apa was alive, the young girl would prop herself on the seat and flip through old copies of *Vogue*, staring at pictures of models with long, shapely legs and hair as gold as the wheat fields that stretched for acres in her village. Struggling to sit in her sari, Sorayya slid on to the chair after the third attempt.

'What do I have to do here?' she asked, with a hint of annoyance.

Bi Jaan gazed in awe at how a gangly village girl had transformed into a graceful woman in a single makeover. 'You look just like that Indian film heroine, Madhuri Dixit,' she said, to assuage her niece's concerns with a comfortable distraction.

Sorayya's face shone with a dimpled smile at what she knew was a compliment from her aunt.

'Everything will be fine,' Bi Jaan told her. Despite her confident delivery, she wasn't convinced herself. Brushing away her doubts about Naureen's intentions, she scuttled out of the room and hurried to the kitchen, in case her services were required.

*

'Naureen, I thought you mentioned that six people would be attending the party,' Dolly said, spinning her fork in a plate of spaghetti. 'So far, only Farid, Saleem, Parveen, Sabeen and I have shown up. Who's the sixth person?'

With a long sigh, Naureen rose from the sofa and searched through her purse for Nazia's blue pocket diary.

'Our sixth guest is on his way,' she said, evading Dolly's question. 'He's Nazia's friend. None of you know him.'

'Ah, a mystery!' Parveen chimed excitedly. 'This party just became a lot more interesting.'

'Wait a second,' Asfand said in a deep, authoritative voice. 'Who is this person, Noori? Why is he coming over?'

'Are you hard of hearing, Asfand Mian?' Parveen exclaimed. 'He is Nazia's friend!'

'Noori,' Asfand said, baffled by the aura of secrecy surrounding the surprise guest. 'How does this person know Nazia?'

'He's probably another one of her lovers.' Parveen nudged Dolly and giggled uncontrollably.

'No, Pino,' Naureen said in a tone that made it clear she was frustrated by Parveen's habit of jumping to conclusions. 'He isn't Nazia's lover.'

'Then who is he?' Saleem asked, rising from his seat.

Naureen put on her spectacles, peeled open Nazia's blue pocket diary and gingerly flicked through its pages. 'Nazia left all of us a note to explain everything,' she said. 'This is her way of answering all your questions. I'll read it out and let each of you draw your own conclusions.' She cleared her throat, turned her head to avoid Asfand's perplexed gaze and began reading Nazia's note.

Hello everyone,

I am grateful to all of you for attending this party. I apologise for leaving this world before any of you got a chance to say goodbye to me.

I'm told death is meant to shock you. The pain of losing a loved one courses through your veins like venom, making you uneasy for days, months or even years. My death will, no doubt, shock you because of the circumstances surrounding it and my strange demands. But I don't want anyone to be saddened by my absence for too long.

I suspect that my end will be silent, quick and painless. But don't you worry about me. I've been raised to believe that all of us will go to a happier place. I'm not afraid of death or the ambiguity of the afterlife. I'm prepared to meet my maker. I'm more worried about all of you.

You're probably wondering why I chose to have a party rather than an extravagant funeral. The fact is that I've always hated funerals. I've never felt comfortable attending funerals where women beat their chests and weep profusely. At the risk of sounding silly, I find it somewhat strange that people waste their time mourning the dead. We fail to comprehend that death is a tussle between the present and the future. It demands change. I firmly believe that no sane individual would like to be mourned after his or her death. It appears somewhat egotistical to expect people to put their lives on hold and lament the passing of a friend, a parent, a lover or a loved one for several days. Even the three-day mourning period stipulated in Islam seems a bit excessive.

I've always believed that the dead should be liberated from our memories. Why should we burden them with our thoughts and grievances? If we chain them to our thoughts, we deprive them of a much-needed release from the tyrannies of our world.

Whenever I shared these views with my friends, they called me an orthodox Muslim who is influenced by bearded maulvis, *and they insisted that I should be more considerate towards people who have lost their close relatives and friends to the jaws of death. However, my beliefs have nothing to do with my religion. In fact, they have a pulse of their own.*

Death disconnects us from the world. I see death as a catharsis that allows spirits to free themselves from the shackles of pain that bind us to this world. We must learn to be selfless about death and let our loved ones go without subjecting them to the pain of wounding us with their absence. I've lived all my life witnessing some form of pain in a city that breeds cold-blooded violence. It's time for me to find an exit that doesn't pull me back into this world. As some of you might have guessed, this party is an exorcism of sorts. It's my way of being forgotten.

Naureen, my younger sister, has always been good to me, despite the fact that I constantly created friction between us over trivial matters. I've discussed my thoughts with her and requested that my wishes are adhered to. She's an excellent hostess, so I imagine that you're being taken care of well.

I know what you're thinking at this very moment. You mustn't forget that I've always been perceptive and can guess what people are thinking before they tell me what's troubling them …

A gnawing heaviness seeped into Naureen's heart, and she fell silent. She'd gone through the letter several times to rehearse for this moment, but still stopped before reading the passage where Nazia wrote about their relationship. In that momentary pause, she found herself plunging into the spiral of a loss she had yet to fully mourn.

An awkward, abrupt silence filled the room. Parveen and Saleem exchanged curious glances, while Asfand's brow furrowed with concern.

From the way the diary shook in Naureen's hands, Dolly feared that she would break down. She rose to her feet and made a feeble attempt to hug Nazia's grieving sister, but plopped down on the sofa when Naureen shook her head vigorously and returned to reading the letter.

Naureen, you're probably wondering why I chose you to give effect to my plans. I admit that our relationship was marred by sibling rivalry, the occasional bouts of rage that I directed towards you, and my frequent attempts to violate your trust. But you're my sister and the only person I can trust in these matters. It has taken me a long time to realise that I've overstepped my bounds and outstayed my welcome in your house. I should have moved out a long time ago. After Sabeen left, I intended to find an apartment near Sea View and live the rest of my life in isolation. But my daughter's departure was followed by my stroke.

I kept it a secret from most people because I dreaded the thought of being pitied. You helped me guard this secret. Despite our many differences, you let me remain in your house, which was especially generous at a time when our relationship had turned sour. Over the next few months, I became mean-spirited, irritable and painfully childish. But your kindness didn't wane at any stage. Bi Jaan and Sorayya were also always there to look after me. Now that I'm gone, I want you to forget that you ever had a selfish, overbearing sister, who was nothing more than a liability. I want this party to be a release, an opportunity for you to move on with your life, without being haunted by the memory of my death. I want you, Naureen, to prepare to erase all doubts and grievances that you have against me.

Asfand, I would rather not say what you're thinking. All I can say is that I've wronged you in many ways. My constant presence in your life made it difficult for you to start a life with Naureen. I was the spectre that haunted your marriage. Now, I need you to eject me from all your thoughts. Please don't bind me to this world as the ghost that disturbs your relationship with my sister.

Sabeen, you're probably troubled by my demise, but I doubt that your grief has made you question Pino's version of what happened. I've missed you, Sabeen. You are the reason that I made some key decisions in life. I decided to move in with Naureen Aunty and Asfand Uncle because I wanted to give you a stable home, where you would feel protected. You were much too young to realise why our old house was unsafe for us. Your father had left us, and his 'enemies' kept turning up at our doorstep, issuing threats and demanding money. I couldn't raise you in such an insecure environment. As you grew older, I sensed you harboured hostilities against me for taking you away from your father's home. You became critical of my choices and vilified me. I've invited you here today so you can understand my choices and forgive my indiscretions. I love you, my darling, and have only ever wanted the best for you.

Pino, I'm sure you're heartbroken. We were childhood friends. But there came a time when our friendship became an ordeal. I'm sorry for allowing circumstances to spiral out of control. I should have known better. When I put pen to paper, I warned myself against commenting on how you sullied my reputation to create a rift between me and Sabeen. For that, I will always despise you, Pino. I'm often tempted to forgive you because I, too, have wronged you in the past. But you've done far too much damage to me. I can't possibly free you from blame. You've been invited to this party so that you can understand the root of your bitterness towards me. I'm sorry if my behaviour has upset you in the past. However, I don't think I deserved to be treated in such a cruel manner. I've invited you here so you can attempt to shatter the illusions that have misguided you for all these years. Free yourself, and me, from them.

Saleem, you must be surprised to receive an invite to this party. Many people will have expected you to be excluded from the guest list. But I wanted you to attend for Sabeen's sake. She may be an adult, but she will seek out parental comfort at this time. I want to give you the opportunity to be there for her. It is in your hands, now, to make this relationship work. Secrets were our undoing, Saleem. Initially, you thought I was too young to handle the truth. During those days, I often wondered if you considered me your wife or saw me as a child whose tantrums you had to endure. Though we outgrew these hiccups, fate threw us into another quagmire. I don't think that you've pondered over the nature of our relationship. Saleem, I want you to think about the choices we made in our marriage – not for me, but for Sabeen.

My dearest Durdana, I don't remember how I got into the habit of calling you Dolly. I think it had something to *do with Farid. When I started working at his newspaper, back in the 1990s, he'd always mention his wife Dolly, who ran her own publishing company. He's the one who helped me muster the strength to approach you with the manuscript of my first book. I was pleasantly surprised when you liked my book. Soon, you became my closest friend and confidante. But I ruined our friendship with that one betrayal that I still cannot forget. I wasn't fair to Farid either, and that left cracks in your marriage. I want this party to provide both of you with a chance to repair your relationship and overcome the pain that I put you through. There is another reason why I've invited you to this party, Dolly. Last month, I sent you my last manuscript, titled Three Different Men. I know it is my final book, because I don't have the courage to use words as weapons anymore. As you prepare to put this book out into the world, I want you to understand what it means to me.*

As per my instructions, Naureen will introduce all of you to the sixth guest of the evening once everyone has arrived and has been served tea and something to eat. His name is Salman Narang and he's a hypnotist. Don't mock me. I haven't got myself involved with a charlatan. In fact, he's a trained therapist with a vast repertoire of healing powers. I came across him a few years ago and he has helped me deal with my anxieties. He managed to unlock hidden chambers of my mind and put my fears to rest. Please let him help all of you overcome the negative memories you have of me.

In order to provide you with an incentive to go through with this request, I've left five sealed envelopes with

Naureen that contain three thousand dollars each. My inheritance and life earnings have found their way into those envelopes. I want you to have it all. Before that, I want you to let Salman hypnotise you and release all those negativities you carry against me. If you do this, I'll be able to move into the next world in peace. Each of you is a narrator of my life's story. I want you to relive that story one last time in an attempt to forget me and heal from my mistakes.

Love,

Nazia Sami

Naureen closed her sister's pocket diary and clutched it tight. Rattled by her mother's letter, Sabeen cupped her hand against her mouth, let out a cry and ran out of the room. Parveen, sobered by what she had heard, straightened herself on the sofa and held out her hand in a futile attempt to stop Sabeen.

'This is absurd,' she said indignantly. 'I refuse to believe that Nazia has written this letter.'

A Time to Forget

Asfand walked over to his wife, took the diary out of her hands and read the entry. Tears filled Naureen's eyes as she watched him go through Nazia's diary. She wondered if the tears were fuelled by sorrow over her sister's heartfelt farewell note or her husband's suspicion.

'This is definitely Nazia's handwriting,' Asfand said, as he flicked through the pages of the diary. 'Naureen is telling the truth, Pino. These are Nazia's words.'

'Salman Narang will arrive shortly,' Naureen whispered, sniffling as she spoke. 'I'll give all of you a moment to talk this over. I want you to do this for my sister's sake.' She lowered herself on her haunches and wept.

Dolly adjusted her sari, knelt on the floor with some difficulty and stroked Naureen's hair. 'Let it all out,' she whispered, struggling to avoid the ache in her knees.

Snubbing Dolly's efforts to console her, Naureen got to her feet and scuttled out of the room with an unusual urgency.

'Sabeen,' she said cried out frantically as she flung the door open. 'Where have you gone?'

Asfand ran after her, baffled by the dramatic turn of events.

'All of this is just preposterous,' Parveen grumbled. 'How can we subject ourselves to this charade? This has got to be a practical joke of some sort. How can Nazia expect us to be hypnotised? The Nazia I knew was practical. She would never agree to this nonsense.'

'I don't understand why I was even invited to witness this drama,' Saleem said. 'This makes no sense to me.'

Unwilling to succumb to the hysteria that had plagued the other guests, Farid tapped a few buttons on his phone, drew it closer to his bespectacled face and peered at the screen. 'I've just run a quick Google search,' he said, after staring at his phone for a few minutes. 'I don't quite understand why Nazia would even consider hypnotherapy as a means of controlling our psyche. If Freud struggled to hypnotise his patients, how would a therapist like Salman Narang succeed at it?'

'I doubt Nazia's trying to *control* our psyche,' Dolly said calmly. 'She just wants us to forget all the terrible things she did to us. I think we should go along with it. For Nazia's sake.'

'I hate to say this, but I think you're right, Dolly,' Farid said. 'None of us really believes in all this hypnosis mumbo jumbo. But it sounds intriguing. It could be fun.'

'I didn't realise that we were here to have fun, Farid Mian,' Saleem responded sternly. 'I expected a *Quran khwani*, not some game. This is absolutely outrageous.'

'Let's not get carried away, Dolly,' Parveen chimed in. 'This is clearly a terrible idea. Hypnotism doesn't work.'

'Actually, it does,' Farid said.

The other guests turned towards him in silence, puzzled by the sudden shift in his views on the matter.

'I thought you said Freud failed to hypnotise his patients,' Saleem said. 'How will Salman succeed in hypnotising us?'

'Well, there are countless possibilities,' Farid replied, trying to sound reasonable. 'A few months ago, we ran a story about a gang of thieves who would hypnotise people at various traffic signals across Karachi. According to our reporter, the gang would masquerade as beggars and windshield-cleaners. They carried a piece of cloth with them, which they used to put drivers in a trance. Apparently, they would instruct the drivers to park their cars in a secluded part of the city, where their collaborators would steal their wallets, jewellery and other belongings.'

'Were they ever caught?' Parveen asked, suddenly curious about hypnosis, despite her dismissal of it minutes earlier.

'Many of the victims came out of their trance after a few hours. By then, it was difficult to identify the gang members. So, no, none of them were caught.'

'Perhaps this Salman Narang is one of the gang members,' Parveen said with smug confidence. 'Shouldn't we try to probe further, instead of agreeing to make ourselves his victims? Your wife is wearing all of her fineries, Farid Mian. Do you want her to go home without her jewels?'

'There's no need to get personal, Pino,' Dolly spat at her. 'All you've done since we got here is criticise me. I'm not going to tolerate your nonsense any further.'

'Oh, what are you going to do? You've already dropped me as one of your writers. What's the worst you can do to me now?'

'Ladies, calm down,' Saleem cut in. 'This isn't the time to bicker. We have bigger problems to deal with.'

Parveen sulked, her smiling face sagging with disappointment at being told off by Saleem.

'Farid Mian,' Saleem said, with a strange equanimity to his voice, 'can you ask one of your reporters to do a background check on Salman Narang? Meanwhile, let's tell Naureen that we're going ahead with this plan. When this man tries to hypnotise us, we should go along with it and pretend that we are in a trance. That will give us a chance to keep an eye on what he says and does.'

'And what if there's nothing against him?' Farid said, the pragmatist within him trying to weigh all their options. 'What do we do then?'

'Then we can just pretend to be hypnotised,' Parveen said. 'You heard what Nazia wrote in her letter. If we take part in this nonsense, we'll get an envelope with three thousand dollars. She doesn't say anything about telling the truth while we're at it. I don't think that's a bad bargain.'

'How can you think of money at a time like this?' Dolly quivered with rage. 'Our friend hasn't even been dead a week and you have your eye on her money. That's shameless, Pino.'

'Don't be so self-righteous,' Parveen rebuked her. 'Neither of us is greedy for a measly three thousand dollars. But, as Farid Mian pointed out earlier, the dollar has shot up to over a hundred and fifty rupees. What's that, anyway? Four or five lakhs? That's our reward for agreeing to Nazia's demands.'

Dolly glared at her, unnerved by the indifference with which Parveen was planning to disrespect Nazia's last wishes.

'The money does sound tempting,' Saleem ventured to say, prompting Parveen to assume that he had been thinking about the envelopes stacked with dollars ever since Naureen had read them the letter. She knew then that Saleem had abandoned his feelings for Nazia. Her silent victory brought a smirk to her face.

'Let's find out what we can about Salman Narang,' Saleem said to Farid. 'If this chap has a clean record … well, we'll do it for the money.'

Farid nodded as he dialled a number on his phone. Astounded by the sudden change of heart in the room, he wondered what Nazia would think of Saleem and Parveen's greed for the money she had meticulously placed in envelopes for them. Nazia wouldn't be pleased about being betrayed again, he told himself. But, when his reporter, Sajid, answered his phone and was told to run a quick search on Salman Narang, Farid knew that he too had become an accomplice to this secret, a bystander roped into committing a crime. *Sorry Nazia,* he thought. *I just can't say no.*

'*Wah,*' Parveen said, still reeling in her drunken state. 'We finally get to see Saleem taking charge of a situation like a good politician. Isn't it strange how we think alike? You and I had the same suspicions about Salman Narang, and we were also sharp enough to think about the money Nazia left us in the envelopes.' She sauntered over to the chair Saleem was seated on, leaned against its arm and patted him on his back. 'Maybe, if you'd married me, you wouldn't have had to run away from your family,' she whispered into his ear.

Saleem flared his nostrils in a derisive scoff, not keen on encouraging Parveen's fantasies about their perceived compatibility. But even this gesture had a softness to it that, Parveen felt, was quite uncharacteristic of Saleem. *Is he finally warming up to me?*

'I hope we're doing the right thing,' Dolly said in an impatient voice that extricated Parveen from her thoughts about Saleem. 'I came here for Nazia. I don't want to disrespect her wishes in any way.'

'*Choro*, Durdana Begum,' Parveen said, as she ambled towards Dolly. 'Don't be so sensitive. If your Nazia wanted to respect you, she wouldn't have made passes at your husband.'

'Pino, be serious,' Dolly said, tears welling up in her eyes and rolling down her lacquered face. 'I don't want Nazia's last wishes to be disrespected.'

Parveen softened, seeing Dolly suddenly look so vulnerable. She nestled her head against Dolly's shoulder, soaking in the whiff of her old friend's perfume, and held her tightly. She knew then that theirs was a friendship that went beyond the barbs they customarily threw at each other. Their differences, though difficult to erase, were surpassed by rare moments of compassion – even if they were short-lived.

'Let Noori worry about her sister's last wishes,' Parveen said. 'You need to enjoy the party and let your husband find out more about this hypnotist. Now, stop crying – it's ruining your make-up.'

Dolly chuckled as she wiped her tears and then rose from the sofa. 'I'll go tell Naureen that we're going ahead with Nazia's plan,' she said, sniffling into her tissue as she left the drawing room.

Parveen trailed behind her, suddenly remembering that Sabeen had stomped out of the room. Naureen had chased after her, and Asfand had run off to console his weeping wife. *What if they'd said something to Sabeen?* Parveen thought.

*

'Why didn't anyone tell me that my mother was sick?' Sabeen asked, her eyes hot with tears and her forehead covered with a sheen of sweat. 'Didn't I have a right to be informed?'

'Your mother didn't want you to know, *beti*,' Naureen said, carelessly stroking a finger against her niece's cheeks to rub away the tears. 'She didn't want you to put your life on hold for her. Nazia wasn't selfish, despite what she said in the letter about herself.'

'That's not a good enough excuse,' Sabeen responded, emboldened by her aunt's low pitch. 'I refuse to accept this explanation.'

'Don't explain anything to her,' Asfand said, disapproval clinging to his words.

Naureen eyed him with dismay and instinctively shook her head.

'No, Noori, this has gone too far,' he continued, his anger churning in his reedy voice. 'I don't see why we have to constantly justify ourselves to her.'

'Asfand, let it be,' Naureen said, holding her husband's hand in a comforting gesture, hoping to stymie the acidic words rolling off his tongue. 'Calm down.'

'I won't calm down!' Asfand wrenched his fingers out of Naureen's clasp and marched over to Sabeen, narrowing his eyes. 'I don't understand you,' he said. 'You believed all the lies that Pino Aunty fed you and walked out on your mother. And now you're complaining about how we didn't keep you informed about Nazia's illness? Maybe, if you had tried to understand your mother when she was alive, things would have been different.'

'I did what I thought was right!' Sabeen exclaimed. 'You're the one who—'

'Asfand,' Naureen interrupted, pressing her palm against his left shoulder, 'this isn't the time and place to discuss such things. Sabeen has lost her mother. Have some sympathy, for God's sake.'

'Did you know that your beloved Pino Aunty was aware of your mother's illness?' Asfand said, pushing Naureen's hand away. 'She knew and she didn't tell you. Have you bothered to ask her about this? Or does Pino Aunty not allow you to question her?'

Sabeen's shoulders slumped and she sat, disarmed by what she had heard. In a daze, she slowly looked around the room, her eyes wide with shock, and then blinked in confusion. She jumped to her feet, wiped the beads of perspiration from her neck with her dupatta and stared questioningly at her uncle.

'This can't be true,' she mumbled.

Dolly and Parveen ambled into the lounge, immersed in a conversation that was conducted in whispers, and smiled at Naureen. Concerned by the dejected look on Sabeen's face, Parveen went over to her and gently hooked her arm around the young woman's waist. Sabeen pushed her hand away, as though she had been touched by a stranger, and sat on a wooden chair next to the kitchen.

What have Asfand and Naureen told her? Parveen pondered for a moment. *Have they told her the truth?*

'Naureen –' Dolly's husky voice resonated through the lounge – 'when can we expect this Salman Narang? It's almost eight p.m. He ought to be here soon, if we're all going to be hypnotised tonight.'

'I'm so glad everyone has agreed to do this,' Naureen said with a grin. 'I'm sure he'll be here soon.'

'We gave it some thought,' Parveen said, setting her gaze on Sabeen. 'If Nazia wanted us to be hypnotised, we can't deny her wishes.'

'I'll do it too,' Sabeen said emphatically, sounding more confident than she had before. 'I'm prepared to do anything for Mama. I owe it to her, especially after I mistreated her for so many years.'

'*Chalo*, that's great,' Naureen said cheerily. 'Now, let's all go back to the drawing room. I'll have Bi Jaan make some more tea while we wait for Mr Narang.'

As the guests went back into the drawing room, Asfand held Naureen's hand and pressed his fingers against her knuckles. It didn't take her long to realise that he had concerns about the evening's events. He always found new ways to obsess over the trivial details and exasperate her with his anxieties.

Instinctively, she cocked her head toward his shoulder and leaned against his ear. 'It's all under control,' she hissed.

'You should have told me about Nazia's letter,' he said, whispering so no one else would hear him. 'I'm going along with this for you. But I'm very confused. Who is this hypnotist, Noori?'

'Be patient,' she said, drawing her hand out of his grasp. 'Like I said, it's all under control.'

'There's no winning with you, Noori,' he said, exhaling noisily and marching back into the drawing room. Asfand knew that it was best to put aside all arguments and allow Naureen to do as she pleased. At this point, his wife was opposed to even a speck of reason and was only going to ignore his advice, regardless of how well-meaning it was.

'I'd like some green tea, actually,' Dolly said as she entered the drawing room.

Naureen nodded, a vacuous smile flooding her face, and went into the kitchen to inform Bi Jaan to prepare some tea.

When she was out of earshot, Parveen nudged Sabeen and stared quizzically at her. 'Why did you say that to them?' she asked. 'You didn't mistreat your mother, do you hear me? These people will make you believe all sorts of things. Don't listen to them—'

'Pino Aunty, did you know Mama was ill?'

The words made Parveen's heart lurch and she felt her face flush. She anxiously fidgeted with her anklet, angling for the right words to clarify her position. 'Who told you that?' she asked, casting a puzzled glance at Sabeen.

'I know it's true, Pino Aunty,' Sabeen said, feisty with rage. 'There's really no point in you denying it. I can't believe you didn't tell me! She was my mother!'

'*Beti*, hear me out, please,' Parveen said, her angry tone suddenly replaced with a pleading whine. 'You've misunderstood the situation.'

'Don't talk to me right now, Pino Aunty,' Sabeen roared. 'While we're here, don't come between me and the things my mother wanted me to do. Is that clear?'

Naureen emerged from the kitchen. 'Is everything all right?' she asked.

Denied the opportunity to explain her position, Parveen was tempted to lash out at Naureen and remind her of the destruction she could wreak with a few peppered words muttered into Sabeen's ear. But she remained silent. Still irked by the confrontation, Parveen didn't want to stoke unnecessary drama that could expose her further.

'Yes, absolutely fine,' Sabeen said in a flippant manner that added to Parveen's irritation.

Sabeen sat on a chair next to Naureen, deliberately avoiding Pino Aunty's gaze. Undeterred, Parveen sipped her tea and watched in silence as Sabeen tried to strike up a conversation with Naureen. The soft cadence of the words they exchanged with one another made her shudder with disgust – a feeling of ultimate rejection. She flinched when she saw Naureen spoon another dollop of spaghetti on to her niece's plate and pour tea into her cup. *This wouldn't have happened if I'd been more vigilant*, she thought.

She hadn't anticipated that Sabeen would shift her loyalties so easily. In mourning Nazia's death, Parveen had allowed herself to drown her sorrows in booze and momentarily forget that she had to monitor Sabeen – and, more importantly, protect herself. She should have considered all the possibilities for disaster this night could threaten. She should have stopped Sabeen from wandering around the house. Childhood memories, the pain of losing a parent and the machinations of her aunt and uncle had polluted her thoughts, steered her away from the invisible boundaries that Parveen had set for her.

She's just like Nazia, Parveen thought as she sipped her tea. *Like Nazia, Sabeen doesn't have even a shred of loyalty towards people.*

'When is this Salman Narang going to arrive?' Parveen bellowed. 'My hair will turn grey waiting for this man.'

Sabeen pulled out her phone and pretended to stare at something on the screen to make it seem like she hadn't heard Parveen's comment.

'No worries – we'll have one of the servants get you hair dye from the nearest shop,' Dolly quipped. 'That will give you something to do while you wait.' She winked at Parveen and smiled at her joke.

Parveen rolled her eyes and looked away.

'I'll just call him to ask where he is,' Naureen said, rising from the sofa and walking out of the room.

Just then, Farid nudged Saleem and pointed towards a message on his phone. 'It's from our reporter, Sajid,' he hissed, trying to be discreet, so Asfand wouldn't hear him. 'He's finding information on Salman Narang.'

Saleem nodded, taking a deep breath as he wondered what Nazia had planned for the evening.

Meet Salman Narang

Naureen swung open the front door and whispered a soft *salaam* to a man in a beige shalwar kameez, standing by the potted plants on her porch.

'I'm sorry to have kept you waiting,' she said. 'Bi Jaan probably didn't hear the doorbell. She's been so busy in the kitchen. I see you kept yourself busy too.' She nodded, with amusement, at the newspaper he had been reading when she opened the door.

He flashed a saber-toothed smile at her, folded the newspaper, removed the reading glasses that were perched on the bridge of his nose and walked in. He tossed the newspaper into a tattered satchel and accidentally dropped his glasses on the floor. Naureen leaned over to pick them up, but he stopped her.

'Don't worry,' he said with a foolish grin as he knelt down. 'I'll get them.'

He was about to retrieve his glasses when a Parker pen and an empty flask fell out of the satchel. While he managed to catch the flask before it clanged to the floor, the pen broke as soon as it made contact with the marble, leaving a thin line of blue ink in its wake. He pulled out a handkerchief from the pocket of his kameez and began mopping at the stains with it.

Naureen observed his movements with a bewildered smile. What had Nazia been thinking?

'Don't worry about that, Salman,' she said. 'I hope you didn't have trouble finding the place?'

Bi Jaan had peeped out of the kitchen door when she heard something fall to the ground.

'Who is this man?' she murmured, warily observing him as he spoke to Naureen. 'I've never seen him visit the house before.'

'No, no,' Salman Narang told Naureen, his grin fading. 'There was just so much traffic. But, tell me, has everyone arrived?'

'They're all in the drawing room,' Naureen said. 'In fact, let's go in and meet them.'

'Not yet,' he replied. 'First, I must see the girl. Is she upstairs in Nazia's room?'

Naureen silently pointed towards the staircase.

'Sorayya?' Bi Jaan muttered to herself, confused by the stranger's request. 'What could he possibly want from her?'

'Before I meet the guests, I must ensure that she's ready,' Salman Narang said.

Naureen nodded as she stealthily led him towards the stairs. 'The door to the drawing room is closed,' she assured the visitor. 'No one will disturb you when you're upstairs with her. Take all the time you need.'

'Thank you. It won't take me too long.'

'I'll do anything to fulfil my sister's final wish,' she told him as they climbed the stairs. 'I stood by her when she was alive and will certainly respect her wishes now that she's gone.'

Salman Narang stared blankly at her, uncertain if he should say something to console her. Bi Jaan winced at the treachery of her words. *How had Naureen Bibi stood by Nazia Apa?* For decades, Bi Jaan had been a silent spectator to several quarrels between the sisters. The seeds of their conflicts had been sown during their childhood. Nazia was always the first to start their arguments, but Naureen's silence did little to quell her sister's fits of rage. As the years passed, the fights became frequent, spreading like a poison that assailed their relationship. The reasons for their disagreements varied, but the squabbles were always loud, belligerent and cruel. When they were younger, Bi Jaan found it easier to mediate between them. But, as they grew older, Nazia and Naureen tacitly disapproved of the old housekeeper's involvement in these matters. With time, Bi Jaan learned to resist the temptation to arbitrate, and she avoided their spats.

With each footstep that clacked against the stairs, Bi Jaan heard her heart pounding faster than usual. She scampered out of the kitchen, stood at the bottom of the staircase and tried to eavesdrop on Naureen's conversation with the stranger.

'Everything is going as planned,' Naureen said. 'Sorayya has been asked to sit in Nazia's room.'

'All right,' Salman Narang said, as impassive as he was before. 'Leave me alone with her for a few minutes.

I'll meet you downstairs shortly and we can talk to Nazia's guests.'

Naureen nodded her assent, robotically turned around and began climbing down the stairs. Seconds later, Bi Jaan heard the sound of a door slamming and her heart sank in despair. Intuitively, she went to climb the stairs, her hands pressed against her mouth to prevent herself from shrieking in fright. A dull ache coursed through her body as she recalled that dreaded moment when she had petitioned Naureen Bibi to hire her niece.

'Sorayya can look after Nazia Apa,' she'd said to her employer. 'My niece looked after her ailing father until the day he died. She'll know how to look after a sick person. She's also excellent at housework.'

Naureen Bibi had been generous enough to keep Sorayya on the payroll, even when it became obvious that Bi Jaan had embellished the truth and saddled them with a clumsy village girl who could neither perform housework nor see to Nazia's needs.

Where is her generosity now? Bi Jaan wondered as she scrambled up the stairs. How could Naureen Bibi let that man go into the room alone with Sorayya?

A distant day flashed through her mind as Bi Jaan climbed the staircase. She recalled the smell of disinfectant at the village hospital and the sight of her brother's bandaged body, mere seconds after he'd died. Hours earlier, as death threatened to envelop him, the old housekeeper's brother had extracted a promise from her. 'Take care of my children,' he'd said. 'Protect them to the best of your ability.' In the long years since her brother's death, Bi Jaan had moulded herself into a perfect guardian and dutifully accepted her responsibilities towards Raqib and Sorayya.

When the children grew older, Bi Jaan's single-minded devotion to them started to waver and was replaced by concerns about her own financial well-being. She had compelled Sorayya to work, to help her reduce the unbearable pressures of earning a living, even though she was just a child. The stranger's presence had lifted the blinkers Bi Jaan had grown accustomed to and reminded her of an old promise that was in danger of being broken.

'Where are you going, Bi Jaan?' Naureen said, her face contorted in worry. 'Go back into the kitchen.'

'Naureen Bibi,' she said, between a few muffled sobs, 'who is that man? Why is he going into Nazia Apa's room, alone, with Sorayya? I should go there and—'

'She'll be fine,' Naureen reassured her. 'That man is Nazia's friend. He won't harm Sorayya, I promise you. Now, go back to the kitchen and make more tea. It's going to be a long night.'

Bi Jaan shook her head, reluctant to listen to her employer and leave her niece alone in the room with a stranger. 'Bibi,' she said, pressing her hands together to plead with Naureen. 'When I brought her to your house, I vowed to protect her honour. Please let me go into the room.'

'Calm down, Bi Jaan,' Naureen said. 'Don't you trust me? I'm telling you that she'll be fine. Stop worrying.'

She jabbed her fingers against the skin on Bi Jaan's shoulders, nudged her down the stairs and led her into the kitchen. 'Go! Make us some more tea!' She bellowed the order at the old housekeeper and closed the kitchen door.

Naureen contemplated locking the kitchen door to prevent Bi Jaan from going upstairs and interrupting Salman Narang's ritual. *If I do that, it will arouse suspicion*, she thought, as she dismissed the idea. *I'll just have to keep an eye on her*.

On the other side of the door, Bi Jaan paced the kitchen floor and willed herself not to cry. I'll need to protect Sorayya, she told herself, as she boiled a pot of water to prepare tea for Naureen Bibi's guests.

*

Sorayya rose from the chair as Salman Narang strode into Nazia's room, hurriedly bolting the door behind him, swivelling his head and grinning at her. Baffled by the stranger's presence and driven by the sudden instinct for self-preservation, Sorayya balled her hand into a fist, preparing to attack him.

'Who are you?' she said, her heart thumping against her chest like a sledgehammer. 'And why are you locking the door?'

'I don't think you know me,' he said evenly. 'I'm Salman – Nazia's friend.'

'Oh,' she said, perplexed as to why he had come into Nazia's room without being escorted by Naureen

Bibi or Bi Jaan. 'Why aren't you sitting with the guests in the drawing room? Everyone is there. I think you should go.'

Salman Narang walked towards Sorayya, his smile wilting at the edges and eyes widening with unexplained anticipation. 'I'll go meet the guests soon,' he said. 'But first, Nazia asked me to talk to you.' He took out a pocket watch attached to a silver chain and dangled it in the air. 'Focus on this watch,' he said, the command spilling out of his mouth with a tenderness that alarmed Sorayya.

'Stop playing this trick on me,' she said, laughing nervously. 'It won't work on me. My brother used to try to hypnotise me as a child, but never succeeded.'

Salman Narang continued to wave the pocket watch in the air, his paan-stained teeth jutting out of his mouth as he smiled.

Shaken with fear, Sorayya gasped at the sight, hoping that someone would sense her absence and drag her out of the room before Nazia Apa's friend harmed her.

'Unlike your brother, I know how to hypnotise people,' he said. 'I have learned from experts.'

'Sahib, I don't understand what you're saying,' she said, visibly hyperventilating, her fear palpable like a hunted animal's. 'Why do you want to hypnotise me? Where is Naureen Bibi? I won't do anything without talking to her.'

'Don't be unreasonable,' Salman Narang said, impatiently grabbing her wrist. 'Do it for your Nazia

Apa. Better still, do it to save your job. You don't want to disappoint your brother by losing your job, do you?'

'Who are you?' she asked, her mouth hanging open in awe. 'Let me out of the room, at once.'

Ignoring her questions and frantic demands to unlock the door, Salman Narang swung the pocket watch in her line of vision. While this was an old method that was seldom used these days, Salman knew it was far more appropriate than employing progressive relaxation techniques, which Sorayya would have resisted at all costs.

'Try to relax,' he whispered. 'Focus on the watch. Don't worry about anything else. You'll gradually feel safer. Just calm yourself down.'

Though she tried to look away, Sorayya was drawn towards the rotations of the second hand of the pocket watch, its thick ticking beckoning her. Overcome with a calm sensation, she fell deeper into Salman Narang's trance. She blinked until the lights in the room seemed to flicker, as if someone were switching them on and off. Seconds later, the room plunged into darkness and Sorayya fell into a deep, dreamless sleep. Salman Narang caught her lanky body before it collapsed to the floor. He propped her up on his shoulders and laid her gently on the bed.

'You will only wake up when I snap my fingers,' he said, moving a strand of Sorayya's hair behind her ear and gently stroking her forehead. 'Don't worry, you're in a relaxed state. No one will harm you.'

Salman slid a phone out of his pocket and typed a text message: *She's ready, Naureen. I'm coming downstairs to meet the guests.*

*

'This is Salman Narang,' Naureen said, awkwardly pointing at Nazia's much-awaited sixth guest, who was standing at the entrance of the drawing room. 'He's a trained hypnotherapist.'

Asfand sat up on the sofa and quietly drank his tea. His gaze shifted from the chandelier to the mauve curtains as he took each pensive sip.

Sensing his discomfort, Naureen turned away from him. *It doesn't matter if he isn't entirely pleased with what's happening,* she thought. *For now, I must focus on my sister's wishes.*

'I never realised that quacks required training as well,' Parveen said, with a deadpan look on her face.

Naureen tossed a disapproving glance at her. Parveen scowled back, emboldened by the memory of her argument with Sabeen. Dolly caught sight of this, smiled apologetically at Naureen and clicked her tongue to silence Parveen.

'Let's not be rude, Pino,' Dolly said, holding her hand out towards Salman. 'Hello. I'm Durdana, Nazia's publisher. You can call me Dolly. Should I call you Salman Sahib? Or should I address you as Dr Narang?'

Salman Narang shook his head, his eyes travelling to her manicured fingernails and inspecting a spidery pattern of veins on the back of her hand. His lower lip trembled involuntarily until he tucked it into his mouth. 'Let's avoid formalities,' he said, timidly pressing his fingers against hers in what appeared to be a reluctant handshake. 'You can just refer to me as Salman.'

Dolly chuckled nervously, confused by Salman Narang's ungainliness and desire to be addressed by his first name only.

'So, what you're saying is that you aren't a doctor?' Saleem asked.

'Just as I'd suspected,' Farid said grimly. 'You're a charlatan.'

'You're mistaken,' Salman Narang replied, trying not to appear too defensive. 'I am a doctor. I just prefer not to be called one.'

'Do you have an office where you meet clients?' Farid continued to grill Salman without pausing to reflect on his explanation.

'Yes,' Salman said. 'I rent a small room in Azizabad, from where I run my clinic. It's near Qadri Pakwan and BBQ Centre.'

'Are you telling me that Nazia would drive all the way to Azizabad to seek your … services?' Saleem asked, staring at him with disbelieving eyes. 'I would ask Nazia to join me at the rallies in Azizabad that were presided over by Bhai himself. She never agreed to do it. But I guess a visit to a hypnotist was reason enough for her to forget her qualms about going to an unknown neighbourhood.'

Naureen winced imperceptibly at Saleem's sarcastic remark. How did he have the nerve to raise questions about Nazia's shortcomings? Had he forgotten that Nazia had defied all wise counsel and parental expectations to marry a man like him? What was Saleem, anyway, before he'd met Nazia? Naureen pondered.

Nazia was the one who'd chosen to marry a Mohajir man ten years older than her who had been affiliated with the All-Pakistan Mohajir Student Organisation and was later part of the MQM. When their mother had learned about Nazia's affair with Parveen's fiancé, she was vehemently opposed to it. But, surprisingly, Saleem's age and her daughter's shameless attempts to break her childhood friend's engagement didn't rankle her as much as Saleem's political leanings.

'How could she settle for a Mohajir boy, especially after what they did to us Pukhtuns?' Amma had complained, outraged by her older daughter's lack of loyalty to her own community. 'Since that Bushra Zaidi was run over by a Pukhtun bus driver, these Mohajirs have been out to get us by burning our buses and paralysing the city with strikes and riots. It's absurd. They haven't even spared the Pashto-speaking refugees coming from Afghanistan. *Tauba hai!*' Much to her mother's chagrin, Nazia didn't waver from her decision to marry a card-carrying member of the MQM. 'You'll marry the man I want you to marry,' Amma had told Naureen. 'Nazia will regret her decision.' While Amma didn't live long enough to see Saleem abandon his family, her older son-in-law's failings weren't a secret. How could Saleem overlook his own failures? Naureen wondered now, as she saw him sniggering at his jibe.

'I can't even imagine her crossing the Clifton Bridge,' Parveen said, smiling coyly as she made it clear that she agreed with Saleem. 'If you read her books, it doesn't seem like she knows Karachi beyond Defence and Clifton.'

'Actually,' Dolly replied, throwing a pointed glance at Parveen, 'her final novel is filled with some charming insights about Azizabad. It's a masterpiece.'

'I'm surprised she was able to understand the nuances of life in Azizabad,' Saleem said, with a condescending grin.

'Well, it seems like her understanding of Azizabad is heavily influenced by you.' Dolly threw an icy stare at him. 'There's a character in the book that is based on you, and his views on Azizabad are quite similar to yours.'

Stunned into silence, Saleem lowered his head and fidgeted with his fingers. Parveen studied his expression, expecting his lips to quiver with rage or worry lines to emerge on his long forehead. Avoiding her gaze, Saleem coughed into his hand and tucked a strand of silver hair behind his ear.

'Nazia seems to have based her characters on real people,' Dolly said. 'Especially the men.' She shot a sideward glance at Farid, who froze, lowering his eyes in an unspoken shame.

A smile returned the glow to Salman's face as he was reminded that he didn't need to get distracted by the cynical remarks and quips of Nazia's guests. Over the next few hours, they would know that Salman Narang wasn't a charlatan, but a trained professional who bore the ability to alter their lives.

'Azizabad has changed for the better since the MQM lost its influence there,' he said, turning to Saleem and standing straighter, his chest puffing a little as he spoke. 'No one comes knocking on the doors of my clinic asking me to attend rallies in support of Altaf Bhai.'

Dolly nodded reassuringly, giving the impression that she was aware of every street and byway of Azizabad, even though its sights, sounds and flavours were foreign to her.

'As you all know,' Salman said in a curt, businesslike tone, 'we're here today because it's what Nazia wanted. But we haven't gathered at Naureen's house to remember Nazia. We're here to forget her. I will help you do this.'

'How do you plan to do that?' Dolly asked.

'The human mind is complex,' Salman said assertively. 'But I firmly believe that the subconscious mind knows the cause and the solution for every problem that it is confronted with. As many of you may already know from Nazia's letter, I'll be using hypnotherapy to understand the workings of your subconscious minds.'

Farid rolled his eyes. Salman turned away from him.

'Some of you are sceptical of me,' he continued, somewhat defensively. 'I understand your reservations. Hypnotherapy has been criticised for many years. But you must understand that hypnosis is a state that we experience on a regular basis. It is a state between sleeping and waking. My job as a hypnotherapist is to help you use this state to overcome your problems with Nazia. I will do this through the use of suggestion. All

I need is for you to cooperate with me, as all hypnosis is self-hypnosis. You mustn't fear anything. You'll be in control throughout the process. Trust me – I know what I'm doing.'

'Will you hypnotise us the way they do in the movies?' Parveen said, chuckling into her palm. 'Or is that something that is reserved for magic shows?'

'Don't be silly, Pino,' Farid shrieked. 'I doubt Salman will wave his pocket watch or a gold locket in the air and expect us to fall into a trance. That would be simply foolish.'

Dolly giggled at the absurdity of the suggestion, and then fell silent when she realised that the question may have offended Nazia's sixth guest.

'Well, that's pretty much how I'll be doing it, actually,' Salman said, ignoring their jibes at the craft that had taken him years to learn and perfect. 'But I have other methods too. It varies from person to person.'

Still mistrustful of Salman's professed skills, Farid shrugged his shoulders, then briskly pulled out his phone and checked if he had received a text message from Sajid. All his inbox offered was a few messages from his mobile service provider about how much of his internet package had been consumed, an automated text from the Pakistan Telecommunications Authority that warned people against sharing pornography and blasphemous content, and the last text he had received from Nazia, some months ago.

Where is Sajid? he thought. Why is it taking him so long to dig up some dirt on Salman Narang?

'That sounds a bit juvenile,' Parveen told Salman, making every attempt to curb the rebellion in her voice.

'Pino,' Naureen said, 'let's not be critical. Salman is only trying—'

'Pino Aunty,' Sabeen cut in caustically, 'I don't think there's anything juvenile about all this. Don't forget, we're not doing it for ourselves. We agreed to do this for my mother's sake. Stop being so sceptical.'

The venom in Sabeen's words stung Parveen. She felt the burning desire to retaliate, but didn't. 'You're right,' she said through clenched teeth. 'We're all doing this for your mother. We shouldn't complain.'

'Sabeen, please don't take Parveen's criticism the wrong way,' Saleem said. 'She's just as upset about your mother's death as you are.'

Parveen stifled a grin, pleased that Saleem had defended her. Through this gesture, it had become clear to her that she and Saleem were no longer adversaries. Parveen knew that their easy camaraderie had something to do with cold self-interest, their desire to inherit Nazia's money. But she also speculated that either a romantic or emotional connection was brewing between them. The prospect frightened and excited her in equal measure, threatening to rekindle all those muted longings for Saleem. Beneath her rough veneer and cunning demeanour, the young Parveen was trying to resurrect herself.

'Oh, please,' Sabeen sneered. 'Let's not give her too much credit.'

Just as Saleem opened his mouth to speak, Naureen impatiently snapped her fingers, demanding silence like a schoolteacher might of an unruly group of students. Saleem turned to face her and then dutifully pressed his lips into a thin line.

'I think we've interrupted Salman for far too long,' she said. 'Why don't we give him a chance to speak?'

'I agree,' Dolly groaned. 'I'm so tired of all this bickering. Why can't we just go ahead with this already, without everyone making snarky comments?'

'Precisely,' Salman said grimly, realising that he had to be firm with the guests. 'I can sense that all of you have your doubts. But this isn't a sham. Nazia used to visit me every week to address the demons of her past. She was overcome with guilt over the terrible things she felt she had done to each of you. This party is her atonement, her way of undoing all the mistakes that she committed. Please be a bit more open to her wishes.'

'I didn't realise she regretted her actions.' Moved by this revelation, Dolly whispered tearfully, 'So she tried at least to take some responsibility, and sought help. If she could do it, surely, we can too.'

'How can you say with certainty that it will work?' Farid interjected, moved by neither Salman's statement nor Dolly's tearful reaction. He was still staring at the screen of his phone, willing a text message bearing incriminatory information on Salman Narang to arrive.

'As I said, you'll need to be open to the idea and believe that it can heal your heart and mind.'

'Don't you worry,' Saleem reassured him. 'We'll definitely believe that it will work.'

'Salman Sahib,' Naureen said, 'why don't we begin? I think we've wasted too much time already.' She opened Nazia's pocket diary, turned the pages and settled on an entry that was towards the end of the book. 'Nazia decided on the order in which you will all be hypnotised,' she said.

'You've got to be joking!' Parveen said, with unintended sarcasm.

Sabeen turned around and eyed her with hostility.

Exasperated by the constant scrutiny of her behaviour, Parveen was tempted to continue speaking. But, when she caught sight of Saleem shaking his head and stealthily pointing at his phone, comprehension dawned on her and she grew silent. Once they had exchanged a conspiratorial stare, she opened her handbag, took out her phone and saw a WhatsApp message from him on the screen. With furrowed brows and a curious smile, she opened the message and read it several times over.

Stop making these sarcastic comments. Let's get this over with and get our share of Nazia's money.

Parveen looked at Saleem and nodded – perhaps too eagerly. She slid her phone back into her purse and feigned interest in the rising pitch of Naureen's voice.

'Nazia wanted Dolly to go first,' Naureen said, looking up from the pocket diary. 'Farid will go next, after which Asfand, Sabeen, Parveen and Saleem will be hypnotised.'

'What about you?' Dolly asked in a reproachful tone that pricked Naureen. 'Surely, you also have unresolved issues with your sister? So, why didn't she include your name in the list of people who have to be hypnotised?'

'Naureen has already gone through hypnotherapy for all her issues,' Salman said, knowing perfectly well that he wasn't telling the truth. Naureen was not on the list provided by Nazia. 'So that won't be necessary.'

Satisfied with this response, Dolly nodded and rose from the sofa with a sense of finality. 'I suppose we shouldn't delay this any further,' she said. 'I'm ready. Where are we going to do this?'

'In Nazia's room,' Naureen said. 'Salman will escort you there.'

Farid frowned at her and shot up from his seat, reluctant to let her go on her own.

'Relax,' Dolly said, waving her hand in the air and walking out of the drawing room. 'I'll be fine. Let's go, Salman Sahib.'

'Don't worry,' Salman reassured the guests as he followed Dolly out of the room. 'You are all in good hands.'

As the door closed, a panic-stricken Farid checked his phone again, desperately urging a response from Sajid.

*

'I'll go check on Bi Jaan,' Naureen said, with an absent-minded smile. 'I told her to get us some more tea. Or, if you're hungry, she can prepare dinner for us.'

'Let me help you, Naureen Aunty,' Sabeen said in a syrupy voice that made Parveen uncomfortable.

Naureen's smile receded and a stern expression flooded her face. I must make sure Sabeen doesn't speak to Bi Jaan, she thought.

'I'll come too,' Asfand said, setting his teacup on the table and springing up from the sofa.

Naureen faced her husband and eyed him in disbelief. From the look in his eyes, she knew that he had questions and doubts that she couldn't erase – not yet. She affectionately held Sabeen's hand and took her into the kitchen.

'I think we'll need tea and dinner, because it's going to be a long night,' Asfand told his guests without moving his gaze from Naureen. 'Let me order some dishes from Cafeela. I hope you like their saag and chicken karahi.'

Without waiting to hear what his guests had to say about the matter, Asfand hurriedly left the room and trailed behind his wife and niece.

'Where has Sajid disappeared to?' Farid said when Asfand was gone, anxiously dialling the reporter's number and holding the phone against his ear. 'Hello, Sajid,' he bellowed into the mobile phone. 'Did you find anything on him?' Farid paused, his face sagging with discomfort and a dismayed look in his eyes. He heaved a gentle sigh and hung up. 'It seems that Salman Narang is not an imposter,' he said finally, pinching his temples with his fingers. 'Sajid wasn't able to find anything against him. Salman is telling the truth. He's a hypnotherapist with a small clinic in Azizabad.'

'You're kidding,' Parveen said, gasping with shock.

'Sajid is trying to find out more about him,' Farid said.

'I see,' Saleem said, his forehead creased in a deep frown as he contemplated what their next step would be.

'Why are we even trying to find any dirt on this man?' Parveen said in exasperation. 'Why does it even matter? We should just do it for the money.'

'I know. I am,' Saleem said with hesitation. 'I do need the money.'

'I do too,' she said, tightly holding his wrist in a cage of her thumb and fingers.

Saleem grinned indulgently.

'I hate to admit it,' Farid said, 'but I could certainly do with the money too. The media is in tatters, and I need to send my son some money to pay his hostel rent in the US. We spent most of our savings on building Dolly a new office space for her publishing house.'

'Children can be such a burden,' Parveen said. 'Thank God I didn't have any of my own. Of course, spending time with Sabeen has made me realise that I should have had children.'

She usually found it difficult to conceal her assorted burdens as Sabeen's carer. But, today, Parveen suppressed the impulse to tell Saleem that his daughter was nothing but a nuisance to her. If she succumbed to this temptation, she stood the risk of damaging her new connection with her former fiancé. At this point, she didn't want to lose her second opportunity to court the man she had never stopped loving.

'What do you need the money for?' Parveen asked Saleem, expecting an effusive response that would leave her more infatuated than she already was.

'I h-have expenses,' Saleem stuttered.

Parveen grimaced, wondering if she should probe further and ask for details on his expenses. Why is he suddenly being so evasive?

'You're right, Pino,' Farid said. 'It was rather silly of us to find out more about him. All of us just need the money.'

'Let's just pretend that we've been hypnotised,' Saleem said conspiratorially. 'We can tell him what he wants to hear.'

'I'm afraid that Dolly might not go ahead with the pretense,' Parveen said. 'What if he actually hypnotises her? What will we—?'

'Hypnotherapy is just a trick, Pino,' Saleem interrupted Parveen, rubbing his hand against her shoulder to comfort her. 'He won't succeed. I'm sure of that.'

The touch of his fingers against the smooth fabric of her kaftan made Parveen's heart flutter with delight. Fearing that her enthusiasm would bring an unnatural glow to her face, she nodded at Saleem, hurriedly picked up her teacup and took a sip.

*

Asfand pulled Naureen towards the staircase before she could walk into the kitchen with Sabeen. Though she was annoyed at being waylaid by her husband – especially because she feared that Bi Jaan would tell Sabeen about Sorayya's confinement – she remained calm.

'What's wrong?' she asked, with a supercilious grin.

'Noori,' he whispered, 'why have I been asked to go through hypnotherapy?'

'Asfand, I didn't decide who was going to be hypnotised,' she said, making an attempt not to come across as defensive. 'Nazia did.'

'You should have told me this before,' he said testily. 'This is preposterous, Noori.'

Naureen clicked her tongue. *This is getting repetitive*, she thought.

'And why have you been exempted from hypnotherapy?' Asfand asked incredulously. 'When did you have it done? I'm surprised that you didn't tell me about it. Why would you keep it a secret?'

'Asfand, you're being very unreasonable,' Naureen said. 'I have no time to deal with your tantrums right now. I'm doing this for my sister. All I need you to do is cooperate.'

With that, she walked down the stairs and entered the kitchen to find Bi Jaan and Sabeen cracking jokes – like they used to before Nazia's daughter left home. The smile on Bi Jaan's wrinkled face shocked Naureen. Had the housekeeper finally overcome her fears for Sorayya's safety, or was she just disguising her pain? Naureen couldn't tell. The atmosphere in the kitchen reminded her of happier days from Sabeen's childhood, when their world was devoid of anguish. *How did everything change so drastically?* Naureen thought. *Where did it all go wrong?*

Friendship Most Foul

'Isn't she the maid who served us tea?' Dolly shrieked in panic when she saw Sorayya sprawled on the bed from the entrance to Nazia's room. 'What happened to her? Why is she lying on the bed? Is she hurt or unwell?'

'Don't worry,' Salman said, his voice dropping to a soothing pitch. 'Sorayya has agreed to help us with the hypnotherapy.'

'Is that so?' Dolly said sarcastically, unconvinced by his rather improbable explanation. 'I'm surprised she even knows what she has agreed to do.'

'Nazia felt having her in the room would help us,' he replied, lowering his body on to the rocking chair with an unsettling ease. 'You'll see.'

Perplexed by the conviction in his words, Dolly glared at him and took tentative steps as she entered the room, her gaze fixed on Sorayya. A strand of the girl's dark tresses was haphazardly tossed against a face luminous in serenity. Something's not right, Dolly thought as she watched her from a distance. Instinctively, her eyes wandered to Sorayya's chest, and she gasped with relief when she realised that she was breathing.

'Oh, I completely forgot,' Dolly said, adjusting the pleats of her sari as she pulled up her leg and removed her sandals at the door. 'Nazia hated it when people wore shoes in her bedroom. She believed it was a sign of disrespect towards people who took pains to ensure that their rooms were clean.'

Salman smiled to show Dolly that he was moved by her gesture. But the uncertain look on her face didn't disappear.

As she sat on a chair next to the bed, Dolly was awestruck by how little had changed since the last time she had been in Nazia's room. The curtains, the books on the wooden shelves, the rocking chair and the bed linen were all the same, and the trinkets Nazia had collected over the years were in the same places she remembered them. Dolly noted that her friend's room hadn't aged, even though she had.

'For a woman who never resisted change, Nazia certainly knew how to hold on to old things,' she said, to ease the hesitation that clung to her heart.

'She was truly special,' he said.

'Salman Sahib,' she blurted, 'surely you realise how odd this is for me? When I came up the stairs, I didn't expect to see a young girl sleeping on the bed.'

'She's not sleeping,' he corrected her. 'She's been hypnotised. I hypnotised her before I met you all.'

'Is that so?' Dolly said laconically, hesitant to show her surprise over Salman's abilities as a hypnotherapist.

'You seem somewhat startled,' he said, laughing. 'Surely you knew I wasn't lying when I said I could hypnotise people?'

'No, no,' Dolly reassured him, disguising her doubts with a smile. 'I believed you. *Waise*, I have a feeling that you've only hypnotised Sorayya to persuade us of your capabilities.'

Salman let out a grunting laugh as he sprang up from the rocking chair and ensconced himself on the bed, a few inches away from Sorayya. Dolly cringed as a new fear settled in her heart. She shuffled over to the bed and sat down beside him, resisting the urge to fling him off the bed.

'Let's get started,' she said with an unmistakable sense of urgency.

Salman turned to face her, smiling dreamily as he looked into her almond eyes. 'Don't worry,' he told her, with a reassuring grin. 'Sorayya's fine. I won't harm her and I won't harm you either.'

She looked him squarely in the eyes, still uncertain if she should trust him.

'Don't take this the wrong way,' he continued, after a brief pause, 'but I noticed that you take good care of your hands.'

'The same hand that you were reluctant to shake, earlier today?'

'I hope you didn't take that the wrong way,' Salman murmured. 'I was slightly baffled by the sight of it.'

'Oh,' Dolly said, a confused look flooding her face as she self-consciously cast her eyes on her hands. 'I didn't realise they were terrifying.'

'No, no. There's nothing wrong with them. Your nails are perfectly buffed and shaped. My wife used to take care of her hands too.'

'Why did she stop?' Dolly blurted the question.

'She died a few years ago.'

Dolly's face registered concern. Her hand covered her mouth to suppress a gasp. 'I'm so sorry,' she said.

'It happened a long time ago,' he said. 'When I saw your hands today, it reminded me of Asifa.'

'Did you turn to hypnotherapy after she died?' she asked.

'I started long before she died,' Salman said. 'I couldn't help myself deal with the pain of Asifa's death through hypnotherapy, though. But I know I can help others manage their pain.'

The soft rhythm of his voice pacified her. With a long exhalation, she placed her hand against Salman's wrist, and flinched as he tightened his grip around hers with his free hand. As Dolly adjusted to his warm touch, she allowed herself to soak in the serenity of it and momentarily forgot all her reservations about him.

'Let's begin,' he said, rising from the bed. 'Why don't you lie next to Sorayya?'

Dolly sprawled herself on the bed, unconcerned about the creases appearing on the perfect pleats of her sari.

Averse to wasting any more time, Salman dangled his pocket watch above her face. 'Can you see the second hand on my pocket watch?' he asked, slowly yet firmly.

'Yes. I can see it moving around in circles,' Dolly said, her eyes fixed on the watch.

'Focus your eyes on it,' Salman said. 'Don't lose sight of it. Allow its movement to help you relax.'

Dolly observed the second hand spinning around the dial, the rhythm of its ticking sound flowing into her ears like a familiar melody – a signal she couldn't ignore. Gingerly, she succumbed to its call, battling the urge to blink as she concentrated on the pocket watch.

'Take a deep breath,' he instructed her. 'But don't look away from the second hand.'

Dolly drew in her breath and let out an audible sigh. The worry lines on her forehead vanished when she exhaled.

'Close your eyes,' Salman said, placing the pocket watch on the bedside table as she complied with his request. 'What do you see around you?'

Though she was sliding into a trance, Dolly was able to detect how absurd his question sounded.

'You've asked me to close my eyes,' she grumbled, with a sardonic ring to her words. 'So I obviously can't see anything.'

'Do you see darkness?' Salman asked grimly.

'Yes,' she said, trying to sound serious so as not to offend him. 'But I can also see patches of orange and red.'

'Close your eyes tightly. What else do you see now?'

'It's completely dark.'

'Does it frighten you?' he asked with concern.

'No,' she said. 'Maybe I'm a bit frightened. But it's nothing I can't handle.'

'Take your time to get used to the darkness,' he whispered. 'Once you're comfortable, you'll be able to conquer any fear and revisit even the most painful memories.'

Dolly mumbled a few mangled words and slowly slipped into a daze. She allowed the darkness to envelop her until the soft echoes of Salman's voice receded into the background, as if she were being pulled further away from him. Her right arm twitched and trembled involuntarily. But Dolly wasn't afraid. The darkness had lulled her into a sense of security that she hadn't experienced in a long time.

'Are you still afraid?' Salman said.

His voice seemed to pierce through her eardrum. She contorted her face in irritation and clicked her tongue.

'Are you still afraid?' he repeated the question.

'No. I'm calm,' she responded.

Salman smiled, gratified by his success in putting Dolly in a trance.

'What's your name?' he asked.

'Dolly,' she said. 'Durdana Farid Afzal.'

'How old are you?'

'Fifty-eight.'

'What do you do?'

'I'm a publishing professional. I run my own publishing company called Spark Press. It's a small publishing house that focuses on fiction. I know many Pakistani publishers aren't keen on publishing fiction. But we have been at it for three decades and pride ourselves on our ability to find Pakistan's local literary idiom.'

'How did you first come to know about Nazia?' Salman asked, weaning her away from the superficiality of her well-rehearsed promotional pitch regarding her publishing house and pushing her deeper towards the core of what he wanted her to talk about.

'My husband spoke about her a lot,' she said. 'She worked at his newspaper and wrote stories that Farid believed ought to be published. He once invited me to his office so I could meet her and help her out.'

'Why don't we go back in time to that day when you first met her?' he said. 'Tell me more about what is happening in your husband's office. What are the first words that Nazia says to you?'

With those words, Dolly was transported to a dusty room. She was seated on a revolving chair, the arms of which had been tucked beneath a mahogany desk. Farid, sporting slicked-back hair and a slim physique, was sitting at the other end of the table, sipping tea, blowing grey smoke rings into the pungent air and yelling into a cordless phone at a reporter who had decided to skip work that day. Accustomed to his fits of rage, Dolly was able to distract herself from her husband's shrill, piercing voice. She looked out through the glass door of his office at the cubicles that were occupied by corpulent old men who slouched on their seats, flicked the ashes from their cigarettes on to stacked copies of newspapers and stubbed their butts on the floor. She was about to look away when she saw a waif-like woman in a green shalwar kameez standing by the bookshelf, browsing through Farid's collection of coffee-table books while she tied her hennaed hair into a chignon. Dolly's curiosity compelled her to stare at the woman long after Farid had slammed the phone against his desk. She didn't even notice him walk over to the glass panel, tap on it and signal for the woman in green to come in. Dolly was only able to break away from her trance when the woman walked into Farid's office, shook her hand and introduced herself as Nazia Sami.

'Nazia says that she's heard a lot about me from Farid Sahib,' Dolly told Salman. 'Then Farid turns to me and praises Nazia's skills as an editor and writer. He asks me to read her manuscript because he believes it's a remarkable work of fiction. Although I'm a bit sceptical of her literary talent, I agree to read her work.'

'What are you feeling about Nazia during this meeting?' Salman asked her.

'I think she's beautiful and quite charming,' she said, with some hesitation. 'I'm instantly drawn towards her, even though I am afraid of her.'

'Why are you afraid?'

'I have a nagging suspicion that she is having an affair with my husband.'

'What makes you feel that way?'

'I don't know. Farid is always flirting with his female colleagues. So I can never tell the difference between those who are his friends and those who eventually become his mistresses.'

'Is she having an affair with Farid?' he asked.

'Not now,' she said dryly, her disgust over the manner in which Salman asked her this question apparent on her face.

'When does it begin?' Salman asked.

'I don't know,' Dolly scowled, frustrated by his line of questioning. 'For now, I just know that I'm infatuated with her during our first meeting.'

'What else can you tell me about this meeting?'

'I tell her to meet me at my office,' she said. 'Nazia has a smile on her face as she leaves the room. It seems to me that she is concealing her pain in that smile. I can't explain why I feel this way. But I know that she doesn't want the world to think that she is weak or vulnerable.'

'What happens when she leaves the room?'

'Farid tells me that she is the ex-wife of former MQM leader Saleem Sabir – the one who went missing a few years ago. He is such a contemptible man. Who leaves a wife and child like that?'

'What more can you tell me about your meeting with Nazia at the office?' Salman asked, veering her thoughts back towards Nazia. 'Does your opinion about her change when you meet her again?'

'No,' Dolly said curtly, as if she were defending herself against an accusation.

'Tell me what happens the second time you meet,' Salman demanded.

Just then, Dolly saw herself gazing out of the window of her old office on Tariq Road. A gentle breeze fluttered through her waist-length hair as she spotted the billboards that dotted Karachi's cloudless skyline, concealing the cluttered façades of buildings. To her right– near the Allah Wali Chowrangi – was a white *TO LET* sign with a telephone number inscribed on it in red. Next to it was an advertisement with an animation of a child in a blue and white striped cardigan, clasping a toothbrush in one hand and a bottle of Dentonic tooth powder in the other. In the distance, she caught a glimpse of the large billboard for Waves refrigerators on Shahrah-e-Faisal, which she crossed every day on her way home.

As she looked downwards, Dolly saw frazzled shopkeepers lowering their shop shutters. Altaf Bhai had called yet another strike in Karachi, even though he had long forsaken it, preferring the comfort of exile to the city's terrors and turbulence. She heard the faint hum of shots ringing out in the air. An angry mob could be expected at any moment, shouting slogans and setting ablaze buses, cars and shops with reckless abandon. Given the speed at which the shops were being closed, Dolly sensed that danger was imminent and made a mental note to call Farid and ask him for updates on the new wave of familiar chaos that had swept through the city.

She went over to lock the main door of her office and prevent any miscreants from barging in. Dolly was convinced that Nazia wouldn't turn up at the office that day. Who would have taken the risk to forge through roads that were littered with burning tyres, torched minibuses and gunny bags filled with mutilated corpses?

But, as she was about to shut the door, Dolly noticed Nazia climbing up the stairs, a black dupatta wrapped around her head.

'She comes to see me – even though there is an MQM strike,' Dolly responded, almost robotically.

'What happens next?' Salman said firmly, coaxing her to remember the minute details of their encounter.

'She pulls out her manuscript from a small bag and I look over it,' Dolly said. 'For the next few hours, I read every word that she has written and realise how wrong I was about her talent. I'm enchanted by her skills as a storyteller. Through her writing, Nazia is able to communicate the fears, frustrations and insecurities that she is otherwise too shy to open up about. The moment I finish reading the book, I tell her that I am going to publish it.'

'What else happens that night?' he asked, expecting her to swim through her mind and remember something that she had forgotten to mention.

'I drop her off at her sister's house, after the situation improves,' Dolly said.

'Do you talk about anything else?' he said, urging her to spool back into the past.

'When we are at the office, Nazia asks if I write too,' Dolly murmured, unwilling to allow the shards of this memory to prick her. 'None of the other writers who I've published have ever asked me this question. They are pompous and self-serving, and don't care that I stay up late at night writing my own book. Nazia is the first person who takes an interest in my book. That day, I show her parts of my first draft.'

'What does she think of the draft?'

'She loves what little she reads of the book,' Dolly said with a grin. 'Nazia encourages me to write more and tell more stories. Every time we meet, over the next few months, she reads a chapter of my book and always praises my work. When I publish her first book, *A Woman Without Men*, Nazia insists that I should read a portion of my own unfinished manuscript at the launch party as well. She believes that women who write shouldn't compete with one another. They must learn to share the spotlight without being jealous of one another.'

Salman opened his mouth to speak, but Dolly continued, sailing through the sea of her memories without being prompted.

'During one of our meetings, Nazia tells me that we're like Vita Sackville-West and Virginia Woolf,' Dolly uttered with a mild chuckle. 'I laugh at the comment and say it is a silly comparison to make because Vita and Virginia were lovers. Nazia stares at me with a smiling face, clumsily puts her hands in mine and kisses them. I know then that we are in love.'

'If she is so ... compassionate towards you, what goes wrong between the two of you?' Salman asked. 'When do you start developing differences?'

Dolly's body stiffened and a gleam of sweat appeared on her forehead. 'Nazia betrays me,' she said, as the memory of an invisible wound resurfaced in her mind.

'Why don't we revisit the exact moment when you felt betrayed?' Salman suggested. 'When does everything change?'

'The day I overhear a conversation between Nazia and my husband at his office,' Dolly answered. 'It is the day after martial law has been imposed in the country, and Farid and I have to go to a wedding. He has a great deal of work to do. He tells me to pick him up from the office so we can go to the wedding together.'

'What do you see when you enter his office?' Salman asked, urging Dolly on with his voice.

'Nazia is telling my husband that the affair has gone on for far too long and has to stop,' Dolly said in a faint whisper.

'How does that make you feel?'

'I'm hurt,' she said, abruptly stopping to heave a sigh. 'Initially, I assume that she is telling him about our secret relationship,' she continued. 'I'm angry and afraid. How can Nazia give us up? I've been honest with her throughout. Nazia knows that we share an intimate connection. I tell her about the problems in my marriage and she discusses all the issues she has with her younger sister, who doesn't have the backbone to stand up to her husband's taunts. But I always assume that she knows our relationship can only go so far. I can't leave my husband and children to pursue a relationship that is socially unacceptable. How can she violate my trust?'

'Do you confront her?'

'I don't need to,' Dolly said in an anguished tone. 'It turns out that I have misread the situation.'

'What do you mean?'

'The moment she tells him that the affair has to end, Farid holds Nazia's hand – in the same way that she had once held mine – and presses it against his chest. He tells Nazia that he simply can't end their relationship.'

'How does that make you feel?'

'I told you,' Dolly responds. 'I feel betrayed.'

Salman decided to mine the dark, distressing possibilities of pain that this memory had produced. 'What do you decide to do, at this point?' he asked.

'I storm out of the room,' Dolly said. 'Instead of going to the wedding, I decide to go home and ring Farid at his office to tell him I'm exhausted and want to rest. Relieved that our plans have been cancelled, Farid tells me he'll be working late. That night, I decide to burn my entire manuscript because Nazia is the only one who appreciates it. The connection that we share is based on deceit. She is not only sleeping with me, but she is also fucking my husband. How can I possibly respect her and value the things that she appreciates?'

'Do you ever talk to her about it?' Salman grilled her.

'No,' Dolly said coolly. 'I just tell her that I feel guilty about our secret relationship and can't continue sleeping with her. I assure her that we'll still be friends and I'll publish all her books. But I never confront her about the affair.'

'If Nazia were right here and you had the opportunity to express yourself, what would you do?' Salman asked, clearing his throat.

'I'm not sure,' Dolly said, with a hint of exasperation. 'I'd rather not say.'

'What if I tell you that she's lying right next to you?' Salman said, his gaze shifting towards Sorayya. 'What if there were no consequences for your actions? What would you do?'

'I would thrash her till her entire body throbbed with pain,' Dolly responded in a frosty whisper. 'I would want her to experience the agony she put me through.'

'She's right next to you, Dolly,' Salman said. 'Do whatever you want to. Get up and strike her.'

As if on cue, Dolly rose from the bed and clenched her hand into a fist. Salman briskly grabbed a pillow from the rocking chair and held it in front of her. Without opening her eyes, Dolly sank her fist into the cushion with a sinister smile plastered on her face. She eschewed her veneer of civility and muttered expletives against Nazia for deceiving her. After each onslaught, a fresh bout of anger boiled within her and she hit the pillow with renewed rage. Seeing that Dolly had shifted uncomfortably close to Sorayya, Salman held the cushion in both hands to shield Sorayya from harm. In a fit of rage, Dolly tossed it out of his hands with relentless force. Before Salman could retrieve the pillow and resurrect the barrier between them, Dolly punched Sorayya's neck. Driven by the instinct to shield the maid from the woman who had expressed concerns about her well-being, Salman clutched Dolly's hand, pulled it away from Sorayya's neck and gently moved her to the other side of the bed. He then noticed the smile sag as loud sobs filled the air.

'It was my fault too,' Dolly said, tears springing to her eyes and moistening her face.

'What do you mean?'

'How could I possibly do this to Nazia?' she said, gently kissing Sorayya's cheek. 'I was the one who betrayed her.'

'What did you do?' Salman asked.

'I … I haven't been telling the truth,' she told Salman. 'I did confront Nazia. The day after I saw her and Farid at the office, I went over to see her and told her that I knew about her affair with my husband. She feigned ignorance until I threatened to expose her by telling Sabeen about her mother's true nature. Nazia begged me not to do such a thing. But I did it anyway. I told Sabeen that her mother was sleeping with a woman. She was too young to understand anything. But the damage was done and the seeds of doubt had been sown in the young girl's mind with that one comment. The tensions that crept into their relationship later had something to do with my telling Sabeen things she didn't need to know and was too young to process properly. Sabeen just became more suspicious of her mother after she found out.'

'Did Nazia forgive you?'

'I think she did,' Dolly said in a pensive tone. 'She never confronted me about it and we remained friends, but our relationship became a professional one only. Over the years, many of her friends who aspired to become writers – including Parveen – approached me through her. I was happy to read their work, and Nazia was grateful for my generosity. I don't know how she did it. I've lived with this guilt for years. I can't tell you how miserable I've felt all this time.'

'You must move on from that guilt now, Dolly,' Salman said. 'Nazia didn't hold a grudge against you.'

'But I held a grudge against her,' Dolly said. 'I still do. I don't know why. It just became a habit to both hate and pity Nazia. I used to backbite about her with Parveen and then feel terrible about doing it. And, now, I'm doing the same thing with her new book. I want to suppress her truth by needlessly censoring her work and removing any details that could present me or Farid in a negative light. I'm a terrible friend.'

'Have you forgiven her for having an affair with Farid?' Salman prodded with another question to pull her into the core of her distress.

'I think I have. I know he still thinks of her. But I do, too. We don't talk about it, but the pain exists. Nazia is the ghost that haunts our marriage and the glue that keeps it from falling apart. I just need to stop being bitter.'

Satisfied with her response, Salman took a deep breath and smiled. Even though Dolly had hedged his questions, he had succeeded in delicately pulling the truth out of her conscience. He was sure he had helped her overcome her anxieties and bitterness towards Nazia.

'Once you open your eyes, you will break out of your trance,' Salman instructed Dolly. 'After that, you will harbour no resentment against Nazia.'

When she regained her vision, Dolly felt a dull ache in her temples. Though she had spilled some of her darkest secrets during the hypnotherapy, she didn't feel self-conscious or ashamed. As Salman escorted her to the door, Dolly realised that Nazia's room looked exactly the same as it had when she entered it. The only difference was that Dolly felt calmer than before, now that the burden of a secret she had carried for years had been miraculously lifted. She exited the room.

Salman adjusted Sorayya's head on a cushion, inspecting her neck for any wounds. 'I'll have to make sure that they don't hurt you,' he said in a frightened whisper, even though Sorayya couldn't hear him. 'Thank God there is no visible wound.' But he worried a bruise would bloom in a day or two.

Salman's thoughts circled back to a conversation he'd had with Nazia when she'd visited his office to inform him about the plans for her final farewell.

'Why does the maid have to be in the room?' he'd asked her. 'And would she agree to being hypnotised?'

Nazia had greeted these questions with silence and a smile. Salman knew to be careful in his questioning of Nazia. She didn't like disclosing information until she believed the time was right, but he had found strategies for probing her in the safety of her therapy sessions with him. It was his job to understand his clients' psyche as he guided them through their past traumas, hopefully arriving at a doorway to peace. Nazia knew this. Yet, she wanted him to brush aside his curiosoities and trust her judgement – a final favour to repay an old kindness. It was no secret that, by allowing him to help her when she did, Nazia had rescued him from penury, a life of endless despair.

Salman recalled the bitter battles he'd waged as a youth against his family when they'd opposed his decision to become a hypnotherapist. Their disapproval initially stemmed from his reluctance to attend medical school and become a physician, as they had hoped. Salman's parents found it difficult to accept that their son didn't want to wear a stethoscope around his neck, examine patients and scribble the names of life-saving medicines into a prescription pad. His interest lay in exploring the invisible traumas that besieged the human mind. From the outset, his parents were displeased by his decision to study psychotherapy, but waited for him to outgrow his bizarre passion. When Salman announced his decision to train as a hypnotherapist, his parents were aghast. 'This is absurd,' Salman's father had scolded. 'You can't possibly do this for a living.' Salman defied his parents and continued to learn the forbidden craft, but their barbs grew more caustic and aggressive. Salman was determined to succeed in his practice and opened up a small clinic from home. But he found his early confidence knocked by a consistent failure to get his clinic up and running. It turned out his parents' attitude to hypnotherapy was not particular to them. In a country where the very weather had become an existential threat, few had the luxury, apparently, of pausing to consider their mental health. Some had even expressed concern that hypnotherapy was a Western incarnation of dabbling with the black arts and jinn. In the end, the pressure to provide for his family obliged him to relinquish his practice after some years and take up a string of odd jobs instead, though the money was barely enough to fulfil his family's basic needs.

After Salman's wife died, Nazia was the one who had restored his confidence in the healing power of his craft. He'd met her when he had found himself being drawn back to hypnotherapy practice and was attending a hypnotherapy conference in Karachi, two years ago. Salman had finally mustered the courage to resume his practice without being buckled by familial pressure. He was struggling to find clients and Nazia, who was battling her own demons, needed a skilled hypnotherapist with ample time at hand to help her emerge from the quagmire of her past. Though their arrangement was based on reciprocity, Salman believed Nazia had taken a chance on him when no one else would.

But can I compromise on my professional standards because of my loyalty to Nazia? Salman pondered now.

He turned towards Sorayya and gently stroked her forehead. 'Don't worry,' Salman said to her, even though he knew she wouldn't remember any of this when it was all over. 'You're in good hands. Everything will be fine.'

Dangerous Lover

'What's so funny?' Naureen asked Sabeen, purging any hint of irritation from her tone. 'What are you and Bi Jaan laughing about?' She patted Sabeen's shoulder and turned to smile at her.

Bi Jaan nervously averted her eyes from her employer's censorious gaze.

'We were just talking about the silly things I did as a child,' Sabeen said, holding Bi Jaan's hand in the same way she used to when she was a teenager. 'Bi Jaan was telling me about the time Mama went for one of her book events and refused to take me along because she said I had shown no interest in reading and would probably get bored. I removed all the books from her shelf and scattered them around the room to create the illusion that I'd been reading them. Do you remember, Naureen Aunty?'

'Oh, yes,' Naureen said, laughing as the memory returned to her. 'Nazia was so angry when she came back home. She vowed never to leave her room unlocked when she left the house again.'

Naureen also had other recollections from that day, but she was reluctant to share them with Sabeen. She remembered how her older sister had thrown herself on the marble floor and wept like a child when she saw her books carelessly strewn about. Sabeen, who had been reclining on the rocking chair, laughed uproariously as she watched her tear-stricken mother assemble the books in a neat pile. 'You little devil,' Nazia had said, her mascara smudged by the tears that rolled down her cheeks. 'All you ever do is destroy things.'

Later, when Sabeen had fallen asleep, Nazia stomped into Naureen's room. Holding a cigarette between her fingers, she asked her sister why she hadn't stopped Sabeen from making a mess in her room. 'It's not like you have any children of your own,' Nazia said, with a curtness that broke Naureen's heart. 'You don't even work. Bi Jaan is always busy in the kitchen. Why does she have to look after the child when you should be doing it?' Naureen had done little to defend herself. Uncertain as to what she could do to placate her sister, she had apologised for not being more vigilant.

Though it had been many years since the altercation, Nazia's words still stung Naureen, reminding her of the miscarriage that she'd had in the first year of her marriage. Asfand, who had been thrilled at the prospect of having twins, was devastated. His grief shattered Naureen's resolve to conceive another child. She couldn't possibly raise his hopes again and then disappoint him – especially when there was no guarantee that the child would remain safe in her womb. She had secretly envied her sister for giving birth. For years, Naureen suppressed her longing for motherhood, enduring all the reproving remarks and stares that were thrown at her for choosing to remain childless, because she feared the pain of another loss. Now, it was too late.

As she made the conscious decision to withhold this memory from Sabeen, Naureen wondered whether things would have been different if she and Asfand hadn't stopped trying after that one misfortune. Her maternal instincts were intact, even though she had no children to lavish them on.

'Bi Jaan was telling me that her niece is working here too,' Sabeen said. 'Was she the one who brought us tea?'

Naureen warily turned towards Bi Jaan and raised her brows, her eyes bearing the question that she wanted to ask her: *What did you tell her?*

Bi Jaan smiled and blinked reassuringly at Naureen, then looked away.

'Yes,' Naureen sighed. 'She looked after your mother until the very end.'

Sabeen nodded, her smile fading at the edges of her mouth. Was her aunt taunting her for not looking after her mother?

Naureen sensed Sabeen's discomfort and realised the reckless implications of her words. She made no attempt to comfort her, because she believed Sabeen deserved to feel some guilt for abandoning her mother. 'Sorayya is a good girl,' Naureen said. 'She did more for your mama than any of us ever could. She—'

'Bi Jaan was telling me,' Sabeen responded, still embarrassed that someone else had carried out the duties that she should have fulfilled. 'I haven't been formally introduced to her. Where is she?'

'Sh-She's …' Naureen stammered. 'She's somewhere around the house.'

'Sabeen *beti*,' Bi Jaan said, watching wide-eyed as Naureen's mouth opened in fear, 'she's running an errand for Naureen Bibi. You'll see her very soon.'

'Ah,' Sabeen said, drumming her fingers against the kitchen counter. 'In that case, Bi Jaan might need some help serving everyone tea. It's going to be a long night. We might as well ensure that we're awake.' She reached for the tray and lifted it in one strong movement, turning with it and sweeping out of the kitchen.

Neither Bi Jaan nor Naureen tried to stop her. Unlike the visitors seated in the drawing room, Sabeen wasn't a guest in their house. This gesture was her attempt to revive the old comfort that she had felt when she lived here. They weren't going to stop her from rediscovering the home she had left behind.

'I didn't tell her anything, Naureen Bibi,' Bi Jaan ardently explained, once Sabeen had left with the tray. 'I won't betray your trust, as long as you tell me what that man is doing to Sorayya in Nazia Apa's room. I keep hearing all these strange sounds from upstairs. I'm worried about her.'

'Bi Jaan,' Naureen said angrily, 'please stop panicking. Sorayya is helping us fulfil Nazia Apa's last wish. We need her to do the cleaning.'

'Is that all?' Bi Jaan asked. She was finding it difficult to believe that someone as clumsy and inefficient as Sorayya would be entrusted with such a task.

'Yes,' Naureen said. 'Stop worrying and asking questions. You and Sahib keep distracting me with questions when I have guests to entertain.'

Bi Jaan muttered an apology, but Naureen only shrugged her shoulders. She walked out of the kitchen, smiling when she saw Dolly climbing down the staircase.

'How did it go, Dolly?' Naureen said. 'How do you feel?'

'Terrific,' Dolly said. 'This Salman Narang is brilliant. From the moment he took me to Nazia's room, to the moment I left, he created a safe space for me.'

'I'm glad,' Naureen said. 'Let's get the next person to go in.'

'I need a cup of tea,' Dolly said. 'This has been exhausting.'

Bi Jaan had eavesdropped on their conversation by peeping through the kitchen door. When Naureen and Dolly returned to the drawing room, Bi Jaan knew that it was safe to climb up the stairs. Determined to protect her niece, she tiptoed to Nazia's door, which had been set ajar, and peered through the opening. She caught sight of Salman and flinched in fear.

He rose from the rocking chair and sped over to the door. 'What do you want?' he asked, with an icy glare.

'Sorayya!' she exclaimed, tears swimming in her eyes. 'I want to speak to my niece. Please don't stop me from seeing her.'

'I'm sorry,' Salman hissed, defensively leaning against the door as if he wanted to close it at any moment. 'You can't see her right now. She's helping us out, here.'

'Please, Sahib,' Bi Jaan pleaded. 'I just want to have one look at her, for my own satisfaction. Don't do this to us. We're poor people and the honour of our women means everything to us. Our honour is all that we have.'

'Don't be ridiculous,' he said nonchalantly. 'No one is taking away Sorayya's honour. She's just helping us.' Adopting a reassuring tone, he said, 'There's no need to panic. I'm a poor man too. I won't let anything happen to your niece. Now, go downstairs. Naureen Madam won't be pleased to see you here.'

Salman slammed the door and Bi Jaan returned to the kitchen before anyone would notice her absence.

*

'So, you don't remember a thing you said to Salman?' Parveen asked. 'And yet, you feel like all your bitterness towards Nazia has disappeared?'

'Yes,' Dolly lied. She recalled everything that had happened in the room, but wasn't comfortable with being interrogated. 'It's remarkable.'

'Are you sure that man didn't drug you?' Farid whispered into her ear. 'If you think he did, let me know. I'll have someone fix him.'

Ignoring her husband's sudden protectiveness towards her, Dolly shook her head and surreptitiously nudged Parveen. Saleem glanced at Parveen, tacitly reminding her not to say anything that would upset Dolly. Parveen moved closer to Dolly, who muttered into her ear, 'I've decided to publish Nazia's book without censoring it too much.'

The smirk on Parveen's face disappeared as a new fear settled into her heart. She was tempted to ask Dolly what had led her to make this decision, but the sound of Naureen's voice interrupted her.

'The first session went well,' Naureen said. 'Let's move on to the next one. But, before that, let me give Dolly her reward.' She foraged through her purse and took out an envelope. 'Here you go,' she said, smoothing out the envelope's creases and handing it to Dolly. 'Please accept this as a gift from Nazia.'

Parveen and Saleem shared furtive glances as the wrapper changed hands.

'I can't accept this, Noori.'

'Use this money to market Nazia's book.' Naureen absent-mindedly patted her on the back and turned to Farid. 'Are you ready?'

Farid rose from his seat and walked towards the door, with an anxious look in his eyes.

'Don't worry,' Dolly urged. 'You'll be fine. Just trust Salman Sahib. He'll cleanse your mind of all doubts.'

Farid gazed at Dolly and gave a little sigh as he left the room with Naureen. Dolly knew from the stolid look on his face that he wasn't thrilled at the prospect of surrendering to Salman Narang's tricks and manoeuvres. Even so, she didn't feel the need to assure him or interfere in his distress. As she poured herself a cup of tea, Dolly lifted her face and smiled.

Parveen noticed the glow in her friend's cheeks. 'What's wrong with you?' she asked, leaning over to whisper in her ear. 'Ever since you came down from Nazia's room, you have been so cheerful and optimistic – like a newly-wed bride. What happened to you upstairs? Was it that good an experience?'

'It was.' She nodded, sipping from her teacup. 'I've never felt more relaxed. It was such a—'

'What's that you were saying about publishing Nazia's book?' Parveen cut in, less interested in hearing about Dolly's spiritual awakening during her session with Salman and more concerned for herself. 'You can't possibly publish it if it presents us in a negative light. Nazia had an affair with your husband. You can't let people believe that she's used that affair as the basis for one of her stories.'

Dolly placed the teacup on the coffee table, coughed into her hand and mopped her lips with a handkerchief. 'That's not the part I wanted to exclude,' she said harshly, her anger fuelled by a fresh bout of self-confidence. 'Don't worry. She doesn't even mention you that much. She never thought much of you, Pino. You're the one who made your presence felt in Nazia's life when you poisoned Sabeen's mind.'

'She wasn't a saint,' Parveen said. 'I don't know why you're overlooking this fact.'

'I admit she wasn't the best person in the world,' Dolly said. 'But she was a good friend to all of us. She forgave us for all the terrible things we did to her. You forget, we wronged her too.'

'Good friends don't snatch their friend's fiancé,' Parveen replied curtly. 'Also, she never forgave me. Didn't you hear what she wrote in the letter? She said I'd done "far too much damage" for her to forgive me.'

'Maybe it's time to undo all that damage,' Dolly said. 'All of us have lapses in our judgement, Pino. Why don't you just let it all go?'

'I can't,' Parveen said, fidgeting with her fingers. 'It's not as easy as you may think it is.'

'I know it isn't easy,' Dolly remarked. 'You just have to try harder.'

Parveen stared at Saleem's gaunt face as he spoke to Asfand. He glanced back at her, his eyes lighting up when he caught her watching him. She envied Saleem's self-assuredness, his ability not to draw attention to himself. Yet, there was a distinct energy, a magnetic appeal about him that excited her.

'I don't need to forgive and forget,' Parveen told Dolly as she settled her gaze on Saleem. 'Nazia wronged me. I have every right to hold a grudge.'

'But you must,' Dolly persisted. 'It's the only way to heal.'

Seething with rage, Parveen turned away from Dolly. What has Salman Narang done to her? she wondered. Why is she behaving in such a strange manner?

*

'Are you comfortable?' Salman asked Farid, who was reclining on Nazia's bed with his eyes pressed shut. 'Are you feeling relaxed?'

'Yes,' he replied coldly. 'But I'm still a bit uncertain about having a maid sleeping next to me. Are you allowed to do this?'

Salman nodded. Earlier, in the drawing room, Farid had been his most vociferous critic and Salman had detected more than a hint of disdain in his demeanour. The moment Farid had strolled into Nazia's room with a scowl on his face, Salman was aware that he wasn't going to be receptive to his methods. He would either evade his questions or offer vague and dismissive answers. Unlike his wife, Farid's hypnotherapy wouldn't be determined by an unwillingness to revisit a painful memory, but by a lack of belief. Salman knew that he had to find other means to draw Farid into a hypnotic daze.

'Why is this making you feel so uneasy?' Salman asked.

'Don't get me wrong,' Farid said, chuckling, 'I'm used to women lying next to me. But I've never had a *maid* sleep on the same bed as me. I have my standards.'

'Is that so?' Salman said, ignoring his condescending remark. 'I'm sure you've lain in bed with someone who's on your payroll before. How is lying next to a maid any different?'

'Oh, yes, it is,' Farid said with a grin.

Salman laughed along with him to make him feel at ease and establish a connection. 'Wasn't Nazia on your payroll?' he asked, steering the conversation in another direction.

'Yes,' Farid said sheepishly, his grin vanishing the moment Salman broached the subject.

'Did you ever share a bed with her?' Salman asked, unconcerned by how bold his question may have come across.

'I think that's an awfully personal question.' Farid responded, enraged by Salman's audacity.

'It is,' Salman admitted. 'But there's a reason why I'm asking you this question. I want to understand your relationship with Nazia.'

'Why?' he asked. 'What do you need to know? Didn't Dolly already tell you everything when you hypnotised her?'

'All stories come with multiples narratives. I'm more interested in hearing your version of the story.' Salman smiled.

'She worked at my newspaper for a few years before she became a full-time writer. She was one of my strongest subeditors and a competent journalist,' Farid said.

'Would you say that you were friends?' Salman persisted, trying to appear warm and unthreatening so he could convince Farid to cooperate with him.

'Salman,' Farid said sarcastically, 'I wouldn't have been invited to Nazia's memorial event if I wasn't friends with her.'

Salman began humming the tune of 'Moon River' by Andy Williams.

'How do you know that song?' Farid piped up, puzzled by how the melody continued to impact him. 'It's from way before your time.'

'I heard it on the radio while I was on my way here,' Salman said evenly. 'Do you like this song?'

'I do,' Farid said, his tone softening as a memory returned to him. 'Nazia and I used to dance ...' He bit his tongue when he realised that the words flowing out of his mouth betrayed his intimacy with Nazia.

'Don't stop,' Salman encouraged him. 'You should talk freely about your memories. You'll feel better once you've put everything out in the open.'

'Why would I tell you about my past?' Farid sneered. 'You aren't my friend or confidant.'

'That's true.' Salman nodded. 'But I can guarantee that your secrets will be safe with me. I won't disclose anything you tell me – before, during, or after the session – to anyone.'

'Are you sure?' Farid said, tempted by the hypnotist's offer not to disclose the details of their conversation.

'I know you're still sceptical of me,' Salman said. 'But I promise that you won't be dissatisfied. I can sense that you have been suppressing your feelings about Nazia for a long time. I want you to trust me, so I can help you process your emotions. This was Nazia's last wish.'

Farid contemplated Salman's proposition for a few minutes, until he let out a sigh. 'Fine,' he whispered. 'But I need to come clean about something before that.' He sat up on Nazia's bed and started crying. 'I only walked into this room because I was tempted by the money Nazia has offered me,' he said, moaning softly as he wiped his tears with a handkerchief. 'I need the money because my children make constant demands on me. But my affection for Nazia is pure. I loved her more than anyone. Before I agree to what you're asking me to do, I need to clarify this, for my own sake – for Nazia.'

'I see,' Salman said. 'I would do anything to protect my wife and daughter too.'

He hadn't expected the ease with which he was able to peel back the layers of Farid's past and expose his deepest vulnerabilities in order to establish a delicate rapport with him. Salman ought to have felt a sense of accomplishment. Instead, he felt a twinge of sympathy for Farid, who had drowned his miseries in silence for years. *I did the same when Asifa died*, he mused.

'I'm glad you got this off your conscience,' Salman said. 'How do you feel after opening up to me about your intentions?'

'A burden seems to have fallen from my shoulders,' Farid replied, the traces of a smile appearing on his face. 'I haven't spoken to anyone about this before. It feels good.'

'Let me know when you want to begin,' Salman said.

'I'm ready. Tell me what I have to do.'

'Lie down on the bed again,' Salman instructed him. 'Close your eyes and allow yourself to relax.'

Farid lowered himself on to the pillow tilted against the bedstead and followed Salman's instructions.

'What's your name?' Salman asked, when he was certain that Farid had slipped into a trance.

'My name is Farid Afzal.'

'What do you do for a living?'

'I'm a journalist. I edit the *Weekly*.'

'Did Nazia work with you?'

'Yes. She was one of my subeditors. In fact, she was one of my strongest subs. Nazia knew how to treat a news story with care. She believed that an editor was a housekeeper, not the owner of a house. Her job was to clean up, not seize control of the entire narrative—'

'Okay,' Salman interrupted, reining in Farid's drifting thoughts. 'When did you meet her for the first time? Let's revisit that moment.'

The first thing Farid remembered about the day Nazia walked into his office for an interview was the whiff of her perfume – a soft scent that spread through the cluttered room. He expected that she would be another one of those well-heeled, convent-school graduates who would make a quick pit-stop in the newsroom while waiting to snag an eligible bachelor. But when she gave him a firm handshake before sitting down on a revolving chair, Farid knew how wrong he had been to judge her on the basis of an expensive fragrance.

'When I first meet her, I can tell she is special.'

'What do you mean, "she is special"?'

'She is gutsy and direct,' Farid said, after a short pause. 'She doesn't conceal anything about herself. During our first meeting, she tells me that she is the ex-wife of

Saleem Sabir, an MQM leader who disappeared, leaving her to look after their daughter.'

'Do you fall in love with her that day?'

'Of course not,' Farid responded testily. 'People don't just fall in love so easily.'

Salman bit his tongue, ashamed at his own foolishness. *Not everyone is like you and Asifa*, he chided himself.

'Feelings develop over time,' Farid added, his tone gentler than it had been before. 'In fact, I can't pinpoint the exact moment when my admiration for her morphs into affection. At first, I see her as a diligent employee and a meticulous editor who has a passion for the news. Most of the reporters are fond of her, because she helps them bring their stories to life. I think the only person who doesn't like her is Shamim.'

'Who is Shamim?' Salman asked.

'He is our crime reporter for Karachi,' Farid said. 'Shamim has a soft spot for the MQM and Nazia always calls him out on it. Nazia doesn't care that the media is being forced to toe the line and become a mouthpiece for the militant party. She makes her reservations about the MQM clear.'

'Let's go back to the day you start falling in love with her,' Salman said. 'When do you know?'

'The day I find out about her special connection with Dolly,' he said uneasily, as if he were insecure about confessing this secret.

'How do you find out? Let's revisit that moment.'

Farid shook his head. 'I can't,' he said. 'It's too painful.'

'Why is that?'

'I'd rather not discuss that moment.'

'And yet, that's the moment when you fell in love with her. Quite strange, isn't it?'

'Hardly,' Farid said groggily. 'It is one of my weakest moments. After many years of being the philandering husband, I realise that my wife is cheating on me. That's the day I understand that I've made a grave mistake in judging my wife. I always assumed that she would be emotionally dependent on me forever. After I discover the truth about her affair with Nazia, the fear of losing Dolly gnaws at my heart.'

'How do you find out about the affair?' Salman repeated his question. 'Tell me about that moment.'

Farid's thoughts wound back to the leafy garden of his old house in Clifton. That morning, he was seated on a chair, reading the newspaper and slurping his tea. He had decided against having his tea in bed, after the driver had complained about Gul Khan, their gardener, who hadn't trimmed the grass in weeks and seldom watered the plants near the servant quarters. Farid had also noticed that the leaves of his favourite money plant had started to wilt. Since Dolly had already left for work and he wasn't expected at the office for another two hours, Farid thought he'd discipline the gardener on his own. His presence had frightened Gul Khan and the gardener had no choice but to dutifully mow the lawn.

As he was about to flip the page of his newspaper, Farid heard the doorbell ring. Startled, he folded the paper and placed it at the other end of the table. The bodyguard dashed out of a rectangular room next to the gate, where he slept and listened to the radio, and opened the door.

'Who is it?' Salman asked, with mounting curiosity.

Farid saw a man clad in a blue suit remove his dark sunglasses as he walked past the long blades of grass that Gul Khan had yet to trim.

'I don't know him,' Farid said. 'But he sits down on the chair next to mine and introduces himself as Asfandyar Shahid – Nazia's brother-in-law. He tells me to call him Asfand.'

'Why is he visiting you?'

'I ask him the same question, after telling the cook to bring him a cup of tea.'

'What does he say to you?'

'He tells me that his entire family reads the *Weekly*, now that Nazia's working there.' Farid chuckled. 'Asfand says our editorials are excellent.'

'Does he tell you about the affair?'

'Not immediately,' Farid whispered. 'He asks me why Nazia has such difficult working hours. I'm used to hearing such complaints from the family members of women who work at the newspaper, so I have a standard answer that always manages to appease them. I tell Asfand that all jobs in the media require journalists to work late, regardless of their gender. But I promise to let Nazia leave a little earlier than usual.'

'How does Asfand respond to this?'

'He apologises,' Farid said smugly. 'Asfand assures me that he hasn't come over to complain about Nazia's work hours. He's just concerned because his sister-in-law's job has led her to neglect her child. It's also inappropriate that she's gallivanting around Karachi with Dolly, especially with all the chaos and kidnappings that are taking place.' Farid paused to stifle a grin. 'I tell Asfand to stop worrying, because my wife and his sister-in-law are capable of looking after themselves if anyone dares to kidnap them. But he's adamant that we must address this situation before it slips out of hand.'

'What is he really worried about?' Salman enquired.

'He tells me something that puzzles me. When Dolly was dropping Nazia home two nights ago, she went up to Nazia's room for a couple of minutes. Asfand and his wife go to sleep early, so Dolly and Nazia knew they'd have some privacy. All they'd have to do is whisper so Nazia's daughter wouldn't wake up. But it appears Asfand wasn't asleep yet. He was climbing up the stairs with a glass of water when he saw Dolly and Nazia hugging, their lips locked together.'

'What else does Asfand tell you?'

'Nothing,' Farid said. 'He says that it is his duty to tell me what he saw, that it is embarrassing for him to even mention this to me. But he has no choice. Asfand assures me that he'll make sure he speaks to Nazia, and he asks me to speak to my wife. I tell him that I'll speak to both Nazia and Dolly, and that he should stay out of the matter.'

'Does he listen to you?'

'Asfand stares at the drooping leaves of the money plant,' Farid said. 'He turns to me and politely says, "You should tell your gardener to water that plant. Sometimes, it's the man who has to step in and make sure things are taken care of." With that, he rises from the chair and leaves.'

'How do you feel after he tells you all this? Do you believe him?'

'I'm furious at Nazia.' Farid clenched his fist. 'I've done so much for her and this is how she repays me?'

'Do you fear losing Dolly to her?'

'I told you before,' he responded irately. 'I am scared of nothing other than losing Dolly.'

'What do you decide to do?' Salman probes.

'I confront Nazia that day at the office,' he said haughtily. 'I tell her everything that Asfand told me. At first, Nazia denies it, but eventually she admits to having an affair with Dolly. She fears that I'll sack her and pleads for mercy. Nazia tells me that she is only working so she can put her daughter through school. She says, if she loses her job, her brother-in-law will make her life a living hell. I tell her that her job will be secure on one condition.'

'What condition is that?' Salman said, his tone firm.

'I tell her that she has to sleep with me as well – at least while she and Dolly are doing it.'

'Why do you ask her to do this?' Salman asked.

'Because –' Farid paused for oxygen – 'I believe it will help me connect with Dolly. I want to be part of their affair, albeit indirectly.'

'Does Nazia agree?'

'At first, she says no,' he said. 'But I manage to convince her.'

'How?' Salman said, struck by the triumph in Farid's voice.

'I threaten to tell her daughter about the affair.'

Salman shifted in his seat, dismayed to realise his earlier assessment, that Farid was just like him, was so wrong. Both husband and wife had shamelessly bullied Nazia into submission, even though they claimed to love her. *How can this be love?* he pondered. *I could never have threatened Asifa in the same way.*

'She agrees –' Farid smiled wanly – 'and we start sleeping together, for a long time.'

'You mean, until Dolly ends their affair,' Salman corrected him, more out of curiosity than a desire to seek clarity.

'No. Even after their affair is over, Nazia and I continue to sleep together.'

'Why?' Salman said, confusion creasing his brows.

'I don't know.' Farid shrugged. 'I think she continues to sleep with me to spite Dolly. But things … change for me.'

Salman wanted to scoff, surprised by Farid's attempts to evade his question. He had spoken so effusively about his affection for Nazia, before he agreed to the hypnotherapy. Why was he suddenly holding back?

'When do they change? Your feelings, I mean.'

'After a few months, our relationship settles into a routine.'

'Are the two of you in a relationship?' Salman quizzed him.

'In a way, we are.'

'Let's go back to the day when the relationship comes to an end.'

Salman's words carried Farid to the precise moment of his discontent. He was dancing with Nazia in his study, his arms clasped around her waist, as though he were afraid of letting her go. The final bars of 'Moon River' wafted through the room. As the dance came to an end, Nazia pulled her hands away from his shoulders and hurriedly sat down on the black settee, as though she had been freed from captivity. She looked radiant in her green silk sari, with pearls dangling from her long neck and her hair tied into a low bun. But he didn't have the courage to tell her that. Their relationship – which was, at first, timid, and later bordered on ruthless carnality – was like a transaction, a form of give-and-take that didn't permit sentimental small talk.

'Where is Dolly?' Salman asked.

'She's visiting her mother in Lahore. After the kids go to sleep, I drive over to Nazia's house and pick her up for a quick meeting. We do this every time Dolly leaves town.' Farid chuckled again as he remembered those stolen moments of bliss.

'And where are you?'

'We're at my house, but Nazia isn't happy. She thinks I've been irresponsible, that my decision to pick her up from her house so late at night and bring her here will raise eyebrows. People will talk and soon Dolly will find out that we're sleeping together.'

'Dolly still doesn't know?'

'No, we've been very secretive about the affair,' Farid said. 'We usually meet at my friend's apartment in Clifton, somewhere near Mideast Hospital. I have a spare key. Plus, he's never there because he works in Saudi Arabia. We can have the place to ourselves.'

'Why have you brought Nazia to your house today? Why can't you take her to your friend's apartment? Is he back from Saudi Arabia?'

'No,' Farid said. 'I want tonight to be different. Tonight, I want to see if we can take this relationship to the next level. For some time now, I've been drawn towards her charisma, her vulnerability that is often disguised in a smile. There's no doubt that we are sexually and emotionally compatible. We're like two strangers who find each other in a bustling crowd. I want to spend hours with her and share my darkest secrets and fears with her.'

'Tell me more about what happens at your house on this evening,' Salman said.

'Nazia's …' Farid paused briefly. 'She's asking me why we decided to dance today, instead of going straight to the bedroom.'

'What are you telling her?'

'I explain to her that today is a special day,' he beamed. 'Today's our anniversary. On this day, three years ago, I interviewed her for a job at the *Weekly*.'

'How does Nazia respond to this comment?'

'She laughs. She thinks I'm being silly. I tell her that I've planned this evening because I consider her to be a vital part of my life. Upon hearing this, Nazia starts to weep and accuses me of burdening her with guilt. She feels terrible about betraying Dolly.'

'Do *you* feel guilty?' Salman asked Farid, struggling to expel all traces of judgement from his tone.

'I do. But Nazia never makes me feel like I'm an accomplice to a crime – even though our affair is a well-kept secret.'

'What happens after Nazia breaks down in front of you that night?' Salman asked dryly, sceptical of Farid's response.

'I tell her everything,' he said. 'I confess to her that I've started developing strong feelings for her.'

'Does she reciprocate your feelings?'

'No, she tells me that it's impossible for her to love me and storms out of my house. The next day, she resigns from the *Weekly*, citing family commitments and the desire to focus on her new book. I warn her that she is making a mistake by leaving her career as a journalist. But Nazia is adamant that she wants to escape the chaos of our secret bond. I tell her she is being silly and even threaten to tell Sabeen about our arrangement if she walks out on me.'

'How does Nazia respond to your threats?'

'She doesn't seem too fazed. As she clears her desk and leaves the office, she dares me to do it.'

'What do you do next?' Salman asked. 'Do you tell Sabeen?'

'I decide to do something even more spiteful,' Farid said. 'Soon after she leaves, I call Asfand and tell him everything about my affair with Nazia. As I dial his number, I'm aware that I'm making a mistake. But I want Nazia to suffer. I want her to understand the consequences of walking away from what could have been a strong and meaningful relationship. I'm confident that she won't be able to stay away from me for too long. Nazia has tried to leave me before, a few months ago, when it became difficult for her to deceive Dolly, and I convinced her to reconsider her decision.'

'What does Asfand do when you tell him about it?'

'I don't know. Once my rage settles, I feel a burning desire to discuss what has happened with Nazia. But she wants nothing to do with me. For years, I write her letters to apologise for my mistake. After the world discards the ink-and-paper route and embraces the keyboard, I write her long emails. By then, my feelings have deepened. Absence has turned my affection for her into a love that knows no bounds, almost an obsession. When she doesn't respond, I send her long text messages.'

'Does she ever reply?'

'I only get a few texts from her,' Farid said, tears rolling down his cheek. 'Nazia tells me not to dwell on the past.'

Salman pressed his thumbs against his eyelids and sighed.

'But how can I not dwell on the past?' Farid said. 'I haven't told anyone about what I did to Nazia, because I still feel responsible. I'm responsible for what Asfand did to her. I wish I knew what he'd done. I'd deal with him.'

'Do you feel an apology is all it'll take to win Nazia back?'

'What I've done can't be erased with an apology. I'll have to live with the fact that I betrayed Nazia. It's one of the many sins I'll be held accountable for when I die.' Farid let out a deep sigh, before continuing, 'Over the years, I've just wanted to hold her, give her the assurance that everything will be all right. It's the least I can do.'

'She's right next to you, Farid,' Salman said. 'You can reach out and do it.'

Intuitively, Farid rolled over on the bed and held Sorayya in a tight embrace, caressing her hair with the flat of his palm. 'I'm sorry,' he whispered.

Salman watched Farid with suspicion, perturbed by his show of tenderness. As he snapped his fingers and brought Farid out of his trance, Salman remembered how effortlessly he and Asifa had shown affection for one another, without making any manipulative demands or inconvenient requests. He glanced at Farid as he rose from the bed, smoothed the creases on his shirt and slipped on his shoes.

'How do you feel now?' Salman asked, even though he was still contemplating whether Farid had ever truly loved Nazia.

'I feel calmer,' Farid said, rubbing his eyes and stretching his arms behind his shoulders, as though he'd woken up from a deep sleep. He fumbled in his pockets for his phone and opened the text message Nazia had sent him. Even now, her cold, calculated words had the power to annihilate him. They were forever seeded into his conscience as Nazia's last revenge for his unforgivable treachery.

Nights to Remember

Bi Jaan waddled out of the kitchen as Farid climbed down the staircase.

'What is happening inside Nazia Apa's room?' she asked him. 'What did you do to Sorayya?'

'I … I don't know,' he stammered.

'What do you mean?' Bi Jaan thundered. 'How can you not know? Weren't you in the room with my niece?'

Naureen scurried out of the drawing room and stood by the staircase with her arms akimbo. 'What's the matter, Bi Jaan?' she fumed. 'Why are you shouting?'

'I don't know, Noori,' Farid said, sounding distraught. 'She keeps asking about Sorayya. I don't know what she's—'

'Don't worry,' Naureen interjected. 'These maids are always up to some mischief. Why don't you go to the drawing room? The food has arrived from Cafeela.'

Farid gave Bi Jaan a suspicious glance and then walked towards the drawing room.

'Also,' Naureen continued, holding out an envelope, 'here's your reward from Nazia.'

Farid took the envelope from Naureen without making eye contact with her, and then walked away.

Bi Jaan smeared the tears flowing down her wrinkled face with the back of her hand and eyed Naureen with quiet scorn.

'I warned you,' Naureen said, gritting her teeth.

'I did what I had to do,' Bi Jaan grunted. 'I was trying to protect Sorayya.'

Just then, Naureen's phone buzzed softly in her hand. She was surprised to see a message from Salman: *Dolly accidentally punched the maid. She's not hurt, though. Should we stop this?* Naureen impatiently typed out a *No*, and clicked off her phone screen after sending the message.

'You must understand,' Bi Jaan said pleadingly, 'she's my brother's daughter. When he was on his deathbed, I promised him I would take care of both of his children. I have to protect them from harm.'

Naureen clasped Bi Jaan's arm and gave it a sharp pull as she dragged her towards the kitchen. The old housekeeper groaned in pain, shocked by Naureen's violent tendencies.

'I told you to trust me. No one is *harming* anyone,' Naureen spat out, flinging open the door and pushing Bi Jaan into the cavernous room. 'Didn't I? How hard is it for you to follow instructions? I guess I'll have to take the situation into my own hands now.'

Naureen slammed the kitchen door and hastily locked it, before Bi Jaan could make any attempt to shove it open from the other side. Ignoring the loud thumping against the door, she slinked back into the drawing room and sat down next to her husband.

'Go upstairs,' she whispered, tapping him on his thigh. 'It's your turn. Don't pay attention to the kitchen door; I've just locked it so we can have some privacy. I don't want the servants knowing anything.'

'Noori,' Asfand said in a low voice, once the thudding against the kitchen door had subsided, 'you're insane. How can you possibly hide anything from Bi Jaan when Sorayya is in Nazia's room?'

'Is everything okay?' Dolly said, from the other end of the room. She gently broke pieces of roti and dipped them into a plateful of saag with great delight. Farid sat next to her, tunelessly humming an old Shamim Ara song.

'Oh, yes.' Naureen grinned. 'I was just telling Asfand to go upstairs. It's his turn.'

'You better hurry,' Parveen admonished him. 'We'll be here all night, at this rate.'

'Let's try to keep each session quick,' Saleem said, yawning audibly. 'I live far away.'

'Oh, yeah,' Sabeen muttered, glowering at her father. 'Where do you live, these days? I wouldn't know, since I've never been invited to see my own father's home.'

Saleem bowed his head and pinched his temples, avoiding his daughter's question and her threatening gaze.

'Don't be silly, Saleem,' Dolly said, laughing. 'Salman can't just keep the session quick. It's all about how soon a person arrives at his or her epiphanies.'

Farid nodded eagerly, as if his wife's explanation were a fact that couldn't be questioned.

'Both of you seem to have suddenly developed faith in this Salman character's abilities,' Parveen taunted them. 'I wonder what he does to people in that room. It sounds like it's better than the best sex.'

Sabeen scowled at Parveen, displeased with her sarcastic remark. Relieved to see that his daughter's rage had been transferred towards someone else, Saleem raised his head and smiled.

'I guess it's time for me to find out,' Asfand said, as he rose from the sofa and staggered out of the room.

'*Waise*, Noori,' Parveen said, as she placed an empty plate on the table and cleaned her hands with a napkin, 'how are things between you and Asfand, these days? I've seen a lot of *khus-phus* between you tonight. You seem very involved with each other.'

Naureen scoffed, reassured that Parveen had mistaken their whispered bickering for a sign of marital bliss.

'I agree, Pino,' Dolly chuckled. 'It's good that the two of you are connecting so well.'

'To be honest, I deserve at least half of the credit,' Parveen joked.

'Is that right?' Naureen feigned surprise.

'Of course,' Parveen said. 'By taking Sabeen away from this house when I did, I made sure that you had one less person to think about. And now, with Nazia gone, you will have all the time in the world to fall in love again.'

'I don't think you can be let off the hook so easily for taking Sabeen away from us,' Naureen said, making every attempt to sound composed.

'*Acha*, and who makes you the person who decides if I should be let off the hook or not? When have you ever made any decisions for yourself? Tonight, you're doing your sister's bidding. But she was the one who always made decisions that you benefitted from. All you ever did was stand by while she did you favour upon favour.'

'Pino, let's not get personal,' Naureen said wryly.

'Why not?' Parveen retorted, still smarting over Naureen's efforts to create conflict between her and Sabeen. '*Arre main kehti hoon*, why not?'

'Pino Aunty,' Sabeen snapped as she jumped to her feet, 'how can you be so insensitive? I refuse to be in the same room as you. I'm sitting in the lounge, far away from all your catty remarks about my mother and aunt.'

'You suddenly care about your mother and aunt?' Parveen snorted as Sabeen quickly walked out of the room. 'I'm surprised.'

'Let it go, Pino,' Saleem said, gently squeezing Parveen's knee. She turned towards him, rubbed a teardrop from her eyes and fell silent.

'Noori,' Dolly said, getting up from the chair. 'If Farid and I are done for the night, can we leave?'

'Sure,' Naureen responded, rising from the sofa and hugging them both. 'Thank you for coming. Nazia would have appreciated everything that you did for her—'

'Don't thank us,' Farid cut in, shaking his head and staring at his wife with a glint in his eyes. 'Dolly and I will always appreciate what Nazia did for us today.'

Dolly turned towards him and beamed. As she walked out of Naureen's house, she was confident that she still loved him, despite his occasional belligerence and their shared obsession with Nazia.

When they got into the car, Farid showed her one of the last messages Nazia had sent him. Dolly's hands trembled as he handed her his phone and she read the words on the screen: *It's over Farid. You ruined what Dolly and I had, and you've certainly tarnished what little you've had with me. Let me be.*

By showing her the text, Farid had tacitly confessed his mistakes to someone who, he knew, would understand his pain. As she looked at the message, Dolly battled the urge to tell him about her brief affair with Nazia, their shared lover. While there was so much she wanted to say to Farid, she feared that she would only be telling him things that he already knew.

Farid placed the key in the ignition and reversed on to Sunset Boulevard. Unnerved by the silence that fell in the car, he focused his energies on gliding past the oil tankers and ten-wheeler trucks that plied the road leading towards Mai Kolachi and the port.

'Why don't we turn towards Gizri?' Dolly said. 'We'll be home faster.'

'You're right,' Farid said, bewildered by her calm reaction to a quiet confession of his mistakes.

'Can I delete the message?' Dolly said, in a tone that made the request sound like a peace offering. 'It's … nothing new to me.'

Farid nodded as he drove along the Gizri Flyover, relieved that they were only a few minutes away from home.

'Is the money in your purse?' he asked her, when they were sitting on a couch on their veranda, a few minutes later.

'Yes,' Dolly said, pulling two envelopes out of her purse and waving them in the air.

'Why don't you count the money and keep it in a safe place?'

Dolly tore the flap of the envelope addressed to her and found a single sheet of paper neatly folded inside. She inspected the envelope by running a finger through it. For a fleeting moment, she threw a flustered look at her husband, hoping that he would be able to explain how the money could have slipped out of a sealed envelope. But Farid had flicked on the television and was engrossed in a boisterous discussion on a talk show about Pakistan's new IMF deal.

'That's strange,' she said. 'There's nothing in this envelope apart from a sheet of paper.'

Farid switched off the television, let out a grunting sigh and arched his brows in consternation. Dolly ripped open the second envelope and her jaw dropped as another piece of paper slipped out of it.

'This is odd,' Farid said. 'Is there something written on the paper?'

'They look the same to me,' she said, hurriedly putting on her spectacles and scanning the sheets of paper, her head turning from left to right as she read each line several times over. With every reading, her face tautened and grew sombre.

'What does it say?' Farid asked. 'Is that Nazia's handwriting?'

'Farid,' Dolly blurted out the words, the trace of a smile playing across her lips as she handed him the letter, 'I think you need to read this.'

A scowl came over Farid's face as he read the note. 'What does this even mean?' he cried out in frustration, while Dolly raised her hands to the heavens and applauded her friend.

'Well played, Nazia. Well played,' she whispered, her laugh drenched in melancholy.

*

When Asfand stumbled into Nazia's room, Salman sensed his fear; sweat streaked his forehead and dripped down to his chin. The sight of Sorayya's body sprawled on Nazia's bed further unnerved him. But Salman knew how he'd ease Asfand into a comfortable state. Using his powers of persuasion, Salman would have to lure him into a good-natured conversation about Nazia and then steer it towards the pain of losing a loved one.

'Sorayya is alive,' Salman reassured Asfand.

'I know,' Asfand answered.

'Do bodies terrify you?' Salman asked, patting his shoulder.

'Don't they terrify you?'

'No; I've seen a great deal of loss,' Salman said glumly. 'Bodies don't terrify me. People do.'

'I suppose bodies remind us of what we've lost,' Asfand said.

'Did you feel that way when you buried Nazia, a few days ago?' Salman asked, in a gentle tone that was carefully honed to gain Asfand's trust.

'I've remained tight-lipped for all these days,' Asfand said stoically. 'I don't want Noori to think that I was rattled by her sister's death. And so, I resorted to being sarcastic and cold, when all I wanted to do was break down—'

'I can understand,' Salman interrupted him. 'I too have lost people who I loved dearly. Let's use this as an opportunity to release these emotions. Honestly, I can relate to your predicament.'

Moved by Salman's compassion, Asfand drew him into the dark recesses of his mind, exposing his feelings and frustrations without being thwarted by guilt, ego, or pride.

'Let's go back to the day you met Nazia for the first time,' Salman said, after Asfand had been hypnotised. 'Tell me what you see.' This one will be easy, he thought.

Within minutes, Asfand was transported to the day he first met Nazia.

'Nazia is sitting on a red sofa in her mother's house, in PECHS,' Asfand said calmly, the memory appeasing his restless thoughts. 'She is wearing a turquoise kurta with a white shalwar and her dark hair has been neatly braided. She looks lovely.'

'Why are you observing every minute detail about her appearance?'

'I'm not,' Asfand said warily. 'I mean, I'm trying not to. My grandmother nudges me and tells me to stop gawking. "You're supposed to marry Naureen, not her older sister," Dadi whispers into my ear when Nazia and her mother go to the kitchen to make tea. "Don't make a fool of yourself. It was already so difficult to get Naureen's mother to agree to meet us. She wanted a Pukhtun boy for her youngest daughter, especially after her oldest daughter shamed their family by marrying a Mohajir. She agreed to meet us Punjabis because she knows that you're a successful businessman, unlike her older son-in-law, who is some Mohajir political leader. And you're spoiling everything by ogling her older daughter? Shame on you, Asfand!"

'Dadi stops to catch her breath and then continues with her tirade: "All you youngsters are ungrateful. When I got married, I never even met your grandfather. We saw each other for the first time on our wedding day and didn't even know what to say to each other for the first few months. Soon after, when India was partitioned and our family home was burned down, we fled Ludhiana and travelled to Lahore to start a life together. That's when our silences came to an end and we learned how to love each other."'

Salman chuckled at the absurdity of Asfand's impersonation of his grandmother.

'I apologise to Dadi,' Asfand continued. 'But I'm still intrigued by Nazia.'

'Do you try to talk to her?'

'I don't,' Asfand said sheepishly. 'I can't – Dadi keeps a watchful eye on me. I make small talk with Naureen, but she doesn't intrigue me as much as her sister does. She tells me about the BA degree that she left unfinished because it didn't appeal to her. She mentions the poems she writes in her spare time. I'm tempted to ask her what she means by "spare time", now that she has shelved her university education. Surely all her time is "spare time". But I try to keep my snarky side under check, lest Dadi accuses me of being cruel to my future bride. She raised me single-handedly after my parents died and I can't possibly defy her.'

'Where is Nazia while you're having this conversation with Naureen?' Salman ventured to ask.

'She's sitting right next to Naureen,' he said, with a crooked smile. 'In fact, she's giggling and prodding her sister, trying to get her to recite one of her poems. Naureen obliges this request and recites a morbid poem about a girl who loses her sister in a car crash. Nazia and I exchange glances and stifle the urge to laugh at her awkward choice of words. Touched by Naureen's sincerity, Dadi announces that she approves of the match and asks the girl's mother to prepare for the wedding.'

'Do you talk to Nazia at any point before the wedding?'

'Only once,' he said. 'On the *mehndi*, she tells me stories about Naureen's childhood antics and laughs excitedly at her sister's youthful eccentricities. Naureen isn't there to defend herself, because women aren't brought to their own *mehndi* ceremonies in some conservative families. I don't care much about these stories, anyway. I'm more interested in hearing the soft cadence of Nazia's voice. That night, I consider the possibility of ditching my bride-to-be for her married sister. If Nazia were single, I wouldn't think twice about confessing my feelings to her. But, with that no-good husband of hers in the picture, I don't stand a chance.'

Salman sighed, allowing Asfand to release his bitterness towards Nazia's husband, despite it feeling like a waste of time. So much vitriol each of them carries, he thought, even as they stand so close to the spectre of death.

'What happens after you and Naureen get married?' he asked.

'My feelings for Nazia take a backseat to a new set of emotions that awaken within me,' Asfand said, with a grin. 'As a wife, Naureen turns out to be quite different from the college dropout who recited terrible poetry during our first meeting.'

'What's different about her?'

'Naureen has a latent talent, a quiet intelligence that draws me towards her. She's perceptive and can locate herself in any social situation without being awkward, which makes Dadi value her even more. Naureen has a huge stack of books on her bedside table that she devours with pleasure. In fact, books are the reason we develop a special bond with each other. She lends me dusty, pirated copies of books and urges me to read them with her. Most of these books are silly romance novels that I find tawdry and boring. But she doesn't care. Noori – as I now call her – uses these books to foster some semblance of love in our relationship.'

Asfand paused to clear his throat, and then grinned as a memory returned to him.

'On Fridays, she drives down to her film-maker cousin Mithu's house, in Sindhi Muslim, and returns with his VCR and tapes of Indian movies. Our weekends are spent watching lovers cavorting around trees and whispering sweet nothings into each other's ears in a mustard field. One day, she insists we watch something slightly different – a film in which two sisters fight over a man. I find it strange because it closely mirrors our reality, even though Nazia and Noori aren't fighting over me.'

'That's an interesting choice,' Salman whispered, looking puzzled. 'Why does Naureen insist on watching this film in particular? Have you done anything to make her suspect that you have feelings for Nazia?'

'I don't know,' Asfand replied curtly, making Salman doubt his sincerity.

'Asfand,' Salman admonished him, 'have you done anything to make Naureen suspicious?'

'Not deliberately. But there are things that are beyond my control.'

'What do you mean?'

'Even though our lives have settled into a comfortable routine, I'm struggling to cleanse my mind of those impure thoughts about Nazia. Those feelings make their presence felt in subtle ways. When Noori talks about her amma's plans to sell their house in PECHS and move in with us, I tell her it's a great idea, because Nazia and her daughter will be able to visit us more often. When Noori tells me about her brother-in-law's frequent disappearing acts, I ask her to invite Nazia to live with us, so she can clear her head for a few days.'

'Does Nazia come to stay at your house?' Salman asked, furrowing his brows in disapproval.

'Not immediately,' Asfand said. 'She only comes to stay with us after her husband disappears and she announces that her marriage is over. Nazia and Noori's amma has been dead a few months, and Noori thinks it would be best if her sister comes to stay with us. Their childhood home – which Amma decided against selling after she realised that Nazia's marriage was on the verge of collapse – is filled with far too many memories that could impede Nazia from moving ahead with life. But Noori and I know the real reason why Nazia has been asked to stay with us.'

'What's the reason?'

'Noori's miscarriage,' Asfand said, with a long, sad sigh. 'It's only been a few months since we lost our twins. We've stopped speaking to each other because it's just too painful to remember a time, not too long ago, when we were eagerly awaiting the arrival of our children. After the tragedy, we no longer watch Bollywood movies or read books together. When my grandmother was around, Noori and I had a shared confidante, someone to remind us that we weren't alone. But Dadi passed away some weeks before Amma's death, and now we have been left to grapple with another void. An eerie silence has settled into our home, making us all the more vulnerable. When Noori asks her sister to move in, she is trying to break the silence, to gain back her strength and mine. Though Naureen doesn't mention it, she's pulling us out of our melancholy.'

'Does it help?' Salman asked, even though he is more curious to know about how Asfand could envisage having children with Naureen when he fancied Nazia. If Salman had done this to Asifa, it would have been an act of betrayal, an unforgivable sin. How could Asfand be so cruel to the women in his life?

'It does initially,' Asfand said. 'As Nazia and Sabeen become part of our household, we forget the silences and learn to distract ourselves from our pain. Or, at least, I do.'

'Why do you say that?'

'I'm the one who learns to move on, faster than Noori does,' Asfand said. 'Noori watches me transform. She is puzzled by my new-found interest in her sister's life. When Nazia starts working at a newspaper, I complain to Noori about her sister's late shifts and new friends. "Why does it bother you?" Noori asks me, somewhat cynical of my intentions. "She's capable of looking after herself." But I continue to reprimand Nazia for the way she dresses when she leaves the house, her friendship with her boss's wife and her neglect of Sabeen. Noori mocks my concern for Sabeen because she claims I do nothing to make things easier for that poor child. But I don't pay attention to her quips and continue to criticise her sister. Noori is perhaps the first one to realise that my criticism is rooted in an attraction to Nazia.'

'Really? How do you know? Does Naureen tell you this?'

'She doesn't need to.' Asfand cleared his throat. 'I just know.'

'Do you tell Noo ... Naureen about her sister's friendship with Dolly?' Salman questioned Asfand, hoping to get a more decisive answer on a sensitive issue.

'No,' he said firmly, digging his nails into the bed sheet. 'I don't want to upset her. But I do tell her that I went to see Nazia's boss about her unsociable working hours.'

'How does she react to your interference?'

'Noori continues to scold me for taking too much of an interest in Nazia's life. "You're obsessed with my sister," she shouts at me that evening. "Why can't you focus on your own priorities and let her rebuild her life in peace?" I assure her that I have our family's best interests at heart, but she isn't convinced by my explanation. From that day onwards, I decide against taking my complaints to my wife. That's why she never gets to know about Nazia's affair with Farid.'

Salman nodded uneasily as he listened to Asfand speak. In their hypnotic stupor, each of Nazia's guests has presented a fragment of her past. Though he didn't realise it, Salman was unravelling the familiar story of a much-despised woman as he pieced together the shards of their memories. It was a story he had heard from Nazia when she was alive, but one that was always weighted against her. Nazia's self-reproach and guilt had led Salman to believe that she had been responsible for ruining so many lives. Now, as he probed deeper into the minds of her accidental victims, Salman wondered whether Nazia was at all to blame for their ordeals. The demons that haunted her guests had little to do with her actions; they were steeped in insecurities that were beyond Nazia's control.

'Do you say something to Nazia when you find out about her relationship with Farid?' Salman asked, his eyes drawn towards his watch.

'I just tell her that I know about her and Farid,' Asfand said.

Salman frowned at Asfand's flimsy response to his question. 'Does she ask you how you found out about the affair?'

'She knows how I know. Over the next few days, she makes an attempt to avoid me. I think she fears that I will ask her questions about her relationship with both Dolly and Farid. But I have no questions to ask her. In fact, I don't judge her for the choices she makes. Unfortunately, it takes her time to realise this.'

'Let's revisit the moment when Nazia realises that she is wrong about your intentions,' Salman said. 'What can you tell me about that day?'

Asfand twitched his eyebrows, flared his nostrils and let out a gentle sigh. His mind painted a portrait of Nazia in a white shalwar kameez, with her hair tied into a braid. She was seated on a sofa in the upstairs lounge, sipping a cup of green tea and leafing through a newspaper or a glossy – as she did every night after Sabeen fell asleep. The door of her room had been set ajar so she could keep vigil over her daughter. It was the night before her book launch and Asfand could sense that she was nervous. That morning, Nazia's new book *Satan's Shame* had been panned in the media, by a male reviewer, for depicting women as saints and chastising men for snatching their smallest joys. Nazia's face contorted as she read the review. Asfand realised that she was angry and would chide him if he approached her.

'I walk over to Nazia,' Asfand drawled, raising his hand in the air to emphasise his point. 'She looks surprised to see me. "Have you come to tell me off?" she says. "Or do you plan to accuse me of committing another mistake?" I pull out a pack of cigarettes from my pocket and offer her one. At first, she doesn't know how to respond to this gesture. I reassure her that I'm not there to start another argument. With a tenuous smile, she lights a cigarette, takes a drag and flicks the ashes into an empty coffee mug. "Why are you being nice to me?" she asks, after the scent of smoke has permeated through the lounge. "Why are you so suspicious of my intentions?" I reply, moving cautiously towards her on the sofa. "This is why," she says, flinging the newspaper in my direction. "All you men are alike." Nazia rises from the sofa and walks towards the window.'

'What happens next?'

'I tell her that I've read the review,' Asfand said. 'I assure her that she has nothing to worry about. "The reviewer hasn't understood the book," I tell her. "I think he isn't aware of the real-life incidents from which you derived your characters." Nazia turns away from the window and stares incredulously at me. "How do you know about the incidents that I referred to in my book?" I sink my back against a sofa cushion and chuckle. "I read them in the introductory note. Where else would I know all this?" She scuttles towards me, still perplexed by my words. "You read my books?" she says. "Of course I do," I declare, with every intention of winning her over with my candour. "I've read all of them." Nazia says, "I don't believe it. Even Noori hasn't read all of my books.'"

'Have you actually read all of Nazia's books?' Salman quizzed him, eager to know if Asfand had lied to Nazia.

'Yes,' Asfand said. 'Noori buys two copies of each book to show that she supports her sister – even though she finds her work pedantic and poorly crafted. She places each copy on a separate bookshelf in the house and tries to show enthusiasm for what her sister does. I doubt she can tell if a copy goes missing. I read them in the dead of night, when Noori is asleep.'

'I see,' Salman said, satisfied by Asfand's response. 'What does Nazia say when you tell her this?'

'She's shocked. We spend an hour talking about the characters in her stories. That night, I rest comfortably because I've made her less anxious about her book launch. However, I'm superstitious about our affinity and want to keep it a secret, especially from my wife. So, I try to make everything appear as it should, without letting Noori feel that my chemistry with her sister has changed. My days are spent criticising my sister-in-law in front of Noori and my nights become less lonely with the help of a new friendship. Nazia is confused by our erratic bond, and it gives her another reason to mistrust me. But, with time, she realises that the arrangement serves us well.'

'Why?' Salman said.

'The more secretive we are about our friendship, the less it will hurt Noori.'

Salman furrowed his brows, slightly puzzled by Asfand's logic. If Asfand had been schooled in the etiquette of a good relationship by a woman like Asifa, he wouldn't have felt the need to be discreet. *When couples keep secrets, it damages their relationship*, she would tell Salman. But Asifa also seemed to find solace in her own secrets, cradling them like children and hiding the pain they caused her from him because she feared it would upset him. As he listened to Asfand speak, Salman recalled how Asifa's decision to remain quiet about her misery as the wife of a useless man who could barely make ends meet had damaged their lives in irrevocable ways.

'What do you and Nazia do every night?' Salman asked now, changing the subject.

'We talk. She tells me about her insecure marriage with Saleem and the problems she's been having with Sabeen. "She just keeps doing strange things to get attention," Nazia says. "Even her teachers are concerned." I ask if she wants me to help her in some way, but she refuses to let me intervene. "Sabeen misses her father," she says. "I don't want her to think that someone else is taking Saleem's place." I don't have the heart to tell her that Sabeen gives me an angry stare whenever she sees me. It's obvious that she knows her mother and I have developed a deep, forbidden connection. One day, she sees us surreptitiously stealing a kiss in the drawing room. Although she knows I've seen her, Sabeen doesn't say anything to me or Nazia.'

'Are you and Nazia sleeping together?' Salman said.

'Yes,' Asfand admitted, without hesitation or the fear of consequences. 'It all begins one winter's night, after we decide to call it a day, hug each other and make our way back into our rooms. But, for some reason, we just can't let go of each other. It's almost as if something is binding us together, pulling us towards an unknown territory that we are both eager to explore. We go into the guest room, lie on the bed and make wild, passionate love – the kind I've never had with Noori. We stay there until we hear the morning azan wafting from the loudspeaker of our neighbourhood mosque. From that day onwards, we sleep together in between our late-night discussions. Sometimes, it feels like our bodies are engaged in a deep conversation. It's magic, a strange magnetism.'

'I see,' Salman said. 'Does Naureen find out?'

'She finds out about our late-night conversations,' Asfand replied, with a sense of relief. 'One night, I see her climbing up the stairs at three a.m. "What are you doing up?" I say. "Nazia and I were just … talking." Noori looks puzzled. "I woke up to drink water," she responds feebly. "I noticed that you weren't in bed." Nazia rises from the sofa and tells her sister that she urgently needed someone to talk with about her writing. "You could have woken me up, Nazia Apa," Noori says. "I didn't want to disturb you," Nazia replies. After that day, Noori never climbs up the stairs, even though I know she's awake, pacing the floor of our room. Noori and I never speak about the nights I spend with Nazia, even when news of our illicit friendship has travelled through the neighbourhood.'

'How does that happen?'

'One night, one of our neighbours can't sleep. She pulls out the binoculars to see if she can spot the North Star in Karachi's moonlit sky – an odd way to put herself back to sleep, but Mrs Imdad was always quite eccentric. It appears that her binoculars don't move beyond the window of our guest room. Nazia and I are very particular about pulling the curtains when we go into the bedroom. But, on the night we are discovered, we forget to do it. Noori hears about it from Mrs Imdad, but rubbishes the rumours.'

'Why doesn't Naureen say anything?' Salman said, more out of concern than shock over her decision to remain wilfully oblivious.

'I don't know,' Asfand said. 'And, frankly, I don't care. I am too preoccupied with my feelings for Nazia to care about Noori. If Nazia wants something, I silently make it happen. A few months into our relationship, she wants me to plant bougainvillea in the garden so she'll have something pretty to look at during her evening walks. I tell the gardener to plant it right away. When she wants me to help her climb into the skin of one of her characters, I never disappoint her. At this point, I am her only friend. It upsets me because I'm responsible for the ugly fate of her relationship with Farid and with Dolly – the two friends who have helped her the most.'

'Do you ever tell her about your role in sabotaging those friendships?'

'I do,' Asfand said, almost with relief.

'How does Nazia react?'

'She's not entirely pleased, but we work everything out, with time,' Asfand said, evading the question with an audible yawn. 'She tells me that Dolly and Farid have hurt her. Nazia tells me that our friendship is a source of comfort for her, after her friends betrayed her trust.'

'When does everything change?' Salman grilled him.

'Everything goes smoothly for many years, until Parveen poisons Sabeen's mind against me and her mother. After that, Nazia and I each find ourselves forced to defend our reputation before the people we love. Noori, who has only silently suspected us after hearing rumours from neighbours, is now forced to confront the truth. She tells Parveen to mind her own business and to stop trying to create problems between Nazia and Sabeen. But Parveen has already succeeded in polluting Sabeen's mind against Nazia. When Sabeen leaves with her Pino Aunty and the chances of her returning appear slim, Nazia retreats into a shell of self-loathing. Our late-night trysts come to a staggering halt as she locks herself in her room. Noori keeps telling me that her Nazia Apa plans to leave in a few weeks.

'Soon after, though, Nazia has a stroke. She survives, but she is no longer the same person that she was before. She spends her days writing in her room, stepping out only for meals and her evening walks. I keep my distance from her because I can't recognise the woman she has become. But I do small things to make her life less burdensome. I insist that the bougainvillea creepers are watered every day, so her walks aren't unpleasant. I send her new notebooks through Sorayya, so she can continue writing – the only thing that gives her peace.'

'Are you satisfied with the way your friendship came to an end?'

'It was an abrupt end to a perfect friendship – a knee-jerk reaction to a calamity that we couldn't control.'

'What do you do after the friendship ends?'

'I continue complaining about Nazia's behaviour to Noori.'

'Why?'

'Because I know Nazia wants me to do that. She wants everything to go back to how it was before we became close. She wants to erase all memory of our friendship.'

'Do you think she expects more from you?' Salman asked, making every attempt to dispel the rancour that might have seeped into his voice. 'After all, you are her closest … friend. Surely you could have done something other than just complain?'

'I do what I have to do,' Asfand snapped, after a short, meditative pause. 'I don't want to get into what I should be doing. I've suffered enough already.'

Sensing Asfand's discomfort, Salman put his hand to his face and decided to conclude the session.

'If Nazia were here with you, what would you like her to do?' Salman faltered as he spoke, anxiously looking at Sorayya as he wondered what she would have to endure this time. Now that Naureen had made it clear that she didn't care about Sorayya's safety, he had to protect her.

'I just want to kiss her forehead,' Asfand said. 'I couldn't do it before the burial.'

Salman heaved a soft sigh, grateful that Sorayya had been spared the cruelty and aggression concealed within professions of love for Nazia that the other guests had demonstrated. As he saw Asfand kiss the maid's forehead, Salman recalled the last time he had kissed Asifa.

It was the night before 12 May 2007, hours before Karachi would turn into a battleground where rival groups would clash with each other. Salman didn't know then that Asifa would wake up the next day, drape a *chaddar* over her body and leave the house with their daughter. He couldn't have imagined that he would spend the following evening frantically dialling Asifa's number, waiting for her to answer her mobile phone and reassure him that she and Zahra had survived the chaos that gripped the city during the Black Saturday riots. When he'd held his wife the night before she left,

Salman didn't know that he would forever be searching for Asifa in the things he saw and the people he met. He didn't know that he would be unwilling to abandon the fantasy of being loved by his wife, when it was clear she didn't want him anymore, as he earnestly tried to prevent her from becoming a ghost.

Ruptures and Resolutions

Sabeen flipped through a copy of *Woman's Own* that she'd found on the coffee table in the lounge, staring through teary eyes at photographs of models clad in the latest couture.

Naureen scuttled into the room and patted her shoulder. 'Don't listen to Pino,' she said, smiling demurely. 'She's always saying the strangest things.'

'I wish she'd respect my mother more,' Sabeen said, tossing the magazine back on to the coffee table. 'I wish I'd known how much she hated Mama. Maybe then I wouldn't have been so much of a burden on all of you.'

'Don't say that,' Naureen cooed, kissing Sabeen's forehead and sitting down next to her. 'We don't think you're a burden. Your mother wasn't burdened by you. She loved you. How could you possibly have burdened her?'

Sabeen slung her arm around Naureen's shoulder and leaned her head against her chest. 'I wronged her, Naureen Aunty,' she whispered, tears coursing down her face. 'I wronged you as well. I didn't realise that my actions would hurt the both of you. I was selfish.'

Before she could say something to console her niece, Naureen caught sight of Asfand trundling down the staircase, his hand pressed against his chest and his eyes moist with tears.

'How did it go, Asfand?' she asked, cavalier and calm.

Naureen's question pulled Asfand out of his stupor. He spun around and faced them, wiping away a teardrop that had coursed down his cheek. 'Oh, it was therapeutic,' he said, unwilling to share what had happened in the room. 'I can't recall what happened there, but it made me feel calmer.'

Naureen beamed, though she was unsure if he was telling the truth. 'In that case, we shouldn't keep Sabeen waiting any longer,' she said, getting to her feet and directing her niece towards the stairs. 'Go upstairs, *beti*.'

Sabeen dutifully ran up the stairs. Though she was reluctant to disobey her aunt's orders, she was taken aback by Naureen's abruptness. Am I being punished for defying Mama? It dawned on Sabeen that there was so much she didn't understand about the people she was expected to trust.

'Noori,' Asfand whispered, 'where did your sister find this man? He's helped me deal with so much of my sadness and guilt. I was initially sceptical, but he really knew how to put my misery to rest.'

'I'm so glad,' Naureen said, releasing her fears in a loud exhalation. 'I didn't think you'd support me.'

'I don't,' he said. 'I still don't approve of this party. Everyone is getting on my nerves. But I'm glad that there was a bright spot to it all.'

Naureen nodded, confused by the composure with which Asfand spoke. *What has Salman Narang done to my husband?*

'Noori,' Asfand said, an unusual warmth seeping into his guttural voice. 'I'm sorry about what happened between me and Nazia. I wish I could undo my mistakes, but I can't.'

Silence.

'Can I ask you something?' he said, when his wife didn't respond to his apology.

'Yes,' Naureen said.

'Did you ever want to have a child, after we lost the twins?'

'What do you mean?' Naureen asked, an ache forming in the pit of her stomach.

Just as Asfand was about to respond, they were interrupted by an urgent pounding at the kitchen door. The incessant knocking was followed by indecipherable cries and alarming shrieks. 'Is that Bi Jaan?' Asfand said, moving towards the kitchen to unlock the door. 'Why is she screaming and why is the door locked?'

'Let her be.' Naureen seized her husband's wrist. 'She's just worried about Sorayya. She thinks Salman Narang will harm her. You go into the drawing room; I'll handle her.'

'Noori, are you sure? Let me reassure her that her niece is safe.'

'No, you go entertain our guests,' Naureen said, as she dragged him away from the kitchen door. 'Go tell Saleem Bhai and Pino about how good your hypnotherapy session felt.'

Frazzled by the day's events, Asfand didn't challenge his wife's dictum and strode into the drawing room.

Naureen waited for Asfand to shut the door before she unlocked the kitchen and confronted Bi Jaan. She was leaning against the counter, clutching a ladle in her fist. It was unclear to Naureen if the ladle was to aid Bi Jaan in cooking or to be used as a makeshift weapon in the old woman's growing sense of paranoia for her niece. The thought of it being the latter irritated Naureen.

'Stop knocking on the door,' she said coldly, moving towards the housekeeper and snatching the ladle from her hand. 'If you don't keep quiet and stay in the kitchen, there will be consequences.'

'Naureen Bibi,' Bi Jaan said as she wiped her tears, 'how can you be so cruel? I've spent my entire life in your family's service. I practically raised you and Nazia Apa. How can you possibly disrespect my niece, after all that I've done for you?'

'Don't flatter yourself,' Naureen said sharply. 'You didn't do anything for us selflessly. You got paid for everything that you did. Please don't make this about you. I'm the one who's lost her sister.'

'It doesn't seem like you care,' Bi Jaan blurted out. 'You wouldn't be having parties where men go into rooms alone with women, if you were sad about Nazia Apa's death. She never liked me, because I was more of a mother to her child than she was. But I loved her, even when she tried to make life difficult for me. Nazia Apa always had a foul temper. But she never meant any harm. You didn't love her, even though she did so much for you.'

'How dare you pass judgement on my relationship with my sister?' Naureen roared. 'I don't owe you an explanation, Bi Jaan. Nazia wanted this party.'

'Nazia Apa wanted Sorayya to go into a room with a strange man?' Bi Jaan said sardonically.

'Yes,' Naureen fumed. 'That's exactly what she wanted. Now, stop trying to go upstairs. Sorayya will be fine.' She paced towards the kitchen door, swung it open and then turned to face Bi Jaan.

'There will be consequences if you come outside the kitchen,' she warned. 'I'm not going to lock the door, because I don't want you knocking frantically like you did before. I want you to trust me, and I'll make sure your niece remains safe.'

With that, Naureen whizzed out of the kitchen, leaving Bi Jaan with a threat that didn't frighten her. Naureen's harsh words had released the old housekeeper from the loyalties that had tied her down and compelled her to prioritise her employer's generosity over Sorayya's well-being. Now that her delusions had been shattered, Bi Jaan cared little for Naureen Bibi's promises. She had left her an unlocked door and Bi Jaan was going to use it to save her niece, even if it came at a heavy cost.

*

'How can we trust Imran?' Saleem said, delighting in the irreverence of his own question.

'There's still a long way to go before we see any *tabdeeli*,' Asfand responded feebly, holding a glass of water in his hand and taking quick sips. Exhausted after a long day, he was struggling to show an interest in anyone – especially someone like Saleem, whom he, for some reason, despised even more, after his meeting with Salman Narang, for disrespecting Nazia. Through his lacklustre responses, Asfand indicated to Saleem his disinclination to having a heated political debate at midnight. Realising this, Saleem threw his hands in the air, flashed an insincere smile at his hosts and became silent.

'I know it's late,' Naureen said in an apologetic tone, 'but it won't be long. I promise.'

'Anything for Nazia,' Saleem said, surreptitiously winking at Parveen as she beamed at him.

Naureen noticed this gesture and fought the urge to shoot a disapproving glance at them.

Parveen's phone buzzed softly. She studied the screen for a moment, visibly puzzled by the call. What could Farid possibly want?

'Don't you want to take that call?' Naureen asked.

Parveen nodded, bounced to her feet and slid out of the drawing room.

Naureen poured another cup of tea for herself, her gaze set on Saleem as he made another attempt to comment on the prime minister's failures as a statesman.

'Hello Farid,' Parveen answered, rather cheerily for someone who had been kept waiting for hours. 'I see you're already missing us.'

'It's not that, Pino,' Farid said. 'I need to tell you something.'

'Did your wife leave behind her earrings?' Parveen quipped, giggling as she traipsed into the lounge and flung herself on to the couch. 'She ought to be more careful about such things.'

'This is no laughing matter, Pino,' Farid fumed. 'Dolly and I just opened the envelopes Naureen gave us. There's no money in them.'

'What?' Parveen cried, abruptly rising from the couch. 'Are you sure? If there's no money in them, then what's our reward for going through the godforsaken hypnotherapy?'

'A letter from Nazia,' he said dismissively, as though he'd been cheated out of his inheritance. 'Dolly and I have received the same letter.'

'What does it say?' Parveen said, disappointed by the turn of events. Over the past few hours, she had harboured countless fantasies about the things she would do with the three thousand dollars that Nazia had promised her. Now that Sabeen was dancing to her doting aunt's tune, Parveen would get to keep the money for herself, instead of spending it on Nazia's daughter. And if things went well with Saleem and they ended up together – after all these years of interruptions from unlikely spouses and unfortunate circumstances – they would be able to consolidate their earnings and plan a future that Nazia had deprived them of.

'I'll send you the letter,' he said. 'It's a silly note. It's true Dolly and I were looking forward to the money –

me more than Dolly – but we've made our peace with it, particularly after meeting Salman Narang.'

Parveen scoffed. Why were they still obsessed with that magician?

Moments after she hung up, Parveen received a pixelated image of the letter. Large chunks of it were poorly photographed; words appeared hazy and unreadable, even when she zoomed in to decipher them. She called Farid back to ask him to send a clearer picture, but there was no response, so she messaged him with her request. Driven by a clumsy curiosity to know what Nazia had written in the letter, she dialled Dolly's number – something she hadn't done since their professional relationship had come to an end. When Dolly didn't answer her phone either, Parveen assumed that the couple was playing a trick on her. In the long years that she'd known her, Parveen had been a victim of Dolly's callous demeanour and careless snubs. Dolly was capable of going to any extreme to deceive those whom she despised. Parveen – the writer she had once nurtured and later forsaken – had always been Dolly's most favoured target. She had kept Parveen away from the literary recognition that she deserved, found devious ways to prevent her from gaining press coverage and stripped her book of the benefits of a wider circulation. The sudden phone call and blurred image of the letter were probably another one of her many attempts to mislead Parveen and ensure that she didn't get what she wanted.

'But what if I'm wrong,' Parveen whispered. 'I can't take such a risk.'

She hurriedly texted Saleem to inform him about Farid's call, then placed her phone on the couch. She propped her feet against the coffee table, rubbed her tired eyes and sighed deeply. Bi Jaan peeped through the door, caught sight of Parveen reclining against the couch and briskly retreated into the kitchen. Parveen noticed that Nazia's old housekeeper – the one who had chased after them when they were boisterous children – had tears coursing down her wrinkled face. Her own relationship with Nazia had been strained by circumstances, but, even so, Parveen felt that she owed a duty towards the people who had continued to love her friend, despite her talent for deceit. She pitied Bi Jaan for having tolerated Nazia's absurdities without so much as a whimper. She deserves an award for being selfless, Parveen thought.

'Bi Jaan,' she said, jumping up from the couch and scampering into the kitchen, 'we haven't had the chance to talk about Nazia.'

'I refuse to speak to someone who disrespected Nazia Apa,' Bi Jaan said, vigorously turning away from her as if she were a stranger.

'Bi Jaan,' Parveen said, shifting uncomfortably close to the old housekeeper, 'I understand that you must be devastated by Nazia's death. She was my friend too and I loved her. I hope you know that you can always reach out to me if you need to talk about her. I'm always here for you.'

'If you were here for me, you'd help me, instead of being part of this *tamasha*,' Bi Jaan snapped, fresh tears travelling down her face.

'What do you mean?' Parveen grilled her. 'I don't understand what you're trying to say.'

'This isn't a funeral!' Bi Jaan shouted, unafraid of the possibility that Naureen may hear her complaints. 'Something is going wrong at this party. Have you ever been to a funeral where strange men take innocent girls into bedrooms—?'

'Wait just a second,' Parveen interrupted her. 'Which strangers are taking girls into bedrooms at this party?'

'Nazia Apa's friend, that man in shalwar kameez, has taken my niece Sorayya into the room upstairs,' Bi Jaan said. 'Naureen Bibi isn't letting me enter the room.'

'I'm sure she's all right,' Parveen reassured her, though she was finding it difficult to believe her own words.

'No,' Bi Jaan said anxiously. 'I have a feeling that Sorayya isn't safe. I'm scared that they're going to harm her.'

Before Parveen could comment on the matter, the kitchen door jolted open and Naureen entered the room.

'There you are!' she thundered.

Parveen and Bi Jaan stood speechless as she poured herself a glass of water and hurriedly gulped it down.

'I've been wondering where you went, Pino,' Naureen said. 'I hope everything's all right.'

'Yes, yes,' Parveen said, hobbling away from Bi Jaan. 'I wasn't getting reception on my phone in the lounge, so I came into the kitchen. After the call ended, I got talking with Bi Jaan. Would you believe that I haven't spoken to her in three years?'

'I see,' Naureen said. 'Come back into the drawing room. Saleem Bhai is taking a swipe at the government's accountability policies. It's quite interesting.'

Parveen nodded, guiltily staring at Bi Jaan as she followed Naureen back into the drawing room.

'Where's your phone?' Naureen asked as they walked through the lounge.

'I think I left it in the kitchen,' Parveen said, turning back so she could use this pretext to continue her conversation with Bi Jaan.

'I don't think so,' Naureen said. She picked Parveen's phone up from the couch and smiled. 'I think you left it here,' she said accusingly, handing the phone over to her.

'Oh, yes,' Parveen said, tapping her forehead with her wrist, hoping that she would seem less suspicious if she feigned forgetfulness. She rushed into the drawing room without making eye contact with Naureen.

Naureen watched her with interest, grinning contentedly as she marvelled at the skill with which she had caught Parveen's lie. If she hadn't left the drawing room when Parveen entered the kitchen, Naureen would never have heard her phone beep, and would never have discovered and deleted the image of Nazia's letter that Farid had sent.

She also wouldn't have seen the text messages that Parveen had been exchanging with Saleem throughout the evening.

'I have to keep an eye on her,' Naureen whispered, knowing that it would be a difficult task.

A Daughter's Requiem

'So, Sorraya was okay with this? It doesn't feel right.'

'Your mother wanted Sorayya to help us with the hypnotherapy,' Salman explained to Sabeen.

'That's my mama,' Sabeen laughed uncomfortably. 'She always knew how to get away with eccentric behaviour.'

Salman chuckled, delighted by the warm repartee that he had struck up with Nazia's daughter. *This'll be a breeze*, he thought. *Or at least it will be easier than my experience with the others.*

'I'm sure her eccentric ways gave you something to laugh about,' he said, smiling.

'Not really.' Sabeen fidgeted with her necklace, unsure if she could trust Salman, despite her mother's confidence in him. 'She had a way of hurting people with her reckless behaviour. She did the same with me. I guess that's why I'm here – to put the memory of her mistakes to rest.'

Salman nodded, his smile disappearing as he led Sabeen towards the bed. 'I had a daughter too,' he told her. 'I understand how difficult parent–child relationships can be.'

'Did my mother tell you anything about me?' Sabeen asked, after a moment's hesitation.

'She never spoke ill of you, if that's what you're worried about.' Salman shook his head. 'Nazia was never the sort to disparage others, especially not her friends and family. She always told me how much she loved you, Sabeen. Nazia wished the two of you could have had a better relationship.'

'I do too,' she said.

A long, awkward silence fell between them, reminding them that they were strangers who had been held captive to each other's company.

'Shall we begin?' Salman said finally.

Sabeen lowered herself on to the mattress next to Sorayya. Salman stood beside her, studying her expression as she shut her eyes and he coaxed her into a trance. Sabeen was slightly older than Zahra would have been. Yet, Salman felt a kinship with her, a mysterious connection that he couldn't explain.

'What's your fondest memory of Nazia?' Salman asked, his tone gentler than it had been with Nazia's other guests. 'Let's go back to that day. What can you tell me about it?'

Salman's question transported Sabeen to a sunny afternoon in the Karachi of her childhood. Dust mingled with the grey smoke emanating from the cars that whizzed past them on the road. A child of four years, Sabeen held her mother's hand, terrified yet intrigued as she soaked in the familiar sights, sounds and aromas, which seemed different when viewed from under the cloth roof of a rickshaw, instead of from an air-conditioned car.

'Mama and I take a rickshaw to our fruit vendor,' Sabeen said. 'I've had a sudden craving for banana milkshake and we've run out of bananas. Mama isn't the sort to deny me anything – especially since Baba started spending more hours out of the house and doesn't have time to play with me. So, she drapes a *chaddar* around herself and insists that I change out of my frock and wear the white shalwar kameez Baba bought me for Eid. "Why do I have to wear shalwar kameez?" I protest. My biggest fear is that I'll look like Nani Amma's maid, Bi Jaan – old-fashioned and boring. Puzzled by my fashion-consciousness, Mama remains adamant that I follow her instructions. "I wear shalwar kameez," she says. "So do Nani Amma and Naureen Aunty. Besides, I've explained this to you before. Baba doesn't like it when we go out without him." When she says this, I stop complaining and run into my room to change.'

'Why doesn't Baba let you and Mama leave the house without him?' Salman said.

'Mama never explains why,' Sabeen responded. 'When she first tells me this, I wonder what we've done to deserve this punishment of being trapped in the house. But, one day, when Nani Amma visits us, I overhear Mama telling her that Baba is in danger and that he's afraid his enemies will harm us too. "I told you not to marry that man," Nani Amma scolds Mama. "He can't even provide his family with two square meals a day. Doesn't he feel ashamed that his wife takes handouts from her mother to feed her child?" My mother doesn't respond to my grandmother's dismissive remarks about her husband. Years later, when the memory returns to me, I wonder if Mama regretted being married to Baba.'

'What happens when you leave the house to go to the fruit vendor?' Salman asked, with a desire to pull a young Sabeen out of her despair.

'Mama hails a rickshaw for us and tells the driver to take us to Bahadurabad,' Sabeen said. 'This is the first time I've travelled in a rickshaw. I've always been driven to and from school in Baba's white Mazda. But the self-assuredness with which she climbs into the rickshaw makes it apparent that Mama has done this before. "Sit on my lap," she instructs me. "And remember, don't tell Baba that we went out." When we reach Bahadurabad, Mama holds my hand and buys half a dozen ripe bananas. She peels one and hands it to me. "*Chalo*, let's cross the road and go to the boutique," Mama says. I seize the edge of her *chaddar* and anxiously descend from the footpath to the road. Mama notices my timid movements and pats me on the back. "Don't be scared," she reassures me. "You can't be scared of the road if you haven't walked on it." She gently holds my hand and we run to the other end of the street amid the din of honking cars and energetic Urdu expletives hurled at us by enraged drivers. In those adrenaline-fuelled moments, I learn something about living fearlessly without stepping back.'

'When does your relationship with your mother turn sour?' Salman asked.

Sabeen's mind drifted to the initial days after her mother whisked her off to Naureen Aunty's house. She recalled the doubled-storied structure, with its gabled roof and brick walls, which always appeared larger than her father's house, but lacked the warmth and pull of memories that could make it feel like home. Sabeen's childless aunt was affectionate from a cold, comfortable distance. Asfand Uncle found ways to aggravate her with his constant nagging.

'I complain to Mama about being lonely in our new home. I remind her of our old house that she has told me to forget, and speak of the dreams I have about Baba's return. At first, Mama listens attentively to me, waiting for the day when my grievances would morph into gratitude for my aunt and uncle. With time, Mama finds herself exasperated by my frequent complaints and reluctance to adapt to my new surroundings. She doesn't want me to set myself up for further disappointment by waiting for Baba to return.

'During our third month in Naureen Aunty's house, Mama slaps me when I insist on being taken back to our old house, and she storms out of the room,' Sabeen said, shuddering as she recalled the memory. 'Bi Jaan, who has just moved in with us, is dusting the antique vases in the lounge when she hears me crying. She rushes over to me and cheers me up by telling me the story of a princess who lives in a huge palace. One day, the princess is forced by the queen to move into a new palace, where she can be safe from all the king's enemies. The princess doesn't want to leave her old palace, but she has no choice. Soon enough, she makes new friends who help her forget her ordeal. That night, I sleep with the assurance that I'll make friends who can help *me* overcome the past. As the years go by, I wait for friends who can fathom my need for comfort and erase the memory of my early childhood with Baba. But the friends I meet at school drift in and out of my life, outgrowing my insecurities and tantrums. Bi Jaan remains my only friend.'

'Do you ever ask your mother why she slapped you?'

'I know why she did it,' Sabeen said, tears flowing down her cheeks. 'I also know why she is always shouting at me. She wants me to be strong. But I keep resisting her attempts to toughen me up. Unlike Mama, I'm not afraid to expose my vulnerabilities. Over the years, she disguises her weaknesses so no one can take advantage of her.'

'How do you know that she disguises her weaknesses?' Salman asked.

Sabeen paused, drew a heavy breath and exhaled gently. The question had perplexed her, pulling her to the core of a mystery that she wasn't prepared to solve. It pained her to revisit and unpack the distressing memories of her mother. So, she opted for what others told her, hoping that it wouldn't do her mother a disservice.

'Dolly Aunty tells me something one day,' she said. 'It's soon after Mama starts working at Uncle Farid's newspaper.'

'What does she say?' Salman said, pretending not to know about the incident.

'She tells me that my mother sleeps with women,' Sabeen said, her lips trembling as she uttered the words. 'I don't understand what she means. But Dolly Aunty's tone tells me that my mother has done something bad. For some months after that, I notice that my mother comes home later than usual, so I ask her where she's been. "I'm at work, *beti*," she tells me. "Oh," I respond accusingly. "Is that where you sleep with women?" Mama is visibly disturbed by my question and asks me where I learned that expression. When I repeat Dolly Aunty's words to her, Mama scolds me for disrespecting her and tells Bi Jaan to take me to another room for the night. I know I've made a mistake when she shouts these orders to the housekeeper. For the rest of the night, I lie on a bed in the guest room, next to my mother's room, with Bi Jaan. Throughout the night, I struggle to sleep. The muffled cries emanating from Mama's locked room are a painful reminder of how a few harsh words can hurt people in irreparable ways.'

'Do you eventually apologise to her?'

'I don't,' Sabeen replied. 'Dolly Aunty's words keep streaming through my mind over the next few years, especially after an incident in secondary school where my classmate Sadia stops speaking to her friend Naila because she kissed her on the cheek. "She thinks I want to sleep with women," Sadia mockingly tells a gaggle of schoolgirls during recess. "Naila is a bloody lesbo!" The rancour in Sadia's words irks me, leading me towards the inconvenient truth that my mother is also guilty of the same eccentricities, that she too is a "bloody lesbo". A deep disgust wells up inside me. When Mama is at work, I pull open her drawers and scan through her diaries for any signs that can confirm my doubts. In the ink-stained pages of her notebook, I discover truths that my mother concealed from me about her married life with Baba, the pain she endured on account of his disappearance. With each entry, my mother paints me a picture of the MQM as a warehouse of violence that defies Baba's blind devotion to the party. Nestled between these entries is a short paragraph about her friendship with Dolly Aunty. Mama writes that their relationship is akin to rain in an arid desert, an escape from the agonies of her past with Baba.'

'How do those diary entries make you feel?'

'I feel sorry for my mother,' Sabeen said. 'But some of her words make me angry.'

'Why?' Salman asked.

'She mentions her affair with Farid Uncle in a few entries,' Sabeen said. 'It was wrong of her to do that to Dolly Aunty.'

'Is that all you are angry about?'

'One of her entries is about a phone call she got from Baba,' Sabeen said in a hushed tone, suddenly remembering that she had to be secretive about reading her mother's diaries. 'If her diary is anything to go by, he came back after many years and wanted to see me. But Mama forbade him from meeting me because, she thought, he'd lost the right to care about me. When I read that, I'm enraged. How could my mother make such a crucial decision without consulting me? The least she could have done was ask me if I wanted to meet Baba.'

'Do you ever ask her why she did that?'

'No. I don't have the courage to. I just keep reading her diaries to find answers to my questions.'

'Does your mother know that you are reading her diary?'

'I'm not sure,' Sabeen said, as she pondered over the question. 'She always keeps the diaries in her drawers. One day, I find her most recent diary on the nightstand. The following week, it is on top of her pillow. The week after that, I notice that she's dog-eared a few pages of her notebook. My child's mind wonders if she wants me to read these entries in particular. This continues for several weeks, until Mama becomes friendly with Asfand Uncle.'

'Why is that?' Salman demanded. 'What changes after she becomes friends with him?'

'She doesn't seem to write her diaries anymore. I keep going through the drawers, searching for new notebooks that my mother may have filled with her thoughts. But I find nothing. I wonder if she's found a new hiding place for them. It takes me some weeks to realise that she doesn't write her diaries anymore. She doesn't need to. The time Mama spent penning her thoughts is now spent with Asfand Uncle. It seems his companionship substitutes Mama's need for a diary.'

'How does that make you feel?' Salman asked.

Sabeen recalled waking up as a teenager to a chilling nightmare about her mother abandoning her. She suppressed a shriek, took a deep breath and switched on the table lamp. After guzzling down a glass of water, Sabeen noticed that her mother wasn't sleeping beside her. Alarmed by her absence, she ran towards the door and peeked out on to the veranda. She gasped in terror when she saw her mother hugging Asfand Uncle and entering the guest room with him.

'I don't know how to react when I see her go into the room with Asfand Uncle,' Sabeen told Salman. 'I am tempted to knock on the door and bring her back into my room under some pretext or the other. But I suspect that she won't come back. As I go back to sleep, I pray that Asfand Uncle dies so that Mama can stop spending her nights with him. But God has a way of ignoring my prayers and doing the exact opposite of what I want Him to do. Asfand Uncle's health doesn't deteriorate, and he continues to spend time with my mother.'

'When do you start losing your patience with your mother?' Salman asked, bringing Sabeen to the vortex of her pain. 'Let's revisit that moment.'

'It all begins when Pino Aunty comes to visit Mama,' Sabeen said. 'I haven't met her before, but Mama says they have been friends since they were kids. Bi Jaan is delighted to see her, even though she later tells me that Pino Aunty is not to be trusted because she always covets everything that Mama has. Even Naureen Aunty comes out of her shell and has a long chat with Pino Aunty – which comes as a surprise to me, because Naureen Aunty only enjoys the company of her worn-out books.'

'What is your first impression of Pino Aunty?' Salman said, coughing.

'I think she should wear more colour.' Sabeen giggled. 'That impression doesn't change when she starts visiting the house frequently over the next few months. She always wears grey shalwar kameez and ties her hair in a messy braid. Even her *paranda* is grey. I don't understand why she'd be comfortable dressing in this manner. When I tell Mama that, she scolds me for being insensitive. "Pino Aunty's husband died earlier this year," she says. "She doesn't want to dress in such a flashy way until a year has passed." As I get to know Pino Aunty, she starts dressing in colourful kurtas and lets her hair flow down her shoulders. She doesn't seem conventionally beautiful, but has a graceful demeanour that adds to her allure.'

'Why does Pino Aunty make you less patient with your mother?' Salman said, steadily losing interest in Sabeen's long-winded monologue. At first, he'd wanted to remain less proactive throughout his session with Sabeen, so she'd have the chance to release all the frustrations she had about her mother. She had initially reminded him of Zahra, but Salman sensed that Sabeen was nothing like his daughter. Zahra had been blessed with a precocious mind and knew how to lend emotional support to her parents with her mere presence.

Over the years, Salman had convinced himself that Zahra had tried to discourage Asifa from leaving, because she didn't want her parents to stay apart. Sabeen was childish, callow and cruel. While listening to her speak, Salman felt the need to chastise her for being insensitive towards a mother who had only tried to protect her. Between his lax attitude towards her during the hypnotherapy and her meandering thoughts, which drifted from her sheltered childhood to Pino Aunty's sartorial choices, Salman felt they were wasting time. He peeped out of the window at the dark, starless sky, and then saw the trucks trundling down Sunset Boulevard. *It's getting late*, he thought. *I need to wrap this session up quickly.*

'Pino Aunty talks to me all the time,' Sabeen said. 'She asks me about my mother. She wants to know what my mother writes and how often she does it. I'm perceptive enough to recognise that she's jealous of my mother's success as a writer. I tell her that I haven't read my mother's books and am not even remotely curious about the stories she writes.

'Soon, Pino Aunty begins asking questions about matters that shouldn't concern her. She asks me if Mama is friends with Asfand Uncle. I lie to Pino Aunty because I don't want her to think poorly of my mother. Sometimes, she brings me sweets and new dresses, and takes me out for long drives. These drives are nothing like my childhood excursions around Karachi with Mama. They leave me feeling somewhat uncomfortable because Pino Aunty repeatedly asks me if I miss my father. "Have you met him since he left?" she asks, as we drive down Shahrah-e-Faisal one evening. "No, I don't think he wants to see me," I lie, in cold denial of what I've read in Mama's diary entries. "But that doesn't mean you don't miss him," Pino Aunty adds. Upon further interrogation, I break down and confess to her that she's the only one who is willing to talk about Baba, since Mama has remained tight-lipped about his whereabouts for almost two decades.

'From that day onwards, I develop a special connection with Pino Aunty. She takes me out a few times a week and tells me everything she knows about my father – or, at least, what she can remember. Nobody questions my growing friendship with Pino Aunty – nobody, that is, except Bi Jaan.'

'Is that right?' Salman blurted out in a grunting whisper, unsure if he wanted to ask a question or make a statement.

'Yes,' Sabeen said. 'She still doesn't trust Pino Aunty. But I tell her that, if Mama doesn't care about my friendship with her own childhood friend, then an old housekeeper certainly has no authority to raise objections.'

'Ah,' Salman said irately, unwilling to forgive the elitist undertones of Sabeen's words. 'How does your relationship with Pino Aunty make you less patient with your mother?'

Sabeen sighed, frustrated by Salman's decision to repeat his question. 'As I spend time with Pino Aunty, I become aware of the mistakes my mother has made. She simply plucked me out of my father's house and moved me to a different setting. She expected me to forget my father as easily as she did. Over the years, I'd come to realise that my mother's relationship with Asfand Uncle stemmed from a desire to find a safe haven for me. Had Asfand Uncle bullied her to sleep with him? I didn't dare to ask anyone this question – even Pino Aunty. I just learned to believe that there was an element of manipulation in their relationship, because it helped me hate my mother less. But Pino Aunty makes me see my mother less as a victim and more as a perpetrator.'

'I see,' Salman said. 'Is that why you believe her when she tells you that Nazia is having an affair with Asfand Uncle?'

'When she tells me about the affair, I pretend that this is the first time I've heard about it. I use it as an opportunity to fight with my mother, to unleash the anguish that I've nursed in my heart since we moved to Naureen Aunty's house. I want her to know that what she's done to me is inexcusable. Mama has controlled my life by choosing who should be in it and who shouldn't. I want her to know that she is wrong to think that I can't make these decisions for myself. While I've grown accustomed to her disappearing acts and midnight trysts with Asfand Uncle, and perhaps also understand her need for comfort, I want Mama to know that she has been a selfish parent. I decide to leave Mama and move in with Pino Aunty. It's my mother's punishment for putting her own need for closure and change before mine.'

As he heard Sabeen's reasons for leaving her mother, Salman wondered if Zahra would have done the same to him for ignoring their family's needs in order to prioritise his profession. Did Asifa take Zahra away from me to spare me the pain of losing her as an adult? He would never know.

'Do you miss your mother, after you move in with Pino Aunty?' Salman asked, temporarily expelling all thoughts about Asifa and Zahra from his mind.

'Every single day,' Sabeen said, with a fervour that brought a smile to Salman's face. 'I read her books for the first time. It unnerves me that I was in the same room with her when she wrote these stories. And yet, each word that she has written in her books alienates me from her. I keep trying to find in them traces of the person my mother was before Baba left. But her books were written after she had purged herself of him. When Mama's books can't offer a glimpse of the woman who sneakily took me to Bahadurabad in a rickshaw, I look for her in other places. I join a group of young women in Karachi who ride bicycles around the city to reclaim public spaces. My reasons for joining them are purely personal. I want to be as daring, courageous and carefree as Mama used to be.'

'Do you think you did the right thing by leaving your mother?' Salman asked.

'No, I don't,' Sabeen said glumly. 'At the time, it felt like the right thing to do. Pino Aunty wasn't the right person to trust, because she manipulated my personal discontents as a way of keeping me away from Mama. She didn't tell me that my mother was ill, and I was racked with guilt when I came to know that Sorayya had fulfilled all the duties that were meant to be mine. I should have been with her until the very end.'

'Do you think you'll ever come back to live with your aunt and uncle?' Salman asked, desperate for her to respond in the affirmative.

'I will,' she said with certainty. 'I must. I can't keep running away from reality. My mother would have wanted me to come back. But I need to find the right moment to return.'

'I think you should move back to your aunt's house,' Salman said, unconcerned by the fact that he was overstepping his bounds and depriving Sabeen of the opportunity to reach a conclusion on her own. It didn't matter that he was trying to steer her thoughts in a particular direction and expecting her to respond to his suggestion. Salman sensed that Sabeen, who had always sought comfort in escaping reality, now needed her family to ease the pain of losing Nazia. What was the harm in ensuring her well-being?

Sabeen nodded her agreement, registering the orders with a lopsided smile.

'Your mama is lying next to you, Sabeen,' Salman said. 'Why don't you turn over and hug her goodbye?'

Though he was wary of any unforeseen behaviour that could harm Sorayya, Salman knew Sabeen would be gentle with the maid. Tears coursed down Sabeen's face as she rolled over, tightly clutched Sorayya's waist, buried her face against her shoulder and wept. Salman rose from his seat, pulled out a handkerchief from his pocket and wiped his tears.

The mere sight of Sabeen sobbing reminded him of a time when Zahra had cried on his shoulder because her teacher had scolded her for not paying her school fees on time. Minutes later, when he drew Sabeen out of her trance, he knew that she was no different from his own daughter.

Another Betrayal

'Can I speak to you, Naureen Aunty?' Sabeen said as she staggered into the drawing room. 'Asfand Uncle, I want you to be there as well.'

Naureen nodded and turned towards Asfand, who seemed eager to excuse himself from Saleem's company. He rose from the sofa, while Saleem continued talking about the sordid nature of Karachi's politics. Asfand rubbed his eyes, stifled a yawn and signalled Sabeen and Naureen to meet him outside.

Parveen shot to her feet, walked over to Sabeen and squeezed her hand. 'What do you need to talk about that you can't say in front of me?' she asked Sabeen.

'Pino Aunty,' Sabeen said, staring coldly at Parveen, 'this doesn't concern you.'

'Pino,' Naureen said, 'it's time for your session with Salman. Also, I completely forgot.' She tucked a small envelope into Sabeen's hand.

'I don't want it, Naureen Aunty,' Sabeen said. 'I don't care about Mama's money.'

'Then I'm sure the envelope won't disappoint you,' Parveen quipped.

Naureen momentarily flinched, and then frowned at Parveen, her eyes daring her to speak further.

'Stay out of my life,' Sabeen said firmly, pointing a finger at Parveen.

Naureen held Sabeen in a tight embrace and reassuringly rubbed her neck.

Responding to her aunt's attempts to comfort her, Sabeen lowered her finger and shrugged.

'Go upstairs to Nazia's room, Pino,' Naureen sternly instructed her. 'It's getting late.'

'Let's go in the garden,' Sabeen said. 'That way, we'll have a little bit of privacy.'

When Sabeen had walked out of the room with her aunt and uncle, Parveen let out a loud sigh and sat next to Saleem. She lowered her neck and pinched her temples, half-hoping that he would offer to massage her shoulders and ease her distress. But he continued to stare at his phone screen, oblivious to her presence in the room. *Has something changed between us?*

'Did you get my text?' Parveen questioned him.

Saleem stared at his phone and hummed, as though he hadn't heard her.

'I asked if you'd read my text,' she reiterated a few minutes after he'd snubbed her.

'I heard what you said,' Saleem snapped. 'Yes, I did see your text. Did you find out what's in the letter?'

'Why are you taking that tone with me?' Parveen scowled in confusion. 'It's not like it's my fault that there's no money in the envelope.'

'I know,' Saleem said brusquely.

'What's wrong, Saleem?' Parveen gently tapped his knee. 'You and I are on the same side. Haven't you noticed how we've been getting along so well? We have great chemistry. But it's not too late, even now, to take our special connection to the next level.'

'Are you out of your mind?' Saleem retorted. 'I don't love you. I've never loved you. What gave you the impression that I was even remotely interested in you?'

'You were so caring and considerate.' Parveen hesitated, her heart racing at a frantic pace. 'I just thought …'

'You thought wrong,' he said grimly. 'I was being nice to you so you'd share your earnings with me. Sabeen would never give me her share. My darling daughter hates me. Anyway, now that we know there's no money, I have no reason to pretend anymore.' He snorted and then returned to his phone. 'I've texted Farid to ask what the letter is all about, though,' he added. 'So don't fret, Pino darling.' He let out a grunting laugh and slapped his thigh. 'Gosh, I can't believe you thought I was falling in love with you,' he said. 'That's bizarre.'

'I thought you'd finally realised how much I've loved you for all these years,' Parveen said. 'You know how devoted I am to you. Saleem, why did you let me believe—?'

'I did no such thing,' he countered. 'Besides, I'm already married and not interested in becoming a polygamist anytime soon. Now, go upstairs. Maybe you'll fall in love with Mr Voodoo-Man in Nazia's room as well.'

Saleem roared with laughter as Parveen stormed out of the drawing room and dashed up the staircase. Though she had been humiliated by the man she loved, she willed herself not to cry – at least, not until she had been duly compensated for the agony and disgrace that she had endured throughout the evening.

*

In the garden, the bougainvillea quivered against a gentle breeze. The distant hum of horns and moving cars along Sunset Boulevard seemed oddly familiar to Sabeen, like an old lullaby that had once put her to sleep. Naureen and Asfand gazed at their neighbours' house, the one with ornate lamps dangling from the balcony, which cast large shadows on their driveway. Tonight, the lamps had been switched off and the din of the generator reverberated through the air.

'It's strange that the Maliks are the only ones who don't have *bijli*.' Asfand spoke loudly, so he could be heard against the whirr of the neighbours' generator. 'The entire neighbourhood usually faces power outages at the same time.'

'I want to move back in,' Sabeen blurted. 'Can I?'

Naureen craned her neck to face her, and smiled. 'Of course you can, *beti*,' she said warmly. 'I'll have Bi Jaan prepare your room tomorrow.'

'I was actually hoping that I could stay here tonight,' Sabeen said hesitatingly, fearing that her request would be denied. 'I'll just go over and get my things. I can't possibly stay away from my mother's home. I need to be with the people she loved, especially because I wasn't there for her when she was dying.'

'Okay,' Naureen said, looking puzzled, yet grinning with pleasure. 'Who are you, and what have you done with our Sabeen?'

Asfand laughed uproariously.

Sabeen's lips stretched into a broad smile. 'I was wrong,' she said. 'I shouldn't have abandoned her. It was all a misunderstanding. Under the circumstances, I feel ashamed to take her money.' She held up the envelope that Naureen had given her and momentarily observed it rustle against the breeze, before returning it to her aunt.

Sabeen extended her hand towards her aunt, who instinctively held it between her palms. Asfand observed this silent exchange with a smile. Sabeen threw an impassive glance at her uncle as she struggled to smile back at him. Even now, she couldn't summon the strength to forgive him. Freeing Asfand from blame wasn't going to be easy.

She knew that she'd have to pretend to be oblivious about her mother's affair with Asfand if she wished to return to Naureen Aunty's house. She would have to be cordial with him to protect her aunt's feelings. *Will I ever be able to forgive him?* Unable to answer the question just yet, she hugged her aunt and nodded amiably at Asfand.

'I'd like to go and get my things from Pino Aunty's house quickly,' she said, dislodging herself from Naureen's embrace and dabbing her eyes with a tissue. 'I'll just get my purse from the drawing room.'

When they returned to the drawing room, Saleem was busily typing on his phone. Sabeen retrieved her bag from the sofa, scurried over to him and smiled. Saleem froze, unsure if he should reciprocate the gesture or disguise his emotions in a blank stare.

'I just want you to know a few things, Baba,' she said softly. 'I'm moving back in with Naureen Aunty. I'm not telling you this because I want you to visit me. I'm just saying it because I need you to know that Naureen Aunty's house provided me with stability when I needed it the most. I can't really forgive you for leaving Mama and me all those years ago. But I must thank you for giving me the opportunity to recognise and appreciate love, especially when it comes from those who aren't our parents.'

Saleem put his phone back into his pocket, rose from his seat and placed a hand on her head. 'Be happy, *beti*,' he whispered tearfully, unable to disguise his regrets about his failings as a father. 'I wish I could have been the father figure your mother asked me to be in her letter. But I see you already have two people who will always guide you.'

Naureen cleared her throat to get Sabeen's attention. 'Asfand will drive you to Pino's house,' she said. 'You can get your clothes and stay in the guest room tonight. It's already 1:30 a.m. and Salman still needs Nazia's room for Parveen's session and Saleem's session. Tomorrow, I'll have Bi Jaan help you settle into your mother's room.'

Sabeen nodded, muttered a polite *salaam* to her father and walked out of the room with Asfand and Naureen.

As they left, Saleem's phone buzzed loudly. He wiped his tears with a handkerchief and let out a deep sigh before he answered the phone.

'Hello, Farid,' Saleem hissed into the receiver. 'Where have you been? Pino tried calling you and Dolly earlier, but there was no response.' He listened quietly as the caller responded to his question, his eyes wide in shock and his mouth suddenly dropping open.

*

Parveen gingerly lay down on Nazia's bed and tucked her elbows into a cushion. She gaped at Sorayya, amazed at how someone could sleep so peacefully.

'Is she alive?' she asked Salman, narrowing her eyes.

'Of course she is,' Salman said impassively. 'I'm a hypnotist, not a murderer.'

Parveen couldn't tell if he was being flippant, or if her question had genuinely offended him. She lowered her neck on to the ruched pillowcase and pressed her head deeper into the cushion.

'Frankly, I didn't know what to expect from you, when I first met you,' Parveen said. 'I decided just to pretend to be hypnotised by you, mumble all kinds of gibberish and walk away with my share of the reward.'

'What made you change your mind?' Salman quipped.

'Circumstances,' she responded vaguely, blinking her eyes to prevent tears from cascading down her face. 'I think I could use an escape from reality, for a short while. I want you to get me to sleep, just like you've put Sorayya to sleep.'

'I'm not here to sing you a lullaby, madam,' Salman said, irritated by her demands. 'I'm here to help you resolve your differences with Nazia. But this is a good sign. Your willingness to temporarily break away from reality will help you enter a hypnotic trance.'

'Then what are we waiting for?' Parveen enquired.

It took Salman a few minutes of intense breathing exercises to lull Parveen into a state of calm. Puzzled by her eagerness to slip into a hypnotic state, he eyed her with a mix of suspicion and apprehension. *Is she faking it?* he mulled. *I have a way to find out.* He leaned against the mattress, gently lifted her hand closer to his mouth and blew on it. When Parveen didn't jump up and shoot him an outraged stare, Salman knew she was in a trance.

'What is your earliest memory of Nazia?' he began.

Parveen nodded slowly and offered Salman a weary smile as she delved into a memory that had eluded her all these years. The first thing she recalled was the date – 4 April 1979. Once the memory had set its parameters in her mind and transported her back in time, Parveen checked the date on the wall calendar that Diya had placed near the kitchen cabinet of their new home – just to be sure. Rumours flew thick that Bhutto Sahib had been hanged. When she heard the news, Diya had settled into their living-room sofa and guzzled a glass of whiskey, as if the death of a prime minister called for a celebratory drink. Parveen had stared blankly at her mother as she cursed Bhutto for his opportunism.

'If he had let Mujib become prime minister, your father wouldn't have had to fight a war in East Pakistan,' Diya told her daughter, in an inebriated state. 'If East

Pakistan hadn't become Bangladesh, your father would be alive today.' Reluctant to hear her mother's laughter morph into tears for her dead husband, Parveen crept out of the living room and strolled into the garden.

'I hear two girls playing in the garden next door,' Parveen said groggily. 'I climb up the palm tree and see Nazia, the louder of the two girls, playing with her sister. They have made tents out of bed sheets and are pounding ladles on steel pots as they pretend to cook. "Apa, you always get to play the princess," Naureen says. "Why can't you play the cook, so I can play the princess?" Nazia shrugs. "Don't be silly," she tells her sister. "I'm the pretty one. Don't you know that the older sister always gets to play the princess?" I laugh hysterically as Naureen sneers at her sister and goes back to beating the ladle on the pots. "Did I crack a joke?" Nazia says, pointing a stick at me. "Yes, a funny one," I respond jubilantly. Perhaps warmed by my comeback, Nazia smiles and waves me over. "Come play with us," she says. I jump down from the tree and land on thick grass.'

'So, you instantly become friends?'

'Yes. It starts with all three of us playing games in the tent for a few months. When the monsoon season begins and the tent is removed from the garden, we start spending time on their veranda, sipping tea and gorging on pakoras that Bi Jaan, the maid, lovingly prepares for us. Naureen is too young and spends her time playing by herself. On those rainy days, Nazia becomes my sole companion, and her house becomes my sanctuary away from home.

'We spend the evenings drawing pictures, doing homework and exchanging secrets. She asks me why I call my mother Diya. "My mother believes that, if I call her by her first name, I won't miss my father anymore," I tell her. Nazia looks confused, so I explain, "If I don't have someone to call Mama, I won't feel the need to have someone to call Baba." I ask her why she's so bossy with her sister. "Noori is a pushover," she tells me. "I'm just trying to make her stronger." I tell her that this is actually just a silly excuse to bully Naureen. With a devious smile, she confesses that she enjoys having the upper hand. But, when it comes to her sister, Nazia has to be a lot more protective because Naureen is impressionable and doesn't realise when she's being exploited. Her candour draws me close to her. Eventually, I convince Diya to let us attend the same school – just so I can spend more time with my new best friend.'

'When do things begin to change?' Salman enquired.

'I think it happens when we each discover that we want to write stories,' Parveen responded. 'Both Nazia and I are avid readers. While she prefers Dickens and Hardy, I survive on a staple of Enid Blyton novels that offer an escape from my wretched life with Diya. But our conflicting preferences don't become a problem until we decide to write a book together. "You write one chapter," Nazia tells me. "Once you're done, give it to me and I'll write the next one. We'll keep doing it until the story comes to an end. When we're older, we can publish it under both of our names. It'll be a novel by two best friends. I'm sure everyone will love it." A week later, I give her the first chapter of a story about a girl named Sanya, who grows up in a mansion with doting parents who always shower her with presents. But, when Nazia gives me the next chapter, I notice that the idyllic life I'd created for Sanya has been blithely distorted. In this chapter, Sanya's father dies on the battlefield, her mother develops a longstanding companionship with whiskey, and Sanya stops receiving presents. As I read the chapter, I wonder if Nazia has sought inspiration from my own life.'

'*Has* she been inspired by your life?' Salman asked.

'I don't know,' Parveen said. 'I try not to think about it. Without further ado, I begin writing the next chapter of our book. In this installment, it is revealed that Sanya's father was only presumed to be dead. He returns from the war and urges his wife to stop drinking. The chapter ends with Sanya's parents buying her presents. Nazia frowns in confusion as she reads this chapter, then pulls out a sheet of paper and begins writing. When she hands me the new chapter, I'm astonished at the way she has swept aside the changes I've made to the storyline by turning it into a dream sequence. In Nazia's installment, Sanya realises that she only dreamed of her father's return and is disappointed to find that nothing has changed in her life. "Why did you do that?" I confront her. "I just wanted Sanya to be happy, instead of being so depressed." Nazia taps her forehead and sighs. "Pino, when will you learn that life doesn't work like this," she says. "There's a difference between reality and fantasy." I tell her to stop giving me unwanted reality checks. Nazia insists that she's being a good friend and will continue to give me reality checks, whether I like it or not.'

'Is this argument the cause of your disagreement with Nazia?'

'No, but it's a big part of it.'

'When do the problems begin?' Salman said.

'It begins a few years later. Nazia and I are sixteen years old. One of Diya's friends has found me a suitable boy. His name is Saleem Sabir. "He's much older than you," Diya tells me one afternoon, as I prepare to go over to Nazia's house. "But he's an enlightened man. He's involved with the MQM, but spends most of his time teaching at Karachi University. I'm sure he won't object to you studying further. You can get engaged after your matric exams."

'When I meet him for the first time, at our house, I realise that the Polaroid I've been shown of my suitor doesn't do him justice. His mullet hairdo and broad smile give him a regal look that no photographer would be able to capture in his lens. He tells Diya that he is actively involved in the MQM, and my mother applauds him for doing a great service for the Mohajirs. Diya is prepared to make him her son-in-law, but Saleem's mother isn't entirely convinced. I think she smells Diya's liquor-shot breath during her visit to our house. "What's that stench?" she asks, as she places her dupatta against her nose. Her husband laughs nervously and nudges his wife to remain quiet. "We simply adore your daughter, Diya Bibi," he says. "I'm sure she'll keep our son very happy." After his father says this, Saleem lowers his head. I wonder if he's blushing.'

Parveen paused suddenly, her words obstructed by a painful thought, and clicked her tongue.

'What does Nazia have to do with all this?' Salman asked, with the intention of coaxing her out of her silence.

'She comes to my engagement party, takes one look at Saleem and declares him unfit for me,' Parveen said, still enraged by Nazia's audacity. 'I tell her that she's being judgemental and cruel. "I'm just telling you the truth," she maintains. "I can tell that this man is going to hurt you. You're much too naive to understand these things." I dismiss her concerns with a shrug. A few weeks later, Saleem breaks our engagement and marries Nazia.'

'Why does he do that?' Salman said, alarmed. 'How does Saleem even get to know Nazia well enough to marry her? Do you introduce them?'

'They meet briefly at our engagement.' Parveen flinched. 'I don't see them speaking to each other during the evening. So, the news of their marriage comes as a surprise. When Diya demands an explanation from Saleem's mother, she says that her son fell in love with Nazia at the engagement. "Young people are making their own decisions these days, *behan*," she tells Diya. "I couldn't tell him to respect my wishes when his heart was set on Nazia. What kind of mother would that make me?"

'The story we hear through the grapevine comes as an even bigger shock than Nazia's marriage. It seems Saleem's mother had reservations about getting her son married off to me because the neighbours have been spreading rumours about Diya. According to the gossipmongers in our neighbourhood, a bearded man in a black shirt and grey pants visits Diya every two weeks and stays with her for an hour. I find the rumours absurd because I can vouch for the fact that my mother isn't having an affair. The bearded man is Diya's bootlegger, Naushad. I don't see what the problem is. Naushad has been coming to our house since prohibition. Ever since General Zia started pushing women into the four walls of their home, people readily feel the need to police the conduct of women.'

'Do you blame Diya for your engagement breaking up?' Salman asked.

'No,' Parveen said curtly. 'I have no expectations of my mother. I'm just stunned by the way Nazia has deceived me.'

'Do you ask her why she married your fiancé?'

'I do,' Parveen replied. 'I go over to meet Nazia, a few days after her marriage. "Why did you do it?" I demand, trying to keep my tears in check. "I did it for your own good," she snaps. "Stop fretting over it. Forget Saleem and move on with your life." Outraged by her insensitivity, I decide to cut her out of my life in the hope that it will help me forget her betrayal – and, consequently, my infatuation with Saleem. I concentrate all my energies on studying for my matric exams and slowly begin to erase the memory of being jilted by Saleem. But fate has other plans. Some years later, I run into Saleem at a shop on Tariq Road. He's holding a toddler – a little girl who has Nazia's eyes and Saleem's curly locks. When he catches sight of me, he turns away and pretends that he hasn't seen me. I walk up to him, greet him with a handshake and put my hand on the little girl's head. Saleem enquires after Diya's health and then hurriedly makes an excuse so he can leave the shop to avoid having an awkward conversation with me.

'As he walks out of the shop and runs towards his car, I notice that Nazia is sitting in the front seat. She smiles at her child and affectionately pinches Saleem's cheek as he tells her something. This gesture makes me wonder if he is telling her about his encounter with me. He places the toddler in his wife's lap and happily drives off. At that instant, my feelings for Saleem reawaken and grow in their intensity. For some reason, I can't get the image of Saleem and his new family out of my mind. It pains me to see Nazia drive away with the man who I was supposed to marry.'

'Is that why you decide to take revenge by turning Nazia's daughter against her when she's older?' Salman intruded, fearing his question sounded more like an accusation.

'No,' Parveen said. 'I try to restrain myself, to keep my feelings in check. Diya insists that I should sit my intermediate exams and then attend university. As the years go by, I obtain a BA in history and political science. Diya introduces me to a man named Wamiq, who runs an export business. We see each other for a few months, until he asks me to marry him. Driven by the faint hope that Saleem will return to me, I reject Wamiq's offer and find someone else to replace him. When the next man gets too serious about me, I ditch him as well. The cycle continues until Diya begins to worry that I'm being too fussy about the qualities I want in a life partner. How can I tell her that Saleem is the only man who possesses the qualities that I want in a husband? Diya wouldn't approve of me chasing after a man who disrespected me by breaking off our engagement.'

'What happens next?' Salman asked.

'I continue to reject potential suitors,' Parveen said, though not without pride. 'Everyone thinks I'm finding faults in the men that I'm introduced to because I don't want to get married. But their criticism doesn't faze me.'

'Do you ever hear from Saleem or Nazia again?' Salman asked. 'Do you try to contact either of them?'

Parveen shook her head. Then, seeming to remember something that she had forgotten to mention, she continued, 'When Saleem vanishes without a trace, I consider calling Nazia, but decide against it. Though his sudden disappearance troubles me, I don't think Nazia will understand my pain or offer consolation. So, I turn to writing – the only pursuit that has helped me escape childhood traumas. I've always sought comfort in folklore and fables to evade reality. In a fit of wild inspiration, I begin working on modern renditions of timeless tales about love. Each story is my attempt to heal, to assuage my restless heart and move on.

'Nobody knows Saleem's whereabouts. Some believe he has defected to the party's breakaway faction or fled the country. Others are of the view that he's being kept in an MQM torture cell, along with the party's dissidents and opponents. I find that hard to believe. While the relatives of other victims of the party's torture cells are protesting and demanding to know their whereabouts, Nazia is moving on with her life and making strides in her literary career. She always remains silent about her husband's disappearance. Rumour has it that they are separated. Saleem's absence is gradually forgotten.'

'Do you forget him as well?' Salman asked. He felt a tinge of sympathy for Saleem. Both he and Nazia's husband had lost their family because of the MQM's violent reign over Karachi.

'No,' Parveen whispered. 'I can't forget him. My only consolation is that he's no longer with Nazia. It makes him suddenly accessible to me, despite the fact that I don't know his whereabouts. Over the years, I continue to nurture my love for him, allowing my feelings for him to metamorphose into hatred, anger and an aching desire for intimacy. But I don't stop living. With Diya's persuasion, I decide to marry Sardar Wajid Ali, a much-divorced Sindhi landlord, who is fond of me, even though I'm obsessed with Saleem. "You've chased everyone from our community away," Diya tells me. "You might as well marry that Sindhi *wadera*. At least he cares about you and is rich enough to keep you happy."

'Sardar Wajid Ali doesn't ask me anything about Saleem, even when I tell him about my ex-fiancé. He's far more mature than my former lovers, who were perpetually at war with the man I couldn't forget. Our marriage doesn't burden me. But he is the most boring man I've ever been with. All he ever talks about are his lands, his Pajeros and his failed forays into politics. But Wajid Saeen slowly begins to play a more avuncular role in my life and revives my interest in our relationship. Every night, he narrates Sindhi fables to me in vivid detail. His words fuel my imagination and shape the base of the stories that I will write – even after he dies.'

'How do you react to his death?'

'I'm shocked,' Parveen said, in a manner that made Salman realise that she's stating the obvious. 'We had developed a special bond that I still can't call love. But Wajid Saeen's death in 2014 reinforces my belief that I'm destined to be with Saleem. He's the only person for whom my feelings haven't changed. He continues to exert a strong influence on my heart.'

'Do you reconnect with Nazia after your husband's death?'

'Yes. She attends my husband's funeral. I'm surprised to see her there, because we haven't spoken in over a decade.'

'What does she say?'

'She offers her condolences and asks me how I've been,' Parveen said. 'I expected an apology from her for betraying me and marrying Saleem, but she doesn't even mention the incident. Instead, she asks me about Wajid Saeen. When the conversation about my dead husband grows morbid, I tell her about my writing. "I'll introduce you to Dolly," she tells me. "She'll help you publish your work." I ask her about Saleem's whereabouts, more out of a desire to know where he is than a curiosity about my estranged friend's marital woes. "I don't know where he is," she explains. "He reached out to me some years ago, but I pushed him away to protect my daughter." I ask her what she's protecting her daughter from. "I did whatever I did for her own good," she says, repeating the words that had forced me to part with her, all those years ago. Her reaction leaves me confused. How can Nazia know what is best for everyone?'

'Do you ask her why she kept Saleem out of her life?' Salman asked.

'No. I'm too scared to ask her anything. But I'm curious to know. Over the next few years, I find ways to rebuild my friendship with her. On Nazia's insistence, her publisher, Dolly, begrudgingly agrees to publish my book. "Let's see if you can sell three hundred copies," Dolly tells me. She and I become confidantes in the months before the book hits the bookstores. During this period, she tells me that her husband once had an affair with Nazia. In exchange, I tell her about my own experience of Nazia's deception. After I share this with her, a new portal opens in our friendship. I feel instantly connected to her. But our camaraderie is short-lived. Dolly drops me once the book comes out. I send her a new manuscript, which she considers too parochial for her taste. When Nazia asks her why she rejected my next book, Dolly tells her she can't risk publishing it because the response to my previous book remained tepid. "Pino's book has barely sold fifty copies," she explains to Nazia. "Your friend should stop writing and go back to being a rich *waderi*."

'Dolly's harsh judgement doesn't prevent Nazia from encouraging me to write, even though I can sense that she derives a sadistic pleasure from knowing that my writing career has sunk. We develop a complex relationship, where I covet her success and she half-heartedly consoles me for my failure. Our professional rivalries aside, Nazia and I are able to revive our lost friendship. She and her sister Noori accept me like an old member of the family. I'm made party to inside jokes and simmering conflicts. "Bi Jaan always monopolises Sabeen," Nazia confides in me, one afternoon, when I visit her. "My daughter's always running after her, asking that no-good *maasi* for advice on what to wear to university and how to handle conflicts with her friends." When I ask her why she feels threatened by the housekeeper, Nazia tells me about her troubled relationship with Sabeen. "She still blames me for leaving her father," she says. I'm tempted to ask her more about Saleem, but rein myself in when she begins to cry. That day, I realise that Nazia's life hasn't been an easy one.'

'If you are so sympathetic towards Nazia's pain, why do you create problems between her and her daughter?'

Salman's question rattled Parveen. Her face hardened and her dark brows twisted into a scowl. 'I have my reasons,' Parveen said defensively. 'I ... I finally see him.'

'Saleem?'

'Yes, of course Saleem. One day, I see him walking down the road, near Boat Basin, in a white shalwar kameez.'

'How do you know it's him?'

'I can tell,' she snapped. 'His hair may have turned silver, but I can't forget his face. It is definitely Saleem.'

'Do you try to talk to him?'

'No; I'm in my car. By the time I park the car and follow him, he's gone.'

'Why does this incident make you betray Nazia?' Salman asked her, confusion in his eyes.

'I ask around about Saleem. I discover that he's returned to Karachi and has been living the life of a recluse. Ever since Nazia forbade him from seeing Sabeen, he's been yearning for his daughter's love. Those who have met him have heard him say that he is willing to go to any extremes to win back his daughter. When I'm told this, I begin to find ways to help Saleem meet his daughter. I try to befriend Sabeen, and realise that her heart aches for her father too. After careful consideration, I decide to win Sabeen over so I can reunite her with her father. This generous act will help Saleem realise that he made a mistake by leaving me for Nazia.'

'How do you go about separating Sabeen from Nazia?'

'I reveal the mother's misdeeds to her daughter.' Parveen sniggered. 'I've been hearing rumours about Nazia's affair with her brother-in-law. I'm not sure how true the rumours are. Since I reconnected with Nazia, I've wanted to ask her if there is any truth to these claims, but haven't found the right opportunity to ask such a personal question. Once, I ask Noori if she's happy with her husband. "Of course I am," she replies hesitantly. "Why wouldn't I be?" The nervous ring to her tone confirms my doubts. And so, I tell Sabeen about the affair and ask her if she'd like to stay with me for a few days, until she's ready to be under the same roof as her mother again. After a heated argument with her mother, Sabeen decides to move in with me.

'The day she arrives at my doorstep, I call everyone in my phone book to tell them that Sabeen is staying with me, desperately praying that someone will tell Saleem of his daughter's whereabouts, hoping he'll come looking for her. For months, I eagerly await the phone call that will reconnect me with Saleem. But the phone never rings. As time passes, my desperation morphs into anger over my foolishness. How could I have been certain that Saleem wanted to reconcile with his daughter? Could it just be a rumour?

'On some days, I seethe with rage about Saleem's absence, when he is the reason Sabeen is living with me. On other days, Saleem's memory haunts me. Meanwhile, Nazia's daughter gets too comfortable in my house and slowly becomes a burden on me. When her father doesn't call for close to a year, I'm tempted to turn her out of my house. But the earnest, if misguided, belief that Saleem will ring me up and seek access to his daughter prevents me from giving in to these impulses.

'Fortunately, Sabeen decides to change her number after she moves in with me, so neither Nazia nor Naureen can reach out to her. That makes it a lot easier for me to hide her mother's illness from her. But all of that is of no use. When Saleem finally calls to ask for Sabeen, he doesn't praise me for trying to reunite him with his daughter. Instead, he's still thinking about Nazia – his dead ex-wife.'

'Isn't it hypocritical of you to use Nazia and Asfand's affair to your advantage?' Salman asked, trying not to appear too reproachful. 'After all, your mother's alleged involvement with a strange man was the reason why Saleem's family rejected you.'

Parveen sighed heavily and began crying. 'I wronged her,' she snivelled, 'and now I'm suffering the consequences. All night, I thought Saleem was my ally. He was paying attention to me, giving me the impression that he was falling in love with me. And I now realise that he was just misleading me to get my share of Nazia's money. It makes me wonder if, by marrying Saleem, Nazia was trying to give me another one of those reality checks she gave me when we were writing Sanya's story. Was she trying to tell me that Saleem was wrong for me?'

'What do you think?'

'I can't say for certain,' she said. 'But there's a strong possibility of that being the case. It upsets me because I haven't been a good friend. All I've done today is found ways to disrespect her last wishes. I criticised Dolly for publishing her book because I feared that Nazia would depict me in a negative light. How could I forget that I was the one who had harmed her through my actions?'

'If you had understood this earlier, would you have treated Nazia differently?'

'I can't say.' She shrugged non-committally. 'She did steal my fiancé. How could I have forgiven her for that? I was young too.'

Parveen's contradictory remarks revealed a complexity to her thinking that Salman had not thought her capable of. He straightened his back, leaned forward and surged ahead with his next question.

'If you hadn't discovered the truth about Saleem, would you have continued to hate Nazia and never made amends?'

'Obviously. Who would want to befriend the villain of their story?'

Salman nodded. Parveen needs more time to process her feelings, he thought. A single session of hypnotherapy wouldn't be sufficient in helping her battle her inner demons. 'If you were given a chance to say goodbye to Nazia,' he said, 'what would you say?'

'I'd fall to her feet and apologise,' Parveen cried, her tone gentler than it had been a few minutes before.

'She's right next to you,' Salman said. 'Apologise to her.'

As Salman watched Parveen throw herself at Sorayya's feet and weep profusely, he remembered how his howling cries had reverberated through his house the day the police brought the bodies of Asifa and Zahra to his doorstep. He would revisit this memory with Saleem, Nazia's final guest for the night, since they had both lost their families due to circumstances beyond their control.

The Man Who Lived

Saleem smiled as he carefully mounted the stairs, tapping his fingers against the handrails and humming an old Pakistani song. He waved at Parveen, who was coming down the stairs with a crestfallen face.

'Had your fun?' he said, patting Parveen's shoulder and dashing ahead without even stopping to hear her response. 'Now it's my turn for fun.'

Ignoring his comment, Parveen lowered her gaze and continued walking down the stairs. *I'll show him fun*, she told herself.

'Pino,' Naureen said, 'I thought I'd share the good news with you. While you were in there with Salman, Sabeen decided that she wants to move back in with us. Asfand's driven her to your house and is helping her get her things. She'll be staying with us tonight.'

'Really?' Parveen said with indifference. 'That's good to hear. I think she's better off with you, anyway. I could never replace Nazia.'

Sensing a drastic shift in Parveen's demeanour, Naureen eyed her with interest, in the hope of finding a devious smile or an angry stare – any trace of her conniving nature. 'I didn't realise that hypnotherapy with Salman would make you so meek,' she said, giving a short laugh. 'What became of the angry, aggressive Pino who was making sly digs at me? I was under the impression that you and Saleem Bhai were up to no good. I also thought you were trying to sabotage Nazia's last wishes, just because we told Sabeen the truth about Nazia's illness. What changed?'

'I need to put aside my differences with Nazia,' Parveen said in dulcet tones. 'I need to forget all the grudges I've held because of those differences. Please forgive me. I was misguided.' Unable to control her tears, Parveen broke down and fell to her knees. She didn't know if she was crying over Nazia's death or because of the shameless cruelty with which Saleem had snubbed her.

Tears pricked at Naureen's eyes as she pulled Parveen up, hugged her and consoled her sister's childhood friend.

'I didn't think she would go so soon,' Parveen said.

'She's left a void in our lives,' Naureen said, between sobs. 'It'll take us some time to get used to her absence.'

The ring of Naureen's phone penetrated the momentary silence that fell between them. 'It's Asfand,' she said, clearing her throat and gazing at her phone screen. 'I'll go take this call in the drawing room.'

She held out an envelope for Parveen.

'You know what's in it,' Naureen said, hastily wiping an errant teardrop that had rolled down to her chin. 'I saw the message Farid sent you. I was going to confront you about it, but now it seems unnecessary.' She lifted the phone to her ear, answering the call, and turned away.

Parveen took the envelope from Naureen, breathed deeply and slipped it into her bag. She threw a look in the direction of the drawing room and, when she was certain Naureen wasn't in sight, sprinted into the kitchen.

'Bi Jaan,' Parveen whispered as she opened the door.

The old housekeeper peeked out of the storeroom with listless, tear-stricken eyes and marched towards Parveen.

'Go upstairs and stand by Nazia's door,' Parveen continued. 'I'll make sure Naureen doesn't leave the drawing room. Saleem has gone upstairs and I don't think we can trust him. Go knock on the door and beg Salman to let you in. You have to save Sorayya.'

Bi Jaan joined her palms and wailed. 'I was wrong about you,' she said. 'Please forgive me.'

'We don't have time for all this,' Parveen snapped. 'Go upstairs at once. *Jao!*'

Bi Jaan ran out of the kitchen and crept up the staircase. Parveen only returned to the drawing room once she heard the housekeeper knock on Nazia's door.

*

'Sahib, please let me in,' Bi Jaan implored, when Salman peeped out of the half-open door.

Salman pressed his eyelids in frustration and let out a heavy sigh.

'I told you,' he said firmly. 'You can't be here. Thank God, Saleem went to the bathroom before we started the therapy. Do you realise what could have happened if he'd seen you? All our efforts to fulfil Nazia Apa's last wishes would have been ruined. Do you want that to happen?'

'I'm not leaving, Sahib,' she yelled at him. 'I'm here to protect my niece. I know something wrong is going to happen to Sorayya.'

'I told you, she'll be fine,' Salman said indignantly. 'Now, go downstairs.'

'Sahib, please don't do this,' Bi Jaan said, her tone stripped of its momentary rage. 'How can I explain to you? She's just like my daughter. I'm sure you'd do the same for your own daughter. Please try to understand. Saleem Sahib might try to harm Sorayya. Would you let something like this happen to your own daughter?'

Bi Jaan's words troubled Salman, reminding him that he had to protect Sorayya – not just on the old housekeeper's request, but also because he was a father. He leaned against the wooden door, glanced at Bi Jaan's trembling face and sighed involuntarily.

'Okay,' he said. 'Wait outside the door. I'll call you in. Till then, trust me. I'll take care of Sorayya.'

Bi Jaan tiptoed into the lounge outside Nazia's room, where she would wait for his signal – even if it took the entire night. Seeing the determined look on Salman's face, she knew that he wouldn't disappoint her.

*

'I have a confession,' Saleem said, falling back on the rocking chair. 'I know that Nazia hasn't left us a three-thousand-dollar reward.'

'I d-don't know what you're talking about,' Salman stuttered, looking Nazia's ex-husband straight in the eye.

'Don't play dumb,' Saleem said. 'Farid told me everything.'

'What has he told you?' Salman said, puzzled by the confrontation.

'I just spoke to him an hour ago.' Saleem's voice dropped to a deeper pitch as he pulled out a packet of cigarettes from his pocket and lit up. 'He told me that there's no money in the envelopes Noori has been handing out. Instead, there's a letter addressed to each of us.'

'So, now you know,' Salman hissed. He stood up, picked up his satchel and slung it over his shoulder. 'I think I should leave.'

'What do you mean?' Saleem said, with a condescending grin. 'Aren't you going to hypnotise me?'

'I assumed that you'd lost the incentive to go ahead with the hypnotherapy,' Salman mumbled.

'Trust me, Narang Sahib,' Saleem chortled, 'the last thing I need is Nazia's money. Maybe Dolly and Farid needed the money. But even they've decided to remain silent about Nazia's ruse.'

Salman stared at him, speechless.

'I don't need to go through hypnotherapy to tell you the things you're going to hear today,' Saleem went on. He paused to take a drag of his cigarette, stifled a cough and then gave Salman a devious stare. '*Waise*, I'm surprised by your reaction. I thought Nazia would have spilled the beans when you put her through this therapy.'

'Spilled the beans about what?' Salman mumbled.

'Relax, Salman,' Saleem said. 'Everything will become clear to you. But first, you must tell me what Nazia told you about me.'

'I can't tell you what she told me, Saleem Sahib. It's a violation of client confidentiality.'

'Did she tell you I'd abandoned my family?' Saleem said. 'Did Nazia tell you I'd staged my disappearance? Did she say that my body had been tossed into a gunny sack or that I'd been tortured to death in one of the party's cells?'

Reluctant to disclose anything Nazia had confided in him, Salman greeted Saleem's questions with a guarded stony silence but he removed his satchel and sat back down. He was ready to hear what Saleem had to say.

'Nazia had quite an imagination,' Saleem chuckled, unperturbed by Salman's reticence, taking it as evidence of his own assumptions being correct. 'It's her imagination that saved me.'

'What do you mean?' Salman asked, perplexed by Saleem's claims.

'I still can't believe Nazia was able to bury this secret in her conscience,' Saleem said. 'I would have thought she'd have blurted it all out during her hypnotherapy. She disregarded our marriage by giving my mother's sari to a maid. Why wouldn't she have told you our secret? That's why I asked Farid to run a background check on you. I wanted to know more about you, so I knew who was carrying my secret. But it seems she took the secret to her grave. I guess there are some parts of the mind that even a hypnotist can't access.'

'What secret?'

'I need to share it with someone, especially because of what Nazia was trying to achieve today.'

'What was Nazia trying to achieve?' Salman asked.

'She was trying to get us to forget her by bribing us with money. But I can't forget her until I can share the secret that she'd buried in her conscience and eventually took to her grave.'

'Go ahead – what is this secret?'

'Let me explain,' Saleem said matter-of-factly. 'Nazia may have mentioned to you that I was actively involved in student politics before I joined the MQM. I was an idealistic student leader, who didn't want to be associated with the violence that had spread like a disease at KU. I simply wanted to right all those wrongs that my family had endured because we weren't rooted in the soil of Sindh, but had come from our so-called "princely states" in India. All I wanted was equal rights for our community. But things started going miserably wrong after 1986. I remember attending a public meeting at Nishtar Park, where armed MQM activists started shooting their guns into the air. I later came to know that some of our activists had smashed the windowpanes of a traffic-police kiosk and had pelted stones at a petrol pump in Gurumandir. While I disapproved of these acts of violence, I decided to remain quiet. But then, Altaf Bhai did something that shocked me. He told the Mohajir youth at a news conference at Hyderabad Press Club to collect arms. Over the next few months, I saw Karachi fall victim to violence, lawlessness and disorder at the hands of my own people. There came a time when the party's top brass demanded arms licences for young activists.'

'What does this have to do with the secret Nazia kept?' Salman asked testily.

'I met Nazia in 1988,' Saleem continued. 'As you may already know, I had been engaged to her friend and neighbour, Pino, for a few months. I had agreed to marry Pino, but I knew that we weren't right for each other. But my parents had been told that, if I got married, the recurring nightmares I'd been having would stop.'

'What nightmares?' Salman blurted out.

'Every night, I dreamed that I was walking down Burns Road with a gun in one hand and blood on the other. When I looked around me, the bodies of innocent children were scattered all over the street, and I had to tread carefully to avoid stepping on a broken limb or a severed head. I'd wake up screaming every night after witnessing this killing field.'

'Why did you marry Nazia, then?'

'She came to see me at the university, a few days after the engagement,' Saleem said. 'Nazia categorically asked me if I loved Parveen. "I don't know," I told her. "Why are you marrying her, if you don't love her?" she asked sternly. Though she looked angry, I didn't feel antagonised. She was determined to protect her friend. I knew I could trust her. I told her about the nightmares I'd been having. "You know why I decided to come back to teach at this university soon after I graduated?" I said to her. "I came back to encourage students not to pick up arms." After hearing what I had to say, Nazia's face was covered in tears.

"I also have nightmares," she confessed, taking my hand in hers. "I see him coming into the room I shared with my younger sister as a child and trying to drag her out of her bed." That's when she told me about her paternal uncle who had tried to rape Naureen when she was eight. Nazia had seen him take Naureen into his room. While she somehow managed to save her sister, she couldn't save herself. When she finally summoned the strength to tell her mother about what her uncle had done, her extended family claimed that Nazia had made the whole thing up. But Nazia's mother didn't pay attention to his excuses, and she stood by her daughter. As a result, the family distanced themselves from Nazia's mother.'

'Nazia never mentioned this during our therapy,' Salman said. 'How do I know if it's even true?'

'I'm not trying to point out the faults in your method,' Saleem said. 'I'm just telling you what I know. Anyway, Nazia and I became quite close over the next few days, and realised that we were in love. "Parveen won't be able to handle you the way I can," Nazia said to me. "She's obsessed with her fantasies and is incapable of negotiating reality." I told her that my mother was suspicious of Parveen's family and would much rather I married someone else, even if it was a Pukhtun girl. Fortunately, when I informally introduced Nazia to Ami, my mother found her delightful. "If this girl makes you happy, marry her," she said. Nazia's mother wasn't pleased with her daughter's decision to marry me, but could do little to dissuade her. A few weeks later, Nazia and I got married in a quiet affair at her house.'

'And the secret, Saleem Sahib?' Salman asked, pressing his hands against his forehead to ease a migraine. Saleem had eschewed the hypnotherapy session, preferring instead to enter into a prolonged and somewhat self-indulgent monologue, so Salman found himself abandoning his usual etiquette and patience, instead snapping, 'I've heard far too many stories tonight. Please make this one brief.'

'I'm sorry,' Saleem said. 'This is a complicated story – so bear with me. After we got married, my involvement in the party increased. What can I say? Politics was akin to breathing for me; I couldn't possibly distance myself from it. By then, the MQM had won municipal as well as national elections, and represented the interests of the Mohajir community. Ethnic and political violence became the norm and the government began to take action. Months before Sabeen was born, Operation Clean-up was launched and MQM activists were targeted. Two years later, MQM's militant wing began a violent campaign of resistance. The party had become a force of terror and many of my trusted colleagues sought a sadistic pleasure in bathing the streets of Karachi in blood. Nazia was troubled by the party's activities and the effect they were having on me. When I started waking up in the middle of the night to the same nightmare of a killing field, Nazia insisted that I quit the party. But I was too deeply involved in the party's affairs, which often kept me away from home for days. If I were to leave now, I would be abducted and killed by my own party members, and my family would be constantly harassed. Nazia wouldn't accept this excuse. And so, she came up with a plan.'

'What plan did she come up with?'

'She told me to go into hiding for a few years. "I'll tell everyone that you vanished and abandoned us," Nazia said. "Everyone will assume that you wanted to escape before the authorities arrested you in a search operation. We'll pretend that our marriage is over. Once you are safe, write me a letter under a pseudonym and I'll also respond under a fictitious name." I told her that running away wasn't going to be easy. "I'll arrange everything," she said. "We'll need to keep everything a secret, for now." Over the next year or so, she asked her mother for money under some pretext or other, and found a way for me to travel to New Zealand. I wrote to Nazia and told her that I'd reached the country safely. Nazia wrote back with a picture of our daughter and a letter in which she told me that some party workers and other dubious elements kept turning up at our house and asking for me. *I've told them we're no longer married*, Nazia's letter stated. *But they still keep coming back. Some of them sympathise with my situation, while others are suspicious of me. I've decided to move into Noori's house. That'll help me keep a low profile. I don't want to raise Sabeen in this way.*

'I wrote to her at Noori's address a few weeks later and told her that I'd started a clerical job at a university. I explained that I couldn't send for her and Sabeen yet, because it would take me years to become financially secure. I encouraged her to get a job till then, because I didn't want Nazia and Sabeen to be dependent on anyone in my absence. Her reply came a few months later: *I've started working at a newspaper*, she wrote. *My life is finally on track and Sabeen is settling into her new school quite well. For now, we're happy in Karachi. I don't want to burden you by coming to New Zealand.* Over the next few months, she told me everything that had happened to her. I knew about her fleeting romance with Dolly and her pact with Farid.'

'Really?' Salman said, surprised to discover that Saleem knew about Nazia's liaisons. 'How did that make you feel?'

'I learned to understand her need to reinvent herself,' Saleem said. 'In a way, she was doing it for me. Nazia started writing controversial books because she knew that they'd make her a different person in other people's eyes. She was no longer the abandoned wife of an MQM defector. She was a celebrity author, who was loved and despised for reasons that had nothing to do with me. Besides, I couldn't hold a few romantic encounters against her. I had a couple of flings myself, which I told Nazia about. She didn't mind.'

'How did you manage to come back to Pakistan?'

'I came back after the Nine Zero raid, when the MQM's power in the city had diminished. I wrote to tell her that I didn't feel the need to hide abroad any longer. I told her that I wanted to come back so I could live in the city of my birth. I was prepared to fight anyone who tried to harm me. Nazia was upset with me for making an impulsive decision that could land me in trouble. I kept assuring her that I'd put on quite a lot of weight and looked nothing like the man I was fifteen years ago. But she didn't listen to me. *I've been telling so many lies to keep you out of harm's way*, she wrote. *For years, I've been writing phony diary entries about you and our marriage because Sabeen, who secretly reads them, needs to know that you aren't to blame for abandoning us. How can you put your life at risk like this? What if they find out that you're back?* Ignoring her concerns, I decided to come back. *I'll be living with a trusted old friend who will keep my enemies at bay*, I wrote in my final letter to her. *Don't worry. I'll never try to reach out to you or to Sabeen.* All I could do was express my gratitude to her for all the sacrifices she had made for me.'

'But why are you telling me all this?' Salman asked him.

'I just spoke to Farid,' Saleem smiled. 'His reporter Sajid sent him a few more details about you. I figured that, since you lost your wife and child on the day of a riot in Karachi and still don't know what happened to them, you'd understand my predicament.'

'If you weren't in touch with Nazia, how did you hear about her death?' Salman said, after a long pause.

'Noori reached out to me. She told me Nazia had given her my number so she could let me know of her death. She also informed me about how Pino had driven a wedge between Nazia and Sabeen. I asked Noori for Pino's number and tried to reason with her. When my attempts to level with her failed, I decided to use Nazia's three-thousand-dollar reward as a way of connecting with her. I led Pino on, allowing her to believe that I was interested in her. I decided that I'd play along for a bit. I figured that, once I had my share of Nazia's money, I'd hand it over to Pino and bribe her to take back all the nasty things that she'd fed to Sabeen about Nazia. When Pino told me that there was no reward, I decided to break her heart at that very instant – just so she'd know how Nazia must have felt.'

'I see,' Salman said quizzically. 'So, you're a survivor. You were able to break away from a party that destroyed so many lives.'

'It's hardly something I can take credit for on my own,' Saleem said quietly.

'My wife was leaving me,' Salman exclaimed, self-consciously wiping the tears that were gushing from his eyes. 'I didn't earn enough to feed our family. She loved me and remained patient, but Asifa knew that I couldn't do much for her. On 11 May, she took my teenage daughter and the two of them left. I don't know what happened. All I know is that their bodies were brought to our house the next day. The police claimed it was an accident and didn't pursue the matter any further.'

'I'm sorry to hear that,' Saleem said, as he distractedly rose from the rocking chair, suddenly fearing that he had said too much. 'But, tell me, why is the maid lying on the bed?'

'It was Nazia's idea,' Salman confessed. 'Sorayya took care of her when she was ill. I think Nazia saw a younger version of herself in the maid. So, she thought it would be a good idea to make her lie next to her guests while they were being hypnotised. It was her way of ensuring that her guests trusted in my abilities. Right at the end of every session, I've been asking each guest to respond to Sorayya as if they were speaking to Nazia.'

Saleem walked over to the bed and glanced down at Sorayya.

Salman moved closer to him, wondering if he had misunderstood the glint in Saleem's eyes.

'She does resemble Nazia,' he said thoughtfully. 'Especially because she is wearing Nazia's sari. Nazia wore it on our wedding night, and her hair ...' Saleem heaved a sigh as he plopped himself next to Sorayya on the bed. 'Do you mind if I also respond to Sorayya like I would to Nazia?' he asked.

'What do you have in mind?' Salman glared at him, confused by this request. 'I was just about to pull her out of her trance.'

'Do me a favour,' Saleem said, as he folded his sleeves above his elbows. 'Go lock the door. You can snap her out of her trance after I'm done with her. It'll only take a few minutes.'

Salman's eyes widened as if someone had opened a portal into a new and dangerous world for him. *How can Saleem expect me to do such a despicable thing?* he thought. *How could God have taken Asifa and Zahra, when a vile man like Saleem has been spared?*

'I can't do that,' he said.

'Don't be such a killjoy,' Saleem said, with a grin. 'Now, go lock the door. Trust me, it won't take long.'

Salman nodded his assent and scuttled towards the door. He turned back and noticed that Saleem was hovering over Sorayya. Before he touched the door, Salman snapped his fingers to awaken Sorayya. Her eyes opened and she rose with a jerk, letting out a scream.

Salman opened the door and signalled for Bi Jaan to enter the room. He stood by the entrance and saw Sorayya run toward the old housekeeper for safety, her screams frantic.

'How dare you try to touch her?' Bi Jaan yelled as she charged at Saleem and banged her fists on his chest.

Hearing the commotion, Naureen and Parveen ran up the stairs and marched into Nazia's room. Parveen let out a faint gasp when she saw Saleem being beaten by Bi Jaan. Naureen rushed over and pulled Saleem out of Bi Jaan's clutches.

'What happened, Bi Jaan?' Naureen hollered. 'Stop attacking him.'

'He was trying to have his way with Sorayya, Naureen Bibi,' Bi Jaan said frantically.

'I can vouch for that,' Salman said. 'He asked me to lock the door so he could violate her.'

Naureen turned to Saleem, incredulous at what she was hearing, and was stunned to find that he was hastily zipping up his trousers, stalled as a part of his shirt had caught in the zipper.

'Saleem Bhai,' she said, her eyes boring into his. 'Get out. At once.'

With a grunt, Saleem, now presentable, left the room.

'Bi Jaan,' Naureen said feebly, unable to find the right words to apologise for Saleem's conduct, 'I'm so sorry.'

'Don't!' Bi Jaan bellowed, pointing a finger at Naureen as she clasped Sorayya in her other arm. 'Sorayya and I are leaving for our village tomorrow. I won't work at a house where my own children aren't safe.' With that, she led Sorayya out of the room.

Naureen lowered herself on to Nazia's bed and watched in silence as they descended the stairs. Tears swam in her eyes, but she blinked them away before anyone could see them.

*

'What did he do to you?' Bi Jaan asked Sorayya, when they had entered the servant quarters.

'I don't know, Phuppo,' Sorayya said in confusion, sipping water from a steel cup. 'All I remember is Nazia Apa's friend coming into the room and showing me his watch. After that, I woke up on the bed with Nazia Apa's husband standing over me.'

Bi Jaan pulled a steel trunk from under the *charpoy*. 'Start packing your clothes,' she said. 'We're leaving tomorrow. I did so much for Nazia Apa and Naureen Bibi. I practically raised them when they were children. And they have betrayed me, disrespected my honour. How can I stay in this house after being treated in this way?'

'What became of your plans to make Naureen Bibi realise that I was an integral part of the household?' Sorayya asked. She said this without the slightest hint of scorn, and Bi Jaan was puzzled by her reaction.

'Are you insane?' she retorted. 'Don't you know what this family tried to do to you?'

'I can't remember anything, Phuppo,' Sorayya said.

Bi Jaan's face registered concern. 'I've been so stupid,' she said. 'You're just a child. How could I have expected you to support your brother, when you haven't even been exposed to the cruelties of this world?'

Sorayya frowned at her aunt, perplexed by her change of heart.

'Don't worry,' Bi Jaan said, suddenly embracing her niece. 'We'll go back to the village tomorrow. I don't know how we'll run our household, but we will find a way.'

Baffled by her aunt's display of affection, Sorayya was reminded of what Raqib had told her about their father's corpse. If Nazia's family was able to host grand parties to celebrate her death, what was stopping her aunt from celebrating another kind of death – the end of the exploitative relationship with Naureen Bibi? At that moment, she decided to use Bi Jaan's vulnerability as an opportunity to tell her something that needed to be said, even if it would hurt her.

'We've carried the burden of Abba's death for too long,' she said firmly. 'That hasn't helped us in any way. Let's not carry yet another burden. Besides, it's time Naureen Bibi started cooking her own food, rather than taking credit for all the effort you make in the kitchen.'

Sorayya kissed her aunt before helping her pack their trunk. The lyrics of her favourite Sunny Leone song whirred through her head. The music that played in her mind drifted her thoughts away from the events of an evening she could barely remember. As she closed the trunk, Sorayya could only recall singing familiar Bollywood tunes with her friends in the wheat fields of a village that would always be her home.

Silence After the Storm

Parveen stood by the entrance of the drawing room and kept checking her watch, wondering if she should leave. Over the last hour, Naureen had prattled on about the embarrassment Saleem's actions had caused her. Salman sat silently on a chair next to her and stared at Naureen with tired eyes, unsure if he should interrupt her.

'Who would have thought Saleem Bhai would do such a shameful thing?' Naureen wailed. Responding to her own question, she launched into a diatribe about how her sister had married a snake who had repeatedly cheated on her and had thrown her into an early grave with his lies and infidelities.

'He probably had his eye on Sorayya when she walked into the drawing room wearing Nazia's sari,' she continued. 'He was also trying to warm up to Pino throughout the evening.'

'Just don't tell Sabeen,' Parveen said in a flat voice. 'It'll give her a bad impression of her father.'

Naureen nodded, taking a deep breath before she finally stopped talking about her brother-in-law.

'I think I should leave,' Parveen said, after she was certain that Naureen had nothing left to say. She hugged her hostess. 'Thank you for tonight.'

When Naureen returned, after walking Parveen out, Salman had risen from the chair and was strolling across the marble floor.

'Do you want me to get you some water?' Naureen asked. 'I don't have any help in the kitchen, so that's all I can offer you right now.'

'Don't worry,' he said. 'I'm good.'

In the silence that fell between them, Naureen noticed beads of sweat on his forehead and sensed that he was anxious.

'I hope you know that I don't hold you responsible for what happened earlier with Saleem Bhai,' she reassured him. 'I just wish we'd predicted that one of Nazia's guests would act like that. You mentioned in your text message that Sorayya had been hurt, but I didn't think something like this would happen. Thankfully, he was the last person to go into the room and most of the guests had already left by the time Bi Jaan created chaos upstairs.'

Salman still cringed at the thought that he had completely misinterpreted Saleem's intentions. He didn't understand what had compelled Saleem to attempt such a shameless act, but he was glad to have been able to protect Sorayya, as he had promised her and Bi Jaan. *If Asifa and Zahra had been alive and knew what I had done today, they would have surely returned to me.*

'Nazia wanted it this way,' Salman said. 'She knew how each of her guests would react. I'm pretty sure she knew what she was doing.'

'I agree,' Naureen said. 'She knew.'

Another interlude of silence hung thick in the air. Naureen yawned, and Salman took it as a cue to leave.

'I wanted to ask you something,' he murmured. 'I hope you don't mind me bringing this up. But, since we're the only ones in the house right now, I thought I'd ask you.'

'Go ahead,' Naureen said, smiling languorously as she sat on a chair.

'Did Nazia go peacefully?' he asked, with his head bowed down. Once the words had streamed out of his mouth, Salman looked up and saw the smile that curved the corners of Naureen's mouth disappear. Had his question offended her? 'I'm sorry,' he said, in the hope of easing the tension that had now settled into the room. 'You don't have to answer that, if you don't want to.'

'What do you mean by that question?' Naureen asked, exhausted by the evening.

'I think you know what I mean,' he said. 'I'm asking if you were able to fulfil Nazia's wish to die peacefully.'

'She told you about it?' she said, her face aflame.

'Yes. Nazia always said she wanted to go on her own terms. She'd spent her entire life trying to tame fate, to woo it into submission. She didn't want fate to decide when she should leave this world.'

'I was with her in the room that night, when she took the pills,' Naureen said. 'I think she wanted me to be with her when it happened. For a few months,

Nazia's attitude towards me had changed. She no longer quarrelled with me the way she had before her stroke. Nazia and I started having long conversations in which she told me everything that she hadn't told me before. She finally admitted to her late-night trysts with Asfand. At first, it was difficult for me to process that my sister had had an affair with my husband under my own roof. I'd laboured under the illusion that she would always protect me. How could she do this?

'Before I could confront Asfand, Nazia told me that she wanted to die on her own terms and needed my help to do it. I finally realised why she had told me about the affair. She knew I had allowed her to stay with me because I felt indebted to her for saving me from Chacha's advances as a child. I'd tolerated her tantrums and stayed calm when we had our spats because I felt guilty for putting her in harm's way. Now, she wanted me to despise her, so I had an incentive to help her die and arrange a party for her.'

As she spoke, tears stung her eyes, and she dabbed a crumpled tissue against them.

'And so, I did it,' Naureen said. 'I helped her go peacefully and allowed myself to grieve by planning this party. Nazia's list of demands gave me an opportunity to climb into her skin and be as calculating as she was. The entire evening was an act that allowed me to walk around in my sister's shoes and understand her intentions. Does it all make sense now? No – it never will. She was her own person, and I am mine.'

With a gracious nod, Salman rose from his chair and gently patted Naureen's shoulder. 'You haven't put yourself through hypnotherapy,' he said, his words coming across as a complaint. 'If you need to process your thoughts and emotions, do give me a call.'

He walked towards the door, then turned back to her and smiled. 'It takes strength to do what you've done today,' he said. 'It wasn't easy to go through with your sister's requests – especially with your housekeeper trying to sabotage everything.'

Naureen let out a quiet laugh as she wiped her tears. 'As you can tell, reliable servants are hard to come by,' she said, touching the tissue lightly against her skin.

'I should get going,' he said, ignoring her comment. 'It'll take me some time to get back to Azizabad.'

Naureen swiftly rose from the chair and went over to shake his hand. 'Goodbye Salman Sahib,' she said. 'Thank you for your help. I'll give you a call if I decide to put myself through hypnotherapy.'

*

Parveen Shah never went to bed without pulling out a book from her shelf and leafing through its pages for at least an hour. Although she was exhausted after a long day, she found it difficult to stray from this ritual. Snuggled under a thin duvet in her air-conditioned room, she decided she was too tired to walk to the bookshelf in the lounge. This was the first time in a long time that she was sleeping alone in the house. Now that

Sabeen was gone, Parveen realised that her presence – albeit burdensome – had filled a void in her life and given her a sense of companionship.

Unwilling to sleep without having read something, Parveen eagerly tore open the envelope and held Nazia's letter in her trembling hands. She switched on the bedside lamp and began reading.

I must apologise for deceiving you. As you may all know by now, there is no money in the envelopes that Noori has given you in exchange for undergoing hypnotherapy with Salman Narang. Most of you are probably feeling short-changed because you were hoping to find a cheque or currency notes stacked into the envelopes. It was wrong of me to mislead you like this. But I had no choice. None of you would have agreed to put yourself through hypnotherapy if there wasn't an incentive.

Nevertheless, I must thank you for doing this for me. After my stroke, I realised that life is transient – a story that must come to an end. My life is a story with many narrators, each with a different perspective on what matters and what doesn't. All of you are the narrators of my story. You've either casually observed me make mistakes or have been directly impacted by my misdeeds. I wanted each of you to share your truths, lies and doubts about me, so you could expunge them from your mind and heal old wounds. At the same time, I wanted you to know that each of you got to see a version of me that was devoid of artifice. I was sincere with all of you, even when you harmed me. For most of you, my choices have remained an enigma. For those of you who understood my intentions, they are as clear as day.

Remembering is part of the healing process. After undergoing these sessions with Salman, most of you will probably claim that you don't remember anything that happened during the procedure. That's a lie, because this only happens on stage shows or television. All of you are painfully aware of what you said when you were in a hypnotic trance. It may take you time to process any changes that you notice in your demeanour, but they will take you a step further towards understanding your pain – and, by extension, mine.

Many of you may have evaded questions or lied to Salman. I can understand why you'd do that. None of you were under oath, so you can't be held accountable for the fictions that you wove about me. Hypnosis can't detect your lies. If you fabricate 'facts', there is no way for them to be verified. And yet, there is a semblance of truth to each of the lies that you may have told – even if they are downright poisonous. I respect your lies, because they bear the truth about how my faults affected you.

As we bid farewell, I'd like all of you to slowly forget me and revel in the relationships that you've managed to reclaim throughout the evening. I wonder if this would have happened if I'd had a proper funeral, where people aimlessly shed tears instead of talking about the pains and problems that divided them. I suppose there was some merit to having no funeral to say goodbye to me.

Nazia Sami

After she finished reading the note, Parveen neatly folded it and placed it in the envelope. She smiled as she switched off the lamp, adjusted her pillow against the mattress and lowered her head on to the silk cover. As the glow from the streetlamp lulled her to sleep, Parveen made a mental note to call Sabeen the following day and apologise for her mistakes. She'd do it right after she returned from Gizri Graveyard, where she would meet Nazia one last time. But, for now, she'd allow herself to sleep before memories of the day's traumas and shocking revelations threatened to keep her up until dawn.

*

The next morning, Naureen sat on the wicker chair in the garden and inspected the bougainvillea creepers, a cigarette tucked between her lips.

Asfand walked into the garden, balancing a small tray crammed with two teacups and a potful of sugar on his palm. 'Sabeen is still asleep,' he said, as he distractedly placed the tray on the table. 'So, I guess it's just going to be the two of us.'

Naureen registered the remark with a nod, her eyes fixed on the bougainvillea.

'*Waise*, I think we can get used to running a house without servants,' he said, stirring a spoonful of sugar into his wife's teacup. 'Noori!' he gasped, when he saw a cigarette in her mouth. 'How many times am I going to have to warn you not to do that?'

Naureen turned to face him and blew smoke rings that wafted above her head. 'Don't let the gardener get rid of the bougainvillea,' she said. 'I know you want to, now that she's gone. But let the creepers remain.'

Asfand nodded as he quietly sipped his tea.

'I wanted the twins to live,' Naureen said abruptly. 'I loved them. After we lost them, I couldn't imagine loving another child. I feared another child would remove the ache in my heart, but the ache was my link to the twins: my love for them. I think I ruined our chance at happiness.' She paused and let out a soft moan. 'I didn't stop you and my sister because I knew how happy she made you. I didn't and don't approve of your relationship, but I understand why you needed it.' Naureen tossed the cigarette butt into an ashtray and buried her face in her palms.

Asfand placed his teacup on the table and knelt on the grass next to her. 'We'll work it out,' he cooed, pulling Naureen's hands away from her face. 'Trust me.'

Naureen looked up at him. 'I'm willing to overlook your affair with Nazia because we've both suffered, but don't ever think that I've forgiven you for it.'

Asfand nodded slowly in comprehension. 'We don't need children to be happy,' he said, changing the subject. 'Now that Sabeen's moved back home, it seems like we already have a child in the house. And you didn't even need to endure stretch marks and morning sickness to get this one. It's a blessing.' He smiled.

'I know,' Naureen chuckled. 'Which reminds me, can you help me tidy up Nazia's room for Sabeen?'

Asfand laughed. 'I doubt we'll ever be able to tidy up the mess that Nazia's guests made in that room last night,' he said. 'But I'll help.'

After he finished his tea, Asfand scurried back into the house, while Naureen sat on the wicker chair and watched the bougainvillea creepers sway in a gentle breeze. After she'd smoked another cigarette, she rose from her seat, strolled along the cobbled path and smiled as she walked past the pink flowers – like Nazia used to. She pulled out Nazia's pocket diary from her purse, kissed it and then held it between her finger and thumb. With a deep exhale, she put a lighter to its cover, flung the diary on to the cobblestones and watched, mesmerised, as small flames licked the pages. The paper curled at the corners and it burst into a mini bonfire, the wind scattering the glowing ashes in flurries all over the garden and beyond.

Glossary

aashiqs – lovers
acha – I see
apa – older sister
arre main kehti hoon – all I'm saying is
baji – older sister
behan – sister
beta – son
beti – daughter
bhai – brother, affectionate form of address for an older
  man
bibi – respectable woman, also wife
bijli – electricity
charpoy – a light woven bedstead
chaddar – large piece of cloth wrapped around head and
  upper body, leaving only the face exposed
chalo – let's go / oh well
chehlum – prayer service held on the fortieth day after
  the death of a Muslim
chokri – girl
choro – let it be
dupatta – scarf worn by women in Pakistan and India
dulha mian – bridegroom

ghusl – full-body ritual purification or ablution mandatory in Islam; in this context, the term is used to describe *Ghusl Mayyit*, the bathing of a Muslim's body before burial

haina – colloquial term meaning, 'Don't you agree?'

hindustani – person from Hindustan, the Persian-language name for India

janaza – funeral prayer, part of Islamic funeral rituals

jao – go

Jinnahpur –an alleged plot in Pakistan to form a breakaway autonomous state to serve as a homeland for the Urdu-speaking Muhajir (emigrated from India during partition community

jora – garment

ka – of

khus-phus – whispering

KU – Karachi University

maasi – maid

maulvi sahib – learned teacher or expert who attends to the religious needs of Muslims

mehndi – traditional wedding party where henna designs are painted on the bride's hands and feet

mian – sir/suffix added to a man's name or title out of respect

Mohajir – Muslim refugees and immigrants, as well as their descendants, who migrated from India to Pakistan in the aftermath of the Partition, in 1947

MQM – Muttahida Qaumi Movement, a political party founded by Altaf Hussain

pallav – end piece of a sari

paranda – a decoration for a braid tassel

PECHS – Pakistan Employees Cooperative Housing Society, an affluent neighbourhood in Karachi

phuppo – paternal aunt

PPP – Pakistan People's Party, a political party founded by former Pakistani Prime Minister Zulfikar Ali Bhutto

PTI – Pakistan Tehreek-e-Insaf, a political party chaired by Pakistani cricketer Imran Khan

Pukhtun – ethnic group, originally from Afghanistan

Quran khwani – a gathering where passages of the Quran are recited

rani – queen

rona dhona – weeping theatrically

roti – round, unleavened flatbread native to the subcontinent

saag – South Asian spinach-based vegetable dish

shalwar kameez – traditional dress, worn by both women and men in South Asia; shalwars are loose pajama-like trousers, while the kameez is a long shirt or tunic

soyem – prayer service held on the third day after the death of a Muslim

tabdeeli – idea of revolutionary change popularised by the PTI, a political party that promised to create a New Pakistan once it assumed public office

tamasha – a spectacle

tauba hai – good gracious; heaven forbid; never again

Umar Marvi – folk tale from Sindh, Pakistan, that appears in Sufi poet Shah Abdul Latif Bhitai's *Risalo*

wadera – informal term for feudal landlord or baron

waderi – informal term for the wife of a feudal landlord
wah – a cry of amazement
waise – by the way
youthias – a pejorative term used for supporters of
Pakistan's former prime minister Imran Khan
zamindars – the formal term for feudal landlords

Acknowledgements

In retrospect, *No Funeral for Nazia* seems to be a premonition of sorts about my mother's death. Shahnaz Imdad Kehar – Naz to her loved ones and friends – encouraged me to use words as a shield and sword. Without her unflagging support, I would never have summoned the courage to write fiction.

I'd like to thank Sofia Rehman, my erudite editor, for the unstinting enthusiasm with which she accepted the novel. Sofia meticulously read the manuscript and highlighted its shortcomings without ever interfering with my creative process.

I owe a great debt of gratitude to Archna Sharma and the entire team at Neem Tree Press for taking on the book and treating it with utmost care.

Aamer Hussein, mentor and friend, read *No Funeral for Nazia* when it was only a 15,000-word Google document. His curiosity about the direction of the story prodded me to complete the manuscript.

It is difficult not to mention the usual suspects, who have made my literary journey less lonesome. I'd like to thank Natasha Japanwala for all the love and appreciation that she's shown my work over the years.

A special thanks to Sidhra, Talha, Abbas, Azfar, Zahida, Aimen and Huma Sheikh for being supportive friends and readers.